PENGUIN BOOKS

CARPENTER'S GOTHIC

William Gaddis' first novel, *The Recognitions*, was
published in 1955; the *San Francisco Review of
Books* later called it "a novel of stunning power . . .
unmatched by any American writer in this century—
perhaps in any century." Wider praise greeted *J R*,
Mr. Gaddis' second novel, which won the National
Book Award in 1976. Both books are available from
Penguin. Mr. Gaddis is the recipient of a MacArthur
Foundation Fellowship and was recently elected to
the American Academy and Institute of Arts and Let-
ters. *Carpenter's Gothic* is his third novel. He lives in
New York.

William Gaddis
Carpenter's Gothic

ELISABETH SIFTON BOOKS · PENGUIN BOOKS

ELISABETH SIFTON BOOKS • PENGUIN BOOKS
Viking Penguin Inc., 40 West 23rd Street,
New York, New York 10010, U.S.A.
Penguin Books Ltd, Harmondsworth,
Middlesex, England
Penguin Books Australia Ltd, Ringwood,
Victoria, Australia
Penguin Books Canada Limited, 2801 John Street,
Markham, Ontario, Canada L3R 1B4
Penguin Books (N.Z.) Ltd, 182–190 Wairau Road,
Auckland 10, New Zealand

First published in the United States of America by
Viking Penguin Inc. 1985
Published in Penguin Books 1986

LIBRARY OF CONGRESS CATALOGING IN PUBLICATION DATA
Gaddis, William, 1922–
Carpenter's gothic.
"Elisabeth Sifton books."
I. Title.
PS3557.A28C3   1986   813'.54   86-800
ISBN 0 14 00.8993 4

The author wishes to express appreciation for assistance given him by the
John Simon Guggenheim Memorial Foundation in the course of writing
this book, and by the John D. and Catherine T. MacArthur Foundation in
completing it.

Grateful acknowledgment is made to Random House, Inc., for permission
to reprint lines from "Wise Men in Their Bad Hours," from *Selected
Poetry of Robinson Jeffers*. Copyright 1924 and renewed 1952 by Robinson Jeffers. An extract from *The Mimic Men*, by V. S. Naipaul, appears on
page 150. Copyright © 1967 by V. S. Naipaul.

Printed in the United States of America by
R. R. Donnelley & Sons Company, Harrisonburg, Virginia
Set in Aldus

Carpenter's Gothic

The bird, a pigeon was it? or a dove (she'd found there were doves here) flew through the air, its colour lost in what light remained. It might have been the wad of rag she'd taken it for at first glance, flung at the smallest of the boys out there wiping mud from his cheek where it hit him, catching it up by a wing to fling it back where one of them now with a broken branch for a bat hit it high over a bough caught and flung back and hit again into a swirl of leaves, into a puddle from rain the night before, a kind of battered shuttlecock moulting in a flurry at each blow, hit into the yellow dead end sign on the corner opposite the house where they'd end up that time of day.

When the telephone rang she'd already turned away, catching breath, and going for it in the kitchen she looked up to the clock: not yet five. Had it stopped? The day was gone with the sun dropped behind the mountain, or what passed for one here rising up from the river. —Hello? she said, —who...? Oh yes no, no he's not here he's... No I'm not, no. No, I'm... Well I'm not his wife no, I just told you. My name is Booth, I don't even know him. We've just... Well if you'll just let me finish! We've just rented his house here, I don't know where Mister McCandless is I've never even met him. We got a card from him from Argentina that's all, Rio? Isn't that Argentina? No it was just a card, just something about the furnace here it was just a postcard. I'm sorry I can't help you, there's somebody at the... No I have to go goodbye, there's somebody at the door...

Somebody hunched down, peering in where she'd stood staring out there a minute before, a line straight through from the kitchen past the newel to the front door fitted with glass, shuddering open. —Wait! she was up, —wait stop, who...

—Bibb?

—Oh. You frightened me.

He was inside now, urging the door closed behind him with his weight against it, bearing up her embrace there without returning it. —Sorry, I didn't...

—I didn't know who you were out there. Pushing open the door you looked so big I didn't, how did you get here?

—Coming down 9W in a...

—No but how did you find it?

—Adolph. Adolph said you'd...

—Adolph sent you? Is something wrong?

—No relax Bibb, relax. What's the matter anyhow.

—I'm just, I've just been nervous. I've just been very nervous that's all and when I saw you out there I, when you say Adolph sent you I thought something's wrong. Because something's usually wrong.

—Bibbs I didn't say that. I didn't say Adolph sent me...
He thrust his legs out from the chair across the hearth from
her where she'd come down to the edge of the frayed love
seat, knees drawn tight and her hands caught together at her
chin, pressed there. —When I saw him last week he told me
where you'd moved, I didn't know what you'd...

—Well how could you know how could we tell you! How
could you know where we'd moved you never, we never
know where you are nobody knows. You just show up like
this with your, your boots look at your boots they're falling
apart look at your, that hole in your knee you don't even
have a jacket, you...

—Oh Bibb, Bibbs...

—And it's cold!

—Well Bibbs Jesus, you think I don't know it's cold? I've
been on the road sixteen hours. I'm driving this moving van
down from Plattsburgh with no heater, I had to cut it out
when the cooling system went. Twice, the whole fucking
thing broke down twice and it just broke down again right
up here, up on 9W. I saw the sign and remembered this is
where Adolph said you moved to so I walked down here.
That's all.

—You look tired Billy, she said in a voice near a whisper.
—You look so tired... and her own hands fell away.

—You kidding? Tired, I mean that fucking truck you
wouldn't...

—I wish you wouldn't smoke.
He threw them, match and cigarette together, at the cold
grate, came forward on a torn knee to pick them up where
they'd hit the firescreen. —You got a beer?

—I'll look I don't think so, Paul doesn't...

—Where is he? I saw the car I thought he'd be here.

—It's broken, he had to take the bus in this morning. He
hates it, Billy...? She was up, calling from the kitchen

—Billy? She looked up to the clock, —he'll be here any minute I just don't want...

—I know what you don't want! He was up talking loud to walls, to the balustrade mounting from the newel at the door, to furniture —Bibb?

—There's no beer, I'm making tea if you...

—You just want me gone before Paul shows up, right? And he was across the room pulling open a door under the stairs on the cellar dark below, jamming it closed and opening another and stepping in without a light, standing over the bowl there. —Bibb? from the opened door. —Can you lend me twenty?

The cup rattled on the saucer, passing. —Oh I should have told you. This one stops up, I should have told you to use the upstairs...

—Too late now... he came out tugging his zipper, —can you lend me twenty Bibb? I was going to get paid when I got the van down there but...

—But what about it, the van. You just left it?

—The hell with it.

—But you can't just leave it there, up there right in the middle of the...

—You kidding? The alternator's shot, you think I'm going to sit up there all night with it? Send that heap out on the road they can come haul it in.

—But who? Whose is it, what are you doing driving somebody's moving van down from...

—Like what do you think I was doing, Bibb? I was trying to make seventy five bucks, what do you think I was doing.

—But you said you just saw Adolph, I thought you...

—Oh come on Bibb, Adolph...? He was down in the chair again, one hand cracking knuckles on the fist of the other. —Adolph wouldn't give me the sweat...

—I wish you wouldn't do that.

—What, about Adolph? He...

—With your knuckles, you know it makes me nervous.

His shrug dropped him deeper into the chair, one hand

seized in the other. —Sit there in his paneled office I have to listen to every fucking nickel he's accountable for to the trust, the estate, the lawsuits the nursing home bills his duty to conserve the assets I mean shit, Bibbs. No wonder the old man made Adolph his executor. He sits there guarding the estate with one hand, dealing out this lousy trust with the other him and the bank, Sneddiger down at the bank. Ask one of them for a nickel he says the other one might not approve this expenditure, I mean that's the way the old man set it up. Just to keep us...

—Oh I know it, I know...

—Just to...

—Well it's almost done, isn't it? It's almost done, by next spring you'll...

—That's the trust Bibb, that's just the trust that's what I mean. That's how he set it up, just to keep us out of the estate, by the time we get there there won't be one anyhow. Twenty three lawsuits Adolph says, they've got twenty three lawsuits by stockholders against the company and the estate trying to get back what the old man handed out in those payoffs. The estate is using every resource at its disposal in dealing with these cases says Adolph, every resource that's Adolph. That's him and Grimes and all of them do you think they want to settle it? Every resource do you think they give a shit if they win it or lose it they just want to keep things going, adjournments postponements appeals they charge the estate every time they pick up the fucking telephone they're talking to each other, like they're all sitting in each other's laps picking each other's noses two hundred dollars an hour every one of them Bibb, they're talking to each other.

—But what dif...

—I mean every time I go in there Adolph has to remind me how they smoothed the way for the old man's retirement when he could have gone to prison instead. I mean why didn't he. He should have gone so should Paul, so should...

—Billy please, I don't want to go over it again, just go

over it and go over it Paul just did what he was told, it was all going on long before he went there anyway. What was Paul supposed to do, they even said it wasn't against the law didn't they? Even the papers, when the...

—Then how come there's all these lawsuits? If it wasn't against the law how come there's twenty three lawsuits, if the old man wasn't as smart as Uncle William he'd be in prison right now but he takes the fast way out like he always did, like he always did Bibb. He crapped on the floor for somebody else to clean up that's all he ever did and there was always somebody there to clean up. There was always Adolph cleaning up that's what he's doing now, that's all he knows how to do. Two hundred dollars an hour he'll keep cleaning up till there's no fucking estate left, you know what he just did? Adolph? He just gave Yale ten thousand dollars did you know that? From the estate, ten thousand dollars for Yale while you're living in this old dump and I'm out driving a broken down...

—But it's not! It's a beautiful old house it's what I always...

—Come on Bibb it's a heap, look at it. Over there in that alcove, take one look at the ceiling and it's ready to fall down, you know what Adolph just spent on those copper roofs at Longview? He just came back, him and Grimes and Landsteiner all of them, they were all down there. You know why? Reviewing the estate's assets Adolph tells me, you know why? right now? It's duck season. Go down there and blow every duck they can see out of the sky and the estate pays every nickel, Adolph doesn't know a twelve bore Purdey from a Sears, Roebuck but he's down there banging away at anything that moves. Conserving the assets they call it, so they decide to spend thirty seven thousand dollars on the roofs, I mean thirty seven thousand dollars. Those copper roofs they're supposed to turn green to go with all that fucking moss hanging off the trees, Longview they call it Longview you can't see ten feet through the...

—Oh I know it I know it...! The saucer rattled the cup and she set it down, —please don't let's keep going over it please!

—All right Bibb, but I mean he could have left it to us couldn't he? Or Bedford, even Bedford, I saw Lilly...

—Leave you Bedford? You think he'd have left you Bedford after that last party you had there? That party when he was off in Washington putting cigarettes out on the carpets and all the broken glass and Squeekie passed out right in his own bathtub? and then somebody painting a hat on his portrait in the library with Day-Glo, you thought he'd leave you the house after that?

—He could have left it to you at least.

—I never liked it. Paul would go crazy at Bedford.

—Paul will go crazy right here. Let Lilly go crazy at Bedford, I saw her coming out of Adolph's office. She was in there trying to get some money to heat the place this winter, she's scared all the pipes will break. Not a nickel, not from Adolph. He always hated her.

—He didn't hate her, he just didn't like the idea of a big country house like that going to a secretary who...

—Who the old man had been screwing for twenty years? so he leaves her a lousy house without a nickel to run it and Adolph jumps right in and pulls out all the furniture? Where is it anyhow, those two big marquetry chests and those chairs from the...

—In New York. It's all in New York, in storage there. We had to rent this furnished, for a while anyhow till they get their things out, or her things, I think it's all hers it's all kind of confused...

—But I mean what are you doing here anyway Bibbs, this broken down little town how did you...

—We just had to get out of New York that's all, we just found this through an agent and took it. You saw me down there the last time I couldn't even breathe, it's filthy, everything, the air the streets everything, and the noise. They

7

were tearing up the street it sounded like machineguns and then they started blasting right on the corner. They were starting a new building right there on the corner and every time it went off Paul went right up the wall, he still wakes up at night with...

—Man like he's already up the wall, he's been up there since he came back whose fault is that.

—Well it's not his! If you'd been old enough to be...

—No come off it Bibb, I mean all that southern officer bullshit of his? that dress sabre with his name engraved down the blade from that halfass military school he went to? And I mean what he told you his father said? his fucking own father? That it's a damn good thing he was going in as an officer because...

—I've told you! It's not, I never should have told you that it's not your...

—I mean how could he tell you! Like how could anybody tell something like that he's already up the wall, he can't get a job he can't even look for one so he pretends he's setting up his own business? I mean he goes in and tells Adolph he's...

—Well he is.

—He's what, setting up his own business where, here? Like what's he going to do, open a laundry? buy you a washboard and...

—Billy stop it, honestly. It's a consulting, being kind of a consultant, I mean it's what he's done before when he was...

—Paul the bagman.

—Please! Don't, start all that... She was up, through to the kitchen. —Twenty? is that enough?

—Bibb...? He followed her in, —I mean you know what he...

—Please I don't want to talk about it... She'd pulled open a drawer, digging under linen napkins, under placemats, —just twenty? You're sure that's enough?

—It's plenty... and as she bent tucking the napkins back

8

he ran a hand over her arm bared to the shoulder, over the bruise there. —This some of Paul's work?

—I said I don't want to talk about it! She pulled away, —here! I, I just...

—Bumped into a bookcase, great... he thrust the bill into a shirt pocket. —I mean you know why he married you, we all...

—All right! I, I just... she came after him to the front door, —I just wish...

—I wish too, Bibb... he pulled the door open, grazing the newel there, and he was out, shoulders hunched against the chill. —You any better up here? your asthma?

—I don't know yet I, I think so. Will you be all right Billy?

—You kidding?

—But where do you, where are you staying, we never...

—Sheila. Where else.

—I thought that was over. I thought she went to India.

—She came back.

—Will you call? Will you, wait will you hand me the mail? I don't want to come out... She reached a bare arm for it, he slapped the mailbox shut and then stopped by the car stalled on the apron there, rocked it with one hand.

—What's wrong with it.

—I don't know, it just doesn't go. Will you, there's the phone, Billy? Please call me...? She came through looking up to the clock, sat down with a shiver. —Yes hello...? No, no but I expect him any minute. Could he call you back when he... Yes any time, this evening yes any time this evening, I'll tell him yes... She hung it up and left her hands there, resting on it, and her forehead down to rest on the back of a hand drawing breath, drawing breath, till she heard the door.

—Liz...?

—Oh. There was a call for you. Just now, a Mister...

—What the hell is he doing out there!

—Is, who...

—Billy, your God damn brother Billy he's out there under the car, what the hell is he doing here.

—Well he just, I thought he'd...

—The usual? came to borrow money? How did he get here.

—Well he, he just showed up, he...

—He always just shows up. Did you lend him any?

—How could I Paul, I've only got nine dollars left from...

—Good, don't. Any calls?

—Yes just now, Mister Ude? He said he'd call back.

—That's all?

—Yes. No I mean there was a call for Mister McCandless, it was somebody from the IRS Paul when can we get this phone thing straightened out, all I do is answer these calls for...

—Look Liz, I can't help it. I'm trying to get a phone put in here under a company name, as soon as the...

—But when they shut it off in New York the bill was over seven hun...

—That's why I'm putting it under a company name! Now God damn it Liz stop pushing me like this the minute I walk in the door, you'll just have to put up with it. Hang up on them, now look what about your brother. Will you see what the hell he's doing out there?

—Maybe he's trying to fix it, the car I mean, he...

—He couldn't fix a rollerskate. I've got to get that thing fixed, this God damn bus what was I, half an hour late just now? Traffic backed up all the way down 9W to the bridge there.

—On 9W? Was there, was everything all right? I mean...

—What do you mean all right, I just told you traffic's backed up for three miles, police cars wreckers the works...

He'd turned from the kitchen doorway to the one opened under the stairs. He snapped on the light there, —Liz? Look don't let him in the house again, just don't let him in. He doesn't know how to live in a house, he doesn't even know how to flush the toilet when he's...

—No wait Paul wait! I told him not to it's stopping up again, don't...

—Well Christ...

—But I told you not to...

—Too late yes, it's all over the God damn floor.

—Paul wait, Billy...? She was up for the door, —Paul? I'll clean it up, Billy what...

—Come out here a second Paul? We might get this heap started... He let the door go without waiting, was down on his back on the broken stone of the apron. —Starter's jammed. Paul?

—Wait a minute...

—Reach in and turn the key when I get under here.

—Wait a minute Billy wait! The whole God damn thing's tipping, this little stick of wood you've got it jacked up on, you can't...

—Can't wait or I won't be able to see anything... he was already halfway under, bootheels scraping the leaves, the broken stone, —ready?

—Wait... The car swayed, he stood back from it reaching in, licked his lips looking down at the dumb angle of the wooden block, the denimed swell of ribs creased under the rocker panel.

—Well turn it!

He stood off as far as his reach allowed, turned the key and stepped back. —My God it started.

—Turn it off!

His hand darted in to the switch, he stumbled back over boots, over knees all coming upright. —Probably torn some teeth off your flywheel, the starter gear hits that dead spot and just spins.

—Well it, anyhow the God damn thing starts.

—Probably sheared your starter gear too, get a new one put in or it can happen again, happen any time... Wind from

the river caught their collars up, brought down a burst of half yellowed leaves from the maple tree on the corner there.
—Thanks, Paul.

—What do you mean thanks.

—Man like I'm thanking you for this good karma you just gave me that's all, I mean you give somebody a chance to do you a favour and that helps out their karma for the next time around, right? So they ought to thank you, right?

—Look Billy don't try to push my, I didn't ask you to do it did I? Crawl under there in the dark this little stick of wood holding it up the whole God damn car could have...

—Like this...? and the sudden thrust of a boot sent the wood shivering, the car crashed down splashing broken stone under the rocker panel. —Why didn't you, Paul.

—Billy God damn it don't...

—Might have been your last chance when it could still do you some good. Here... he'd reached in to pull the keys from the ignition, tossed them over —kids find the keys in it they'll take it for a joyride and leave it in a ditch. An old heap like this Paul, it wouldn't even be grand larceny.

—You would have wouldn't you! Been me under there, wouldn't you! He was down on one knee brushing leaves aside for the keys, —good karma someday Billy God damn it, I'll show you good karma! But the wind threw his words back to him, blowing up from the river, blowing the leaves up in flurries where his fingers raked them aside, smashed wing, muddied mantle barely distinguishable in the protective coloration of death, he straightened up with the keys looking down the hill where the figure hunched smaller against the wind, and then he stooped to pick up the bird by a leg and hold it away as he turned for the door.

—Paul? I thought I heard the car start. Is it fixed?

—Till the next time.

—What's that you've, oh!

He carried it past her to drop in the trash. —Where's the whisky.

—In the refrigerator, you...

12

—What the hell is it doing in the refrigerator.

—You put it there last night.

—Well why didn't you take it out... The refrigerator door banged against the counter. —He's crazy Liz. That God damn brother of yours, he's crazy.

—Paul please he, I know sometimes he...

—Sometimes! You know what he just did out there?

—I thought he fixed the car, you said...

—He ought to be locked up Liz. He's dangerous. Is this glass clean? He ought to be in Payne Whitney with your uncle strutting around in a cutaway, Uncle William strutting around Payne Whitney with no pants on.

—Like the night you folded up all your clothes and put them in the refrig...

—Liz that never happened! It never happened, it's something you read someplace.

—I thought it was funny.

—Nothing's funny. When did Ude say he'd call back.

—He just said later. Who's Mister Ude.

—Reverend Ude. He's a client. Did you bring in the mail?

—It's, yes it's somewhere, I think I put it...

—Look Liz, we've got to get a system. At least you brought it in, good. Now there's got to be a place for it. If I'm going to get any kind of an operation going here we've got to get a system, I've got to know where the mail is when I walk in, you've got to get a pad there by the phone so I can see who...

—No it's there, there behind the bag of onions when I came in I...

—See that's what I mean. I mean if I'm going to run any kind of operation from here I can't be looking for the mail under a bag of onions. Did my check come?

—I didn't look, I don't...

—God damn bank, somebody in there with a lien they're probably freezing everything I... Paper tore, —listen to this. Dear Customer...

—Paul?

—Does taking ten percent off any initial purchase at the finest furniture specialty store in America sound attractive to you? If so, you'll be happy to know that the...

—Paul what just happened out there. With Billy, you said...

—Nothing. Nothing Liz he's crazy, that's all, he ought to be locked up for his own good, what the hell do we need furniture for. This God damn bank look at it, three payments behind on that loan they're threatening to wipe me out now they're trying to sell me furniture. All we've got is furniture!

—I just wish we did. I just wish I could look up and see something of mine sometimes, those two marquetry chests could go right in the...

—Look they're not going anywhere without paying the God damn storage bill, get all that stuff in here where the hell would we put it.

—We could, someday if we could take out that wall in the living room onto the porch? just open it all up and put in an arch there right out onto the porch and glass it all in, the whole porch, and that old piano from Longview we could...

—Pull out that wall the whole God damn house would fall down Liz what are you talking about, rent somebody's house you want to start knocking walls down? Paper tore.

—I just said, someday...

—Gustav Schak MD, two hundred sixty dollars. Who the hell is Gustav Schak.

—The one I saw last week, the one Jack Orsini sent me to and I had that terrible...

—One visit? Two hundred sixty dollars for one visit?

—Well they did those tests I told you, how awful his nurse was shouting at me I could hardly breathe, that spirometry test I was right in the middle of a spasm and she was shouting at me about...

—Spirometry eighty dollars. CC one hundred dollars, what the hell is CC. Comprehensive consultation, what the...

—Well I don't know Paul! It was all so confused, I felt so awful and his nurse was so rude and he was in such a rush he was leaving for a golf vacation in Palm Springs, I hardly saw him for ten minutes. He got me in as a favour to Orsini, because they need to know what these tests say when I see this specialist next week, this Doctor Kissinger I'm seeing next week and Doctor Schak is sending over the...

—Yes all right Liz, all right but Christ. Two hundred and six...

—I can't help it! I, I don't know what else to...

—All right look. Just send him twenty five dollars and write payment in full on the check. Can you call Orsini?

—I did. He's in Geneva. Some big convention of neurologists or something in Geneva.

—So he goes over, reads a paper, gets in a little skiing at Kitzbühel, stops at Deauville to check out his horses, takes the whole God damn thing off his taxes and he's back in town just in time for another giant publishing party, another giant paperback success...

—But he's been kind to me Paul, he's always been generous with...

—Generous? after the way your father set him up? Look I want to talk to him Liz, the next time you hear from Orsini I want to talk to him.

—I wouldn't Paul I just wouldn't, if he thinks you're interfering with that research thing Daddy set up for him he'll be furious I know he will, he'll be...

—I'm not interfering with a God damn thing, that's not what I want to talk to him about now God damn it Liz don't tell me what to do! He brought the bottle tipped over his glass, —what's that one.

—This? She handed it over, —I can't even tell what country it's from.

—Zaire. Who the hell do we know in, wait. Here, it's for McCandless, stick it up in the door there with the rest of his, where the hell is my VA check... Paper tore, —from those insurance bastards. In order to complete their records in this case pending trial they would like you to make an appointment for a medical examination relevant to your claims against this God damn airline what the hell are they...

—I don't know! I've had seven of them, ten I don't know how many it was four years ago, I don't even remember where I told them it hurt, I can't even...

—Well I can... the paper crumpled in his hand, —bastards. I can tell them, dizziness, headaches... He smoothed it out on the table. —Your failure to complete this appointment may jeopardize your claim for injuries sustained in, I can tell them.

Her head had sunk into her hand where she held it, pulling a deep breath, stood abruptly with a step to the sink for a paper towel blowing her nose there, again with a hollow urgency, looking out. Streetlight brought down another leaf or two on the terrace. —When do you want to eat, she finally said.

—Give me some ice while you're up, will you?

She stood there, looking out. —Paul?

—Who do you know in Eleuthera.

—Nobody she said, the paper towel knotted tight in her hand, turning for the harsh chromo of boats on green water. —Oh it's Edie, a card from Edie.

—She still dragging that Indian around?

—I don't know. I just so long to see her.

—Well I can live without her, I'll tell you that.

—I just wish you wouldn't always have to say that, she's the only, Edie's always been my best friend always, she always...

—Look after the way Grimes fixed me up what do you expect me to...

—That wasn't Edie! Do you think she tells her father what to do? she even knows what he does? That was you and Mister Grimes and the company after Daddy, did I ever tell Daddy what to do? Did anybody ever blame me for Daddy?

—All right Liz but God damn it, Edie saw what happened didn't she? when your father was out and Grimes moved up as chairman? Grimes got what he wanted didn't he? did he have to push me out too? Couldn't Edie, your best friend

Edie couldn't she even put in a word? Right now couldn't she? One word from Grimes to Adolph, one word anyplace one word from Grimes to this God damn airline he sits on their board, he sits on the board of their God damn insurance company too this one, this one right here the one that wrote you this letter, Grimes pulled it off before didn't he? that policy VCR had on your father? Some question how your father met his death and they dig in their heels, Grimes takes off his VCR hat and puts on his insurance company hat, they pay off the twenty million without a whimper, VCR cash flow picks up their stock jumps a few points and there's Grimes back in the driver's seat, whole thing was God damn strange Liz. That twenty million coming right when they needed it did you get me some ice?

She steadied a hand on the chair, sat down and said —no, near a whisper.

—I mean it's yours it's going to be yours, one word to Adolph to release a few thousand we'd be out of the hole, it's just taking part of what's ours out a little ahead of time, part of what's accumulated in the trust we won't even miss it when the whole thing comes through it's nothing, a few thousand, one word to Adolph and we'd be...

—Well he won't. Billy just talked to Adolph and he won't even...

—Billy that God damn Billy! What the hell does he do with it, he gets as much from the trust every month what does he do with it! You see him just now? he walks into Adolph looking like that what's Adolph going to do, dig into the trust for you and there's Billy with a dirty hand out? What the hell does he do with it! Liz?

—What.

—I said he gets as much as...

—Well what do we do with it! The paper towel came apart in her hands —what do we do with it, we get as much as he does Paul what do we do with it!

—No now wait Liz that's, wait. We're trying to do something, trying to do something Liz trying to live like civilized, get out of the God damn hole here live like civilized people Liz I'm trying to build something here, have something to show for it he just wants to show his contempt for it, for everything, worse the use he can find for it the better that's what he does with it. Rock bands, queers, spades out there dealing drugs and all this Buddhist crap you know he just tried to pull that on me again out there? that karma crap he got from those Tibetan creeps he had following him around? Same thing Liz the same God damn thing, that greasy little burr head monk in the red blanket doing him a favour taking his money same God damn thing, giving him a chance to show his contempt for the money, show his contempt for the people he gives it to and the system it came out of like all these God damn kids parading around with their guitars and their hair dyed pink they'll scam, con, deal, the worse fraud they can skim a few dollars off of the better the one God damn thing they won't do is work for it, did he ever earn a nickel? work one God damn day in his life?

—Well he has Paul, he has, that's why he was here just now he'd been driving a...

—Borrow some money, that's why he was here just now wasn't it? tried to borrow some money?

—Well but that's not the...

—What I'm telling you Liz, what I'm trying to tell you. Work for money means you've got some respect for it, he just wants it to show his contempt for anybody that works for it, anybody trying to do something, trying to put things together, build something like your father did we both know that's what it's about Liz, what the whole God damn thing is about. I came in there your father could see I'd go in and do the job, that I could step in and size things up, see the big picture and take a few risks to bring it off everything your God damn brother will never do, won't even try to that's why he's still getting back at me, getting back at your father, getting back at anybody who's trying to do the job just get out of the hole here. Get that alimony load off my back they've scheduled the hearing, that should be any day

18

now just these bills, all these God damn bills... He raised the glass and brought it away, pulling a hand over his mouth —tell me how I always get this glass with the chip in the rim? Liz?

—What.

—I just asked you the, problem I just think you don't really listen to me sometimes, don't really get in there and back me up trying to tell you what I'm trying to do here, trying to put the pieces together your God damn brother in there pulling them apart I'm getting things going Liz, three or four things I've got a spade in here from Guinea says he's in parliament there, polo coat grease spots down the front of it he's got the State Department sending him around to look at prisons and broilers, get their prison system out of the tenth century and set up broiler production may have to take him out to Terre Haute broiler farms and a big federal prison right down the road work it in with this other big client, big drug company's got these animal nutritionists from Europe want to see pigs, Terre Haute's got to be pigs get them out there and show them the pigs and this Ude, this Reverend Ude you said called? Nickel and dime radio station going right into nationwide television global coverage he's already moved in on these African missions, spread the gospel get things moving he's already got this Voice of Salvation radio station right out there Liz, old stamping grounds move in take a few risks and bring it off just get out of the hole here, all these God damn bills here look at them bank loans, storage, travel cards, Diners Club American Express lawyers doctors, ask what we do with the money that's what we do with it, one visit two hundred sixty dollars for one visit that's what you...

—I can't help it Paul! If you, do you think I like it going to doctors? Like going to, like you going to restaurants? Plane tickets, car rentals motel bills hotels that's what all this is do you think I...

—Look, just once. Let's try to get this straight just once, Liz. I'm trying to get something going. You don't get something going over a ham sandwich and a beer. You don't take the Greyhound bus and stay at the Y when you're digging up new accounts. You don't nickel and dime unless all you're after is nickels and dimes and you won't even get those now look, I've got a couple of...

—Put it out, Paul.

—What?

—The cigarette. Put it out.

Instead he swept up his glass and turned abruptly through the doorway, in to stand before the empty fireplace drawing smoke, blowing it out, staring back at the wet rag on the wet floor under the stairs. —Liz...? He threw the cigarette smoking into the grate. —Got to do something about this God damn toilet. Liz?

—What.

—I said we can't live like this. Try to live like civilized people your brother comes in here pisses all over the floor we can't even...

—All right! Just leave it, I'll clean it up just leave it.

—Anyplace he goes, somebody cleaning up after him every God damn place he goes. You clean up, Adolph cleans up that's all Adolph's ever done is clean up after him. That car wreck in Encino? and Yale? He's kicked out of every school he gets near so they buy his way into Yale, you know what he told me once? that they'd held him back in eighth grade because he was such a great hockey player? You know God damn well why they...

—Paul what's the point! You shout at me, Billy shouts at me as though I could do anything, as though I'm to blame what's the point! It's almost over, a few more months he'll be twenty five what's the point of...

—The point Liz, the point is he ought to be locked up, he ought to be locked up till he's twenty five or he'll never be twenty five. The point is this trust brings in about five percent, Adolph says he can't invest for income what about Grimes? He sits on the board of the bank that's co-trustee doesn't he? One word from Grimes, do you think he'd say

20

one word for any of us? with Billy in there? that party they found Squeekie passed out naked in your father's bathtub when she was fifteen do you think her father's going to raise a...

—Oh Paul that was a story, that never happened it was just a story that somebody...

—That Edie, she's Edie's sister isn't she? Isn't that how we knew, from Edie? after your father called Grimes? You think Grimes would raise a finger for any of us after that? Adolph can't invest it for income he has to invest for long term growth, one word from Grimes to his God damn bank it could be bringing in twelve percent, fifteen, you think he'll say it? With Adolph handing it right out to clean up after Billy, that Indian Mexican whatever she was Adolph paying her off and this Sheila, buying a ticket to get her and her guitar and dope and mantras and the rest of her Buddhist junk on a plane to India, long term growth what long term? Some next generation that's going to look like a God damn zoo? Billy out there sticking it into anything that walks and Adolph right behind them pulling down their skirts and paying them off so they won't put a monkey in the family tree and we can't even do that, we can't even...

—Paul it's not my fault! It's, it's not my...

—I didn't say that. I didn't say that Liz. I didn't mean...

—But you did you do! You always do you, I go to the doctor every time I see a doctor you blame me for the bills even the plane crash, you even blame me for that you...

—Liz stop it...! He put down his emptied glass, coming round the table. —How could I blame you for the plane crash.

—Well you do. Every time we go to bed, that lawsuit you started against them with mine every time we...

—Liz don't, look. I'm sorry. I didn't mean...

—You're always sorry, you always, no don't. Don't, just give me that napkin, don't you're messing my hair...

But he came down, closer, his breath stirring it, —Liz? Remember that first time? after that funeral? When I leaned over in the car and told you I was crazy about the back of your neck and...

—No please... she pulled away, cringed lower, his hand on her bared shoulder —you're hurting my...

—Well what the hell are you wearing this thing for! He was back out of reach, a hand out for his glass, —you haven't worn it since summer.

—But what, I just...

—Show off your bruise? Sleeveless thing to show off your God damn combat badge to the neighbors and anybody who...

—I don't know any neighbors!

—And your brother what about your brother, your...

—I said I'd bumped into a bookcase. When do you want supper.

—A bookcase... He held the bottle over the glass, held it the way he poured drinks, two handed, one holding the bottle up and away against the other forcing it down, forcing the neck down over the glass, and —a bookcase, he muttered again at the sink for a splash of water, turning past her through the doorway. —Where. What bookcase. Will you show me one God damn bookcase? Everything else here but a bookcase it's like a museum, like living in a museum. Liz...? He'd got as far as the door and he turned on a lamp there, something Japanese under a silk shade that cast the reflection of his unfinished face in the glass-framed sampler hung above it. —Did that agent tell you when they're getting this stuff out of here? Liz?

—They just said his wife's supposed to come for it.

—That means we've got to live with every stick the way she left it? Pictures, mirrors, plants all those God damn plants in the dining room watering all those plants? He raised his glass, brought it down half emptied coming across the room to put it on the mantel his hand's breadth from a china dog there, and no larger. —Looks like she'll be here any minute, whole place looks like she walked out for lunch and expects to be back for dinner... He ran a finger over the china dog, brought it up close and it snapped in his hands. —Liz? Got to get somebody in here to clean... he fitted the halves together, placed them back and came down blowing on them, pressing them close, blowing again and brushing away with his hand, taking his glass, —that list he left? The plumber, electrician, firewood, some woman on it who comes in and cleans? He'd reached the alcove where he raised his glass and finished it, stood looking down the black crown of the empty road and then ran a finger over the pane and looked at it. —Get her in here to wash the windows, so smoked up you can't see out... He turned with the emptied glass, —know where that list is? Get her in here to clean things up, see if she can oww...!

—Paul?

—Does this coffee table have to be right in the middle of the God damn room here? Bang my leg every time I walk past it.

—Where else can it go? There's no place to...

—Got to get this toilet fixed.

—Well what shall I do! I told you I called the plumber and they have to get in that room to reach some trap in the drain.

—Tell them to break the lock. Just tell them to break the God damn padlock. This McCandless, Argentina Zaire wherever the hell he is, look at these smoked up windows he's probably in a cancer ward someplace what are we supposed to do. He rents us the house with that room locked off and a lease that says he reserves access to his papers in there, what do we do? Sit here waiting for him to show up looking for an old laundry ticket while your brother stands here pissing all over the floor? You know where that list is? Just call and tell them to break that padlock and get in there and fix the God damn drain... He was back standing over the bottle, —they can put on a new lock and give the key to the agent, if McCandless ever shows up she can hand it over.

—You'll have to leave me cash.

—Let them send the bill to the agent.

—For the cleaning woman, she...

—You sure this is all the mail? He sat down again, sweeping it toward him, —my VA check, where the hell is it... Instead he found the newspaper. —What about supper.

—There's that ham, what's left of it.

—See this thing in the paper? these gooks adopting dogs and eating them?

—Please, put it out Paul. I'm having trouble breathing.

—We spend five dollars a week here feeding somebody else's cat while these slopes walk into the ASPCA and go home to a dachshund barbecue. See this gook in there patting a Saint Bernard on the...

—Paul, put it out.

—All right! He jammed the cigarette into her teacup, —takes it home to the kiddies whole God damn family eats for a week, can't even...

—They can't help it! She was suddenly up, past him into the living room where she simply stood.

—What? What do you mean they can't...

—I just wish you didn't have to keep calling them slopes and gooks, it's all such a long time ago and you can't call them that, all of them gooks... She bent down for the rag on the wet floor, —the ones who were our friends the ones who...

—Liz God damn it I was there! They're all gooks all of them, every God damn one of them I was there Liz...! and his hand, in a sudden tremor reaching for the telephone, knocked over the glass. —It's probably Ude.

She came on to the trash, caught breath dangling the wet rag that moment before she dropped it in where the feathers, mottled? or just mud spattered, still shone in brownish pink at the throat. It was a dove.

Climbing the hill from the river, stopping for breath, an old dog fell in beside her as she started to climb again, every effort of hers caught up in its plodding step, head carried low going white down muzzle and flews, elbow and hock gone hairless and callused, its dry black coat thinned toward the tail. Almost to the top she stopped again, one hand steadied on a pale of the fence as she drew the other across her forehead, and noticed the dog's nails were done bold ruby red. They crossed the road together side by side, as though they had crossed it side by side together many times before right up the crumbled brick to the front door where the dog crowded against her knee, left staring out there as she closed the door behind her.

25

Somewhere, the roar of a vacuum cleaner dwindled to a whine. —Hello? she called, —hello? Madame Socrate...? At her elbow a blouse in pale green batiste rag remnant, pearl buttoned, draped the newel. A pail of water barred the kitchen doorway. —Madame Socrate? And she extended a hand to the massive floral print descending the stairs, bare feet in a clatter of vacuum cleaner accessories. —I'm, I'm Mrs. Booth, Eliz...

—Madame.

—Yes, well... her hand dropped, —bonjour... she stepped aside. —I'm glad you could come is everything, ça va?

—On a besoin d'un nouvel aspirateur.

—Yes a, a what, quoi?

—On a besoin d'un nouvel aspirateur, Madame.

—Oh yes. Oui.

—Celui-ci est foutu.

—Of course yes the, the vacuum cleaner oui yes it is quite an old one isn't it mais, mais c'est très important de, qu'on nettoyer tout les, le dust vous savez le, le dust? Parce que mon asthma...

—Madame?

—Yes well I just mean, I mean vous faites du bon travail quand même... she backed off, —I mean it's an awfully warm day and you've done a lovely job quand même...

—Oui Madame.

The equipment clattered by and she bent to catch her calf where she'd hit it against the coffee table, sank to the edge of the frayed love seat. Ash lay spilled from the fireplace in a fine grey fall on the hearth. Across the room, a delicate length of cobweb joining the alcove's draperies caught the sun striking through from the dining room. —Madame Socrate? Vous avez fini ici? cleaning in here, I mean?

—Madame? from the kitchen.

—Ici? cette salle, c'est tout...

—C'est pas sale Madame!

—No I didn't mean, not sale not dirty no, salle, I mean, I

mean chambre, cette chambre? c'est fini?

—Oui Madame.

When the telephone rang she was standing at the mantel piecing together the china dog. Through the dining room, she almost went down crossing the kitchen floor awash with the woman on hands and knees dipping the green batiste in wide sweeps from the pail. —I'm sorry... she got by, and then —hello...? No, I... He's not here no, I don't know how to reach... hello? Hello? She hung up, brought her feet to the chair rung as the pail sloshed closer, —honestly! Why people are so rude!

—Madame? from the floor there.

—These people looking for, qui cherchent Monsieur McCandless. Est-ce que, est-ce qu'il y avait des, des téléphones, I mean any calls this morning? ce matin?

—Oui Madame, beaucoup.

—But I mean, you mean there've been lots of calls? She stared at the blank pad beside the telephone, —but who. Who were they?

—Je sais pas Madame.

—But I mean who were they for, then. I mean, pour Monsieur McCandless you mean? Ce matin?

—Il était fâché, oui.

—What?

—Ce matin, oui. Il était fâché.

—Who. Qui.

—Ce monsieur oui, le même qui est venu ce matin.

—What, looking for him? Somebody came here looking for him you mean? Monsieur McCandless?

—Monsieur McCandless, oui. Il était fâché.

—Yes well you said that, he was angry you said that, but I mean who. Qui.

—Monsieur McCandless, oui... The wet swath swept closer, underfoot, —cette pièce là, il ne pouvait pas entrer. Il dit qu'on a changé la serrure. Il était fâch...

—No now wait wait, attendez. He was, you mean Monsieur McCandless était ici? here? He was here?

—Ce matin, oui Madame.

—But he, I mean why didn't you tell me! What did he...

—La pièce là... with a wet thrust at the door behind her, —il se fâchait parce-qu'il ne pouvait pas entrer quand il est venu ce mat...

—Yes well you said that, and he was fâché because he couldn't get in I mean why didn't he call? They put on a new lock last week when they fixed a pipe in there why didn't he call, the agent has the key he could have gone to the real estate agent couldn't he? Did he leave any message or anything? Where we could, où on peut lui téléphoner? or if, when he'll be back? S'il retourner?

—Non Madame.

—Well I don't know what he expects us to do... The pail lurched closer and she got up, got by it, —he didn't say anything? Rien? I mean where we could, où on peut lui trouver? She turned in the doorway, —where these people can call him? I mean I'm a little fâché myself... Steadied against a dining room chair she slipped off her shoes and her steps, shorn of purpose, took her back to the living room, to the mantel. —Madame? Madame Socrate...? She pressed the broken dog together, —ce chien? Qu'est-ce que arrive avec ce chien que, que c'est cassé?

—Madame?

—No nothing, never mind. Rien... She'd turned her back on it, turned her steps irresolute as her gaze fallen vacant where words abruptly snared it, seized upon its own privation shaped here to no purpose,

LOSS OF $412 MILLION, A RECORD, REPORTED BY GENERAL MOTORS

yesterday's headline or the day's before, of no more relevance then than now in its blunt demand to be read, building the clutter, widening the vacancy, driving it elsewhere, anywhere, the still embrace of the armchair there beyond the hearth to flee even that for the front door's glass paneled symmetry.

—Madame?

—Oh! I, you startled me...

—Vous parliez du chien, Madame? Out there on the brick, the old dog hunched scratching a callused elbow with those red nails. —Je ne connais pas ce chien Madame.

—It's not, never mind, ça ne fait rien it's just, it just acts like it lives here no wait, wait I've meant to ask you. Ces meubles? all this furniture? I mean on dit que c'est le, les meubles du Madame?

—Madame?

—Du Madame McCandless oui, qu'elle vient pour le, to move it all out I mean? pour le retrouver?

—Sais pas Madame.

—Because it's all, I mean some of it's quite lovely isn't it it's, c'est comme un petit musée isn't it. I mean ces chaises? they're rosewood aren't they, I wouldn't leave chairs like that for tenants you don't even know, and this vase? It's Sèvres isn't it? n'est-ce pas? Because everything goes together so beautifully, I've never been able to make a place look so, just look so right. Even these... she bent to blow at petals nodding in pink silk, it might have been cyclamen, stood away from the puff of dust. —Madame? Madame Socrate...? From the kitchen the rush of a torrent of water, the clatter of the pail in the sink. —She must have left suddenly, did she? all of a sudden? Or she wouldn't have left everything out like this... And back in the kitchen doorway, —Madame? C'est combien du temps que elle, que Madame McCandless, I mean how long she's been gone?

—Madame? The pail came to the floor.

—How long she's, quand elle est partie?

—Sais pas Madame.

—No but if you've been working for them, I mean you must have some idea when she, quelque idée...

—Sais pas Madame.

—But... she stood there, silenced by the back turned to

29

her, the sullen ease of the arm wiping down white surfaces, the stove, the sink, the sill and there beyond it discoloured leaves filling the terrace in broken sunlight through the haphazard limbs of a mulberry tree, and then abruptly —elle est jolie?

—Madame?

—Is she, ce Madame McCandless, est-ce qu'elle est jolie?

—Sais pas Madame.

—No but I mean you must know if she's pretty, belle? Is she, if she's young? I mean vous connaissez ce Madame puis...

—Connais pas Madame.

—But she, you don't know her? Vous ne connaissez I mean you don't even know her? But that's, I mean that's odd isn't it, n'est-ce pas?

—Oui Madame.

Back in the living room she picked up the newspaper, put it down and picked up the field guide to birds where she studied the ragged crest and squat self importance of red breasted merganser. She had never seen one.

—Madame? in the kitchen doorway now, squeezing on worn pumps.

—Oh, oh you're finished now yes, un moment... Through the dining room she got the kitchen drawer open digging under napkins, under placemats, —that's, c'est vingt cinq dollars?

—Trente dollars Madame.

—Oh...? She came up with another five.

—Et la monnaie pour l'autobus Madame.

—Oh the, your carfare yes, yes combien...

—Un dollar Madame, deux fois cinquante.

—Oui... she got her purse, —et merci...

—Le mardi prochain Madame?

—Next Tuesday yes well, well no. No I mean that's what I wanted to speak to you about, I mean qu'il ne serait pas nécessaire que, that it's maybe it's better to just wait and I call you again when I, que je vous téléphoner...

—Vous ne voulez pas que je revienne.

—Yes well I mean but not next Tuesday, I mean I'll telephone you again I hope you understand Madame Socrate it's just that I, que votre travail est très bon everything looks lovely but...

—J'comprends Madame... the door came open, —et la clef.

—Oh the key yes, yes thank you merci I hope you, oh but wait, wait could you, est-ce que vous pouvez trouver le, les cartes... with a stabbing gesture at the mailbox, —là, dans le, des cartes...? And with the mail clasped to her she still kept standing, watching the steady lurch of the floral print down the hill, the splash of lipstick red hibiscus against the shoal of leaves cast up along the black current of the road rising toward her from the river, her chin sunk in an effort for breath. When she raised it again the telephone had stopped ringing. She closed the door, stepped back from the disheveled burst of red in the glass-framed sampler hung there thrusting her hair back, piercing that staled semblance to the entire alphabet laid out beneath the glass in needlework repose and the reproof of consecrated leisure, the mundane desolation in the lines of verse stitched below: While we wait for the napkin, the soup gets cold...

She came into the kitchen with the halves of the china dog from the mantel, found glue and stood there at the sink pressing the pieces together. An ear snapped off, and she walked more slowly to the trash, her thumb to her lips with a fleck of blood. Here in the top of the trash lay that harsh glimpse of boats off Eleuthera and, down wiping it clean of coffee grounds, a torn piece of a letter in a generous and unfamiliar hand drawn out in severed fragments, anyone's fault, the last thing I, for you to believe me, what else to do. Deeper down, under the wet batiste remnant shorn of its buttons, she found the torn half of the envelope with the Zaire stamp URGENT PLEASE FORWARD, picking it through till the phone brought her up with her thumb to her lips, tasting blood, —Mrs who...? No I'm afraid not, I'm not... Well it's

a very small street and I mean I don't even know who lives...
No now listen I can't join your march against cancer, I don't
like cancer I don't even like to think about it that's all, now...
yes you're welcome goodbye.

Movement brought her eyes up, arrested by the clock; all
that moved was the dapple of the leaf-filtered sun on the
kitchen's white wall, still as breathing till she turned for the
radio which promptly informed her that Milwaukee had
topped the Indians four to one, but not of what game they
were playing, and she turned it off, poured a glass of milk
to carry up the stairs where she turned on the television and
slipped off her blouse, sunk against pillows.

> Where can I change dollars?
> Dónde puedo cambiar dolares?

She moved her own lips.

> Can I change dollars in the hotel?
> Puedo cambiar dolares en el hotel?

Her lips moved with those on the screen.

> At what time does the bank open?
> A qué hora...

—A qué hora... Even here, where the leaf-broken sun
climbed from bared shoulder over her parted lips, the movement continued on the lids closed against it, penetrated in
diffuse chiaroscuro where the movement composed the stillness and herself sealed up, time adrift as the sun reached
further, shattered by the telephone. She spilled the milk
reaching for it.

—Who operator...? Yes it is, speaking yes, it's me speaking I mean who's the call from, who... Oh! Yes put her on
operator yes, Edie? How wonderful yes where are you, are
you back? I got your card from Eleuth... oh. No I'd just so
hoped to see you... You mean you're there now with Jack?
I thought he was in Geneva, his office told me he... Oh
honestly Edie, did you...? Well didn't everyone tell you that's

what would happen? just like that frightful little Burmese who ran off with all your... Oh I hope not no, wait I can't hear you...

She came stretching the line off the foot of the bed where a mouse was flattening a cat with a sledgehammer and turned it off. —What? No it's, it was just some noise in the street Edie when will you be back...? Oh I wish I could I don't see how, we're just getting settled here and Paul's been so busy with all his... No it's a house it's a beautiful old Victorian house right up on the Hudson with a tower, there's a tower on the corner it's all windows that's where I am now, you look right out on the river and the trees, all the leaves are... No not yet we've just rented it, not from anybody I mean nobody we know but you'd love how it's furnished it's all, rosewood chairs and sideboards and the draperies in the alcoves all heavy silk lined and gold and the loveliest lamps and silk flowers I can't wait for you to see it it's just, c'est comme un petit musée, tout... Oh Edie, does it? really...? No well sort of practicing I guess yes, I mean the woman who came in to, today, who came in to lunch today yes a lady I've just met here, she's lived a lot in Haiti and came over for lunch and all we spoke was French, I haven't really... No I know there are just loads of interesting people we just haven't been here that long but Paul you know Paul meets everyone, he's been so busy with all his new clients there was a big story about one of them in the paper today and Paul thinks the next... what? No, honestly? He hasn't mentioned it to me but I mean what did your father say... Oh Edie honestly... Yes well Paul is sort of southern, I mean when he really wants to be but he's never even seen Longview and he knows how your father feels about him, I can't imagine what he thought he could, wait a minute...

The box of tissue was out of reach and she was up for it and back, —Edie...? sopping up the spilled milk, —no it's, it's all fine Edie honestly Edie it's fine, it's not really Paul's fault he's just, he gets short-tempered sometimes and things haven't gone that well for him since Daddy but he's really trying hard to... No, no it's just so much better with all this clean air after New York and thank Jack for that lovely man he sent me to, that Doctor... who? You mean the girl we knew at Saint Tim's? Oh how awful... yes and after that terrible boy with the motorcycle how really awful... No I know it Daddy always said that, he always said her father was the best senator money could buy but when we were in Washington he always... No, against her father? he's running against Cettie's father...? Oh I know it yes, you've met him down there? but I mean isn't he black...? Oh Edie honestly, you mustn't... No of course I won't I won't tell a soul but your father will simply die if he ever... Oh Edie honestly...! No I know it doesn't, but... Where, with Squeekie? I thought she was in Hawaii with that bass player she found in... oh how awful, really...? No I know it's just money but it's still rather awful, she just always believes whatever she... No he's still around, he was here last week he showed up driving a moving van someplace but you know he and Paul can't stand the sight of... No it's not just that it's that and the estate and all the lawsuits and the trust, Adolph and the trust I can't wait for it to be over, he's just so angry at everybody and he's got this girl Sheila she's all beads and her hair's an inch long and everything's Buddhism and dope and their friends, I mean I thought Buddhism was supposed to be getting freed from desire and selfishness and all these ego things they've got one friend with filthy hair eight feet long piled on his head like a cowpie that's what they call him, Cowpie, he's from Akron I mean I've never seen so much bickering and egos it's just all so depressing it's just so sad Edie, it's really just all about money and it's just so sad. I mean even this girl's father, Sheila's father, he's got a dry cleaner's down on the east side and pays her rent where Billy's living he thought Billy was rich and just blames him for everything, when she went off to India he tried to... what? Oh Edie I'm sorry I didn't mean to go on so, it just all gets... I know it yes I know it but... No she's still in that nursing home Jack found for her nobody sees her, nobody goes to visit her she doesn't know you if you do, she just seems to sleep and Adolph complains about the bills and nobody... No I'm fine Edie honestly, I'm fine I just told you nothing's the matter, I've been... I haven't no, I mean it was going to be sort of a novel but I haven't worked on it since we got here I haven't written a word I haven't even looked at it I've, I've been so busy with, with people here a cancer charity and I'm, I mean I've even started Spanish lessons I just started them, just now when you called, I'd just come back when you called...

She pushed the milk-sodden heap away and brought a fresh tissue to her face, —Edie? I just so long to see you I wish you could visit, it's all so, it's such a beautiful day it's so gentle and warm for fall and the leaves are turning all yellows, all greens and yellows with the sun on them and there's one, one right down on the river with some red that's, that's just... Oh I hope so Edie I hope so, you were sweet to call but it's costing you a fortune, we'd better... Edie? goodbye...

She sat studying the blood fleck on her thumb until cries from the street brought her to the windows, boys (for some reason always all of them, boys) shambling up the hill below her on gusts of bold obscenities turning her back for the hall, the stairs, down getting breath at an alcove window. On the corner opposite, the old man from the house above bent sweeping leaves into a dustpan, straightened up carrying the thing level before him like an offering, each movement, each shuffled step reckoned anxiously toward an open garbage can where he emptied it with ceremonial concern, balanced the broom upright like a crosier getting his footing, wiping a dry forehead, perching his glasses square and lifting his bald gaze on high to branches yellow-blown with benisons yet to fall. She fled for the kitchen. Phone in one hand, the other flurried pages of the directory till she stopped, and dialed. —Yes hello? I'm calling about, do you have flights to Montego Bay...? Yes well I don't know exactly which day but, I mean I just want to know the fare... What? Oh, round trip I guess, yes. I mean it would have to be round trip, wouldn't it...

From the terrace, where she came out minutes later, the sun still held the yellowing heights of the maple tree on the lower lawn's descent to a lattice fence threatening collapse under a summer exuberance of wild grape already gone a sodden yellow, brown spotted, green veined full as hands in its leaves' lower reaches toward the fruitless torment of a wild cherry tree, limbs like the scabrous barked trunk itself wrenched, twisted, dead where one of them sported wens the size of a man's head, cysts the size of a fist, a graceless Laocoön of a tree whose leaves where it showed them were shot through with bursts neither yellow nor not, whose branches were already careers for bittersweet just paling yellow, for the Virginia creeper in a vermilion haste to be gone. She looked up for the cry of a jay, for the sheer of its blue arc down the length of the fence and then back to lark bunting, red crossbill, northern shrike, lesser yellowlegs fluttering by on the pages of the bird book opened on her lap while here, in the branches of the mulberry tree above her, nothing moved but a squirrel's mindless leap for the roof of the house and she sat back, her stained face raised bared for the sun gone now even from the top of the maple, gone this abruptly behind the mountain with not even a cloud in what sky these trees allowed to trace its loss leaving only a chill that trembled the length of her, sent her back in where she'd come from.

Stark through past the newel a figure stood outside the front door where a knock still seemed to echo, something sharper, more insistent, brisk as the close-cropped head cocked at her approach.

—Yes...? she opened the door on brown speckled tweed, —what...

—McCandless? He stood drawn up there in ochre trousers to barely her height.

—Oh, oh come in yes I'm so glad you came back, we...

—Is he here?

—Who. I mean I thought you...

—McCandless, I just told you. Is this the house?

—Well yes this is his house but...

—Who are you, his latest?

—His, his latest what, I don't...

—First time I ever knew him to have a redhead. Is he here?

—I don't know where he is no and I'm not, I don't know who you are but I'm not his first redhead his, his latest anything, we're just renting his...

—Just relax now, I don't want the details. When was he here last.

—He was here this morning but...

—Where did he go.

—I don't know! I don't know where he went I didn't see him I don't even know him! And now wait no you're not coming in. . . she strained the door against the point of his boot.

—Just hold on now, hold on... the round eyes darted past her, down the front of the blouse she'd pulled on, back to hers, —no difference to me what he's dipping his dingus in these days, I just stopped by to talk to him. You just give him a message when you see him, will you? Tell him Lester stopped by for a talk?

—But I don't see him and who, Lester who...

—You just tell him Lester... the toe of the boot withdrew, —he'll know... and she got the door closed, watched the brisk strut of spindly ochre legs across the black crown of the road, still standing there when a black car pulled away from the hedge above in a swirl of leaves and flattened the dustpan on the turn down the hill. Back in the kitchen, the radio alerted her that thirty five million Americans were functionally illiterate and another twenty five million couldn't read at all and she snapped it off, filled a jar to water the plants and spilled it in a lunge for the phone, for a pencil, for anything handy to write on, —yes just a minute... she opened the bird book and got down the number under red breasted merganser. She was back up in the bedroom but-

toning a fresh blouse when the downstairs toilet flushed.
—Paul...?

—Who is it.

—Paul is that you?

—Now look Mister Mullins, I can't help you... he'd already seized the phone. —He's not here, he doesn't live here, I don't know where he is and I don't want to know, if you... Well why the hell didn't she just stay in India! There's not a God damn thing we can... yes I'm sorry too, goodbye!

—Paul you didn't have to be so rude to him, the poor man's just...

—Liz I'm sick and tired of the poor man! There's not a God damn thing we can do for the poor man and his crazy daughter the sooner he gets that through his head the better. He says she was supposed to go to some ashram two weeks ago he hasn't heard from her since, out there in the woods with your God damn brother seeking enlightenment all she's doing is getting laid, if they want to drag around wearing mantras and ringing bells what the hell are we supposed to do about it? Go right on cleaning up after your God damn...

—Yes but, well I mean if you could just try to be... she'd come round behind him to switch on the light, —to sound a little bit reassuring...

—What the hell is there to reassure him about! They're up in the woods shooting dope banging on their guitars like that night we had to sit through them playing down in that empty storefront they hung up some yellow rags and called it a temple? Sounded like a fire in a pet store what the hell's reassuring about that... He was up with an empty glass in his hand, —minute I walk in the door it's the same God damn thing, cleaning up after your brother the minute I pick up the phone...

—Paul! what, that grease on your face and your shirt's, what happened...

—Cleaning up after your God damn brother I just told you! The car right in the middle of the West Side Highway the God damn car stalled I could have been killed out there trying to start it, I told you he couldn't fix a rollerskate didn't I? Bunch of spades in a tow truck finally showed up and hauled it in took me for every God damn cent I had on me, in there for an hour trying to call you what the hell was going on? Busy busy busy what the hell was going on?

—I'm not... she sat down, eyes lowered to his hand straining the bottle over the rim of the glass, —I don't know, I...

—An hour Liz, I tried to call you for an hour. What the hell was going on!

—Well it, Edie called.

—For an hour? Edie called for an hour?

—Well she, I mean it couldn't have been a whole hour she just wanted to...

—Liz it was an hour, one solid God damn hour I couldn't reach you nobody could, that whole list I gave you? these calls I've been waiting for? State Department calling about this spade with his prisons and chicken factories did they call? and these pigs? Drug company bringing in these nutritionists for a look at these pigs did they call?

—No they, I mean nobody called about...

—How do you know they didn't. Look. You're on the phone for an hour with Edie, somebody calls they get a busy how do you know they called Liz I'm trying to get something going here, line up these clients tell them to check with my home office and you're talking to Edie? Just some support Liz, just backing me up till I get things off the ground that's all I ask isn't it? Sit around the house here you haven't got a God damn thing to do all day you can't just do that? Take this Reverend Ude, still scraping the red clay off his shoes he's got to have somebody that can step in there and get the job done, nationwide television a media center his Africa radio Voice of Salvation got all the God damn pieces he needs some good clear hard headed thinking in there to put them together, got him in today's paper's what he's supposed to call me about, if he thought he's hooking up with somebody's operating out of a back kitchen office files under a bag of onions think he'd ever call back?

—But he did Paul, I mean that's what I...

—What you what. He called and you're on the phone to Edie? Biggest break I've got going, he calls and he can't get through because you're talking to Edie what did she want.

—She just, I told you she just called, she's on a trip and...

—Her whole God damn life's a trip. He put his glass down empty, —why doesn't she just buy Eleuthera and slam the door.

—She's not even there, she's in Montego Bay. She bumped into Jack Orsini coming back from Geneva and he took her to Montego Bay.

—Didn't I tell you? Reads a ten minute paper in Geneva, stops at Eleuthera to pick up your flaky blonde they hop over to Montego Bay to sit around the pool and he writes the whole God damn thing off as a medical conference, isn't that what I told you? Did you tell her I want to talk to him?

—Well she, it wasn't really the...

—I told you last week, the next time you hear from him I want to talk to him did you tell her that?

—Well not, yes I told her yes, yes she said he'd call you. She said he'll call you when he gets back, she...

—I mean this is important Liz, I mean this is what I mean about these phone calls, getting these important phone calls if we're going to get things going around here. Adolph told me Orsini's trying to hit the estate for another hundred thousand, did I tell you? Adolph says...

—Oh Paul honestly, Adolph says... She was swinging wide the refrigerator door, —didn't I ask you not to get into that it will just make things worse...

—Look don't get ahead of me Liz! You're always trying to get in there ahead of me, here put some ice in this will you? Orsini's sitting on this eight million dollar foundation your father set up for him now he comes up for another hundred thousand operating expenses, tells Adolph he wants to keep things going to carry out your father's wishes what happened to the eight million? Straps a few people down and puts them to sleep, checks their eye movements to track down their dreams now he needs a hundred thousand to publish their findings, I mean what the hell happened to the eight million? Look, Orsini may be looking around for an investment that's all. Some idle cash looking for a quiet place to hide out, straight business that's all, if he wants to spend his time lying around the pool with some spaced out...

—All right! Just, just stop calling Edie a flaky blonde. When do you want dinner, there's this chicken thing.

—Oh come on, Liz. What's she doing playing tickledick in the hot tub with Jack Orsini, put some water in this will you? I thought she got married, that Indian creep last winter called himself a medical student with the long dirty diapers I thought she was Mrs Jheejheeboy, where the hell's Mister Jheejheeboy?

—Well she's not Mrs Jheejheeboy I don't know where he is, they're separated. Now do you want dinner?

—Just like to see the look on her father's face when he paid off Mister Jheejhee...

—He doesn't even know about it.

—Know about it? Grimes? He pays off every time she ties the can to one, only time he got off free was the Burmese that took off with all her traveler's checks. Just like he paid off your brother Billy to keep his hands off Squeek, every time...

—Well he doesn't. Edie has her own money, she has her own money she can't wait to get rid of it.

—Should have had a shot at Edie myself.

—Why didn't you.

—I'm kidding Liz look, all I'm...

—Did you?

—Look I didn't know her. I didn't even know her till I met you.

—All right then after. What about after.

—Liz come on... he tripped against the table leg, —what would I...

—No please Paul, stop it please… she ducked away at the stove. —Do you want that broccoli with this? from last night?

—What do you mean then, she's got money she wants to get rid of! He was back at the table, where he stamped down his emptied glass. —Catch Grimes setting up a trust where she could dip into principal whenever she…

—Paul you don't listen. I told you when it happened you just never listen, that terrible old aunt died she had in Saint Louis Aunt Lea everybody hated her, she kept living till ninety six just for spite just to be mean. She wouldn't part with a penny she wouldn't even die when it would do anybody any good Edie always hated her, she had to go out and stay with her sometimes when she was little and when she left Edie two or three million I don't know how much, Edie was so mad she's just been trying to run through it to get back at her. Do you want broccoli with this or not.

—All right look, just tell me one thing. Liz? The bottle neck shuddered on the rim of the glass and he steadied it, forcing it down, —just one thing. Here's your pal Edie your best friend Edie trying to unload a couple of million, right? Here we are so far in the hole we can't see out the top, now will you tell me why the hell it never occurred to you hit her up for a few…

—Because there are things you just don't do Paul! Especially with best friends there are things you just don't ask from best friends that's why. Because I don't want her to think you can't do what you, I want her to think you can do all these marvelous things you're doing what I tell her you're doing that we don't need help hers or anybody's that's why! Because she thinks you're just marvelous that you're brilliant doing these investments and things because she, because I didn't marry Mister Jheejheeboy that's why!

—All right listen. Just listen. I just told you we're looking for investors. She's got some extra cash, she thinks I know what I'm doing fine, she can put in half a million, straight business no best friends no anything, a good tax angle her money's safe now what's wrong with…

—Oh everything Paul, everything now you've made me burn the broccoli. She doesn't want tax angles she doesn't want it safe she just wants to spite that old woman, she...

—Liz the old woman's dead!

—That's not the point! If she wants to run through it if she wants to just give it to people like this Victor Sweet she met down there why shouldn't she. Do you still want this broccoli?

—Like your brother and his greasy Buddhists same God damn thing, why the hell would she give money to Victor Sweet.

—Because he needs it for politics, he wants to be in the Senate and he needs it to get elected just like anybody that's why.

—No, come on Liz. Victor Sweet? He'd run for dog catcher. He's never got near a...

—Well Edie says he's charming, she said he wants peace and disarmament he's read a lot and he's sincere and he really wants to help his people, she met him at a party down there and she says he's charming.

—Liz he's sentimental and woolly minded, the black vote won't touch him he couldn't lead ants out of a paper bag, he can't even get himself nominated if he wants to help his people what the hell is he doing at parties in Montego Bay?

—He's trying to raise money to get nominated to get, I don't know I don't care. Here. You don't have to eat the broccoli.

—Fine where's the ice did you, Liz? Where you going.

—No place. Just in here.

—But what...

—It's the smoke Paul, it's your cigarette it's just the smoke.

—Yes all right but, Liz? waving the smoke about with one hand, garnishing the broccoli with ashes stamping the thing out on the edge of the plate with the other, —Liz? You're not going to eat?

—I don't know. Maybe later I don't know.

—Then why did you, I mean I didn't say I wanted to eat

right now either... Both elbows on the table he pursued a chicken remnant across the plate, —Liz? You said Victor Sweet wants to run for senator? You mean in Washington against Teakell...? He speared it flaked with ash —like running against a stone wall, Teakell's been in there for thirty years he's got everything behind him from the Administration to people like Grimes, Edie's father that old bastard Grimes you think that's why she's doing it? give him another ulcer? Get next to Teakell I'd be out of the woods... He speared another piece clear of the broccoli, —think she even knows who Teakell is? Liz? Feel like I'm in here talking to myself.

—You are.

—What? I said do you think Edie even...

—I don't know anything about it Paul. We just talked about Cettie, she told me Cettie's been in a horrible accident, burns and just, just all too terrible...

—Who Cettie who.

—His daughter! Senator Teakell's daughter, she's been...

—You mean you know her? you know his daughter?

—I just told you, we were all best friends at Saint Tim's, she...

—No now wait, wait... he came through brandishing the dripping fork —listen. Get next to Teakell we're out of the woods, could she put in a word?

—Could, what do you...

—Teakell Liz, Teakell, one word from him and we're out of the woods... he caught the bite off the fork, chewing —what I've been talking about for a week, this hole Ude's got himself in with the networks can't pay his bills and they're trying to push him off the air, what I've been talking about raising some investment he's trying to set up his own satellite tv operation and there's Teakell holding these hearings on broadcast licensing, his own hand picked man running the FCC Liz do you think she could talk to him?

—Think, who could...

—This daughter, you just said you knew his...

—I said she's in the hospital she's covered with burns! They flew her down to that burn center in Texas they don't even know if she'll live!

—Well you, then he'll probably visit her there maybe she can put in a, Liz? He came after her waving the fork —where you...

—I don't know where I'm going! She was backed against the sink, —that she's lying there in agony all you can think of is putting in a word, you don't think of her of, you don't know what it must be like lying there in a hosp...

—Wait Liz. Wait... His glass came down hard on the table, emptied again, —you know how long I laid there? How many weeks I laid there blown right up the gut watching that bottle of plasma run down tubes stuck in me anyplace they could get one in? Couldn't move my legs I didn't know if I had any, God damn medic breaks the needle right off in my arm taped down so it can't move can't reach down, dare reach down and see if my balls are blown off, my balls Liz! I was twenty two!

—No I don't want to talk about it... She tore off a paper towel, got no further than twisting it between one hand and the other still backed against the sink there —I, I'm tired Paul I'm going upstairs, I'm sorry the broccoli...

—No it's fine, wait... He speared a dispirited flower, —I get any calls?

—You asked me that Paul, I told you Reverend Ude called, he...

—Why didn't you tell me, been trying to reach him about that story in the paper did he see it?

—That's why he called, to ask if you'd seen it, he...

—Just told you Liz, I put it there.

—You? put it there?

—I placed it, what this whole thing's all about, I go in there a media consultant get him in the public eye nation-wide's what I've been talking about, get in there and do the job where is it, have you got it?

—It's here somewhere, I brought it home but why you'd want to get him in the public eye nationwide with a story about...

—Can't you see Liz? can't you understand? Networks trying to push him off the air I get him some exposure in the print media shows these politicians like Teakell the support Ude's got out there in the boondocks thirty, forty million of them Liz they vote. Born agains, creationists, two seeds in the pod Baptists working on an Israeli tie in with these Jews for Jesus even got a few snake handlers from West Virginia every God damn one of them's a vote you think Teakell doesn't know that? Election year down their throats you think every God damn politician in sight doesn't know it? Not one political pie Teakell's thumb isn't into, Intelligence Committee Agriculture Armed Services he's got more seniority than Rip Van Winkle, keeps his name on the front page out there fighting Marxism with his Food for Africa program here's Ude moving in with his Africa missions, Voice of Salvation radio spreading the gospel all the same God damn thing Teakell knows where the votes are. One word from him Ude's satellite transmission gets off the ground where's the paper, get that newspaper story thought I'd give it to Adolph see if he can get past Grimes where is it, where's the paper.

—It's, I'll find it but I can't imagine what you think you're getting past Mister Grimes honestly, why you called him Edie said you'd called him, she said you called him about Longview about taking over Long...

—What I'm talking about Liz God damn it what I've been talking about! Been talking about investment haven't I? Raising investment? Adolph the banks all of them trying to get the estate settled? There's Longview down there soaking up money sixteen hundred acres of it, main house twenty four rooms five outbuildings twelve counting the slave quarters, turn those into guest cottages you could put up a hundred visitors, hold conferences turn that carriage barn into a media center, put in a movie theatre get his broadcast licensing

46

approved set up his global transmission system what the whole thing's all about, Liz. This Bible school he's got going down there on the Pee Dee river some old Quonset huts and a string of used school buses, he started off with a rinky dink fifty watt radio station letters coming in from all over the God damn sun belt every one of them with a nickel or a dime in it? Gets on big time television he can't pay his bills because the money's going to his Africa missions so the networks make that an excuse to push him off the air. One word from Teakell to the FCC he sets up his own operation, one word from Teakell to Grimes we can raise the investment, clean up Longview and raise the investment you think Grimes could see that? Rasping old bastard he lectures me on the prudent man law, as trustees we must ask if this is an investment the prudent man would make hasn't got a God damn thing to do with the prudent man, he still thinks I'm the one that blew the whistle on those payoffs you know what he tried on me? Some press leaks on VCR and some hushup deal he's sitting in on in Brussels tried to string me along and see what I knew, tried to pin me down on the...

—Well why you even called him in the first place. You know what he thinks of you here, here's the paper honestly, why you want your Reverend Ude in the public eye nationwide with a boy drowning it's more than...

—Liz you don't listen, not talking about a boy drowning I'm talking about my press release on Ude's big Afric, what boy drowning.

—The third or fourth page there's a picture of him, he was baptizing a nine year old boy in the Pee Dee river and the...

—No now, now wait what... the broccoli flower trembled on the fork, —Christ... in a flurry of newspaper, —Jesus Christ. Why didn't you tell me. Look at that, same God damn picture of him I gave it to them myself look at that! God damn it Liz why didn't you tell me.

—Paul I told you he...

—And you didn't tell me there's two of them! Wayne

Fickert, boy named Wayne Fickert and an old man he was holding both their heads under when the current Christ, two of them? You didn't...

—I didn't read it all, I just said that he'd...

—He called you said he called, where's the number, he leave a number?

—He did yes, I wrote it down but...

—Well where! God damn pad was here by the phone, that's why the pad was right here by the phone.

—I know it I spilled water on it when I, that's why I wrote it down somewhere else but I can't...

—Well think Liz! Think! He was up seizing the phone book, a paper napkin, the paper towel she'd wrung limp, anything where a number might have been scribbled down, backs of envelopes, —the mail, this the mail? You didn't tell me you brought in the mail.

—Well it's right there Paul, it's right there in front of you it's nothing but bills anyway, bills and something from Christian Recovery for, oh wait, wait there's one there for Mister McCandless isn't it? With the beautiful stamp that's all I noticed, from Thailand, it must be...

—I'll take care of it, he muttered thrusting envelopes this way and that, turning them over.

—There it is, I'll just put it...

—Said I'll take care of it! and he turned it face down, planted an elbow on it —now will you just find that God damn phone number? where you wrote it down? Paper tore,

—Dan-Ray Adjusters these bastards, look. Be advised that we are not depositing your partial payment check to that God damn Doctor Schak, be advised that we shall instruct his attorney to proceed against you for the full sum plus court costs, interest and look Liz, somebody here named Stumpp he says they're taking you to court for, Liz?

—What she murmured, indistinct, her lips stayed by the blue felt pen she held pressed against them, her dull gaze on the shaggy crested profile of Reverend Elton Ude crowded by headlines BOY DROWNS IN narrowing the clutter, the

48

pen came down —I'm trying to think where I...

—Will you listen to me? Trying to tell you they're taking you to court here, anybody comes to the door don't open it. Stumpp serving a summons on you some seedy process server comes to the door tell them a mile away, some down at the heels hopeless looking bastard they get seven dollars a summons he has to hand it to you, has to touch you with it, see some burnt out case out here on the doorstep you open it and all he says is Mrs Booth? hits you with the paper and that's it, don't open the door. You find that phone number? paper tearing in his hands —there, finally got here didn't you see it? Tell me there's nothing but bills been waiting for my disability check for a week I thought their computer had lost me Liz thought you were on the lookout for it, one God damn thing we can depend on thought you knew that, I thought you knew that Liz... paper tearing, —Doctor Yount. OV fifty dollars who the hell's Doctor Yount.

—That was, nothing no I'm just trying to...

—Think Liz! Think! Where the hell's that number, said you wrote it down someplace... he had the smeared vista of small boats off Eleuthera, waving it —get something going here Christ Liz how the hell can I get anything going if you write down numbers and lose them spend the rest of the day on the phone with Edie? Leave the pad right there by the phone so you can, who else called. Any other calls? Liz?

—A lot of them.

—What?

She kept her eyes down where the pen tip flicked, fluttered blue on the newspaper, widening the vacancy, —Madame Socrate said there were a lot of calls this morning.

—But the, who? Who the...

—Madame Socrate is the woman who came in to clean Paul, the woman you wanted me to get to come in and clean. She said there were a lot of calls this morning but she's Haitian and doesn't speak any English and didn't answer them.

—But she, but why didn't you answer them! What...

—Because I was in New York, Paul... the pen quivered at

49

the paper, —I drove into New York with you this morning
do you remember? to see Doctor Kissinger? When I got there
he hadn't received my records from Doctor Schak so I went
over to Doctor Schak's office, and Doctor Schak was still on
vacation, and his nurse his bitchy nurse screamed at me and
said they'd sent the records over and she called Doctor Kissinger's office and then she said she hadn't sent them and
she would and she couldn't give them to me without Doctor
Schak's permission and I went back to...

—Look Liz this has nothing to do with...

—It has to do with me! I went back to see Doctor Kissinger but they said he was leaving for Europe and I could hardly
breathe and I made a new appointment and I, I came home
I, I got the subway up to the bus and, and came home on
the bus.

—Now well look Liz I didn't mean...

—You don't you never do, the whole hideous trip for
nothing that subway I could hardly breathe you never do
you, Cettie lying there half burned to death you don't even,
even...

—Oh Liz, Liz...

She dropped the pen, getting breath, gazing blank at the
newspaper picture there, suddenly her chair scraped back,
banged the wall. —Where's that bird book, that's where it
is yes where is it, here... on the sugar canister where she'd
thrust it when she served his plate, she thumbed it through
—here... she splayed the pages on red breasted merganser,
—here's the number, your Reverend Ude here, I knew I'd
written it somewhere.

—Wait... he was already dialing, —Liz?

—I'm going up.

Rounding the newel, —Hey Elton? this you old buddy...?
pursued her up the stairs, and down the hall —mysterious
ways, now that's for sure... She swept the door behind her
with a thrust of her hip, her only light the livid aura of the
television screen come to life at her touch with a mantled

figure descending into swirls of mist. On the hilltop above sat the rising moon; pale yet as a cloud, but brightening momently, and she unfastened her skirt, opened her blouse, and was back on the edge of the bed with a damp washcloth. A horse was coming. It was very near, but not yet in sight; when, in addition to its tramp, tramp, there came a rush under the hedge, and close down by the hazel stems glided a great dog, whose black and white colour made him a distinct object against the trees. The horse followed, a tall steed, and on its back a rider, and as she slipped off her blouse man and horse were down; they had slipped on the sheet of ice which had glazed the causeway. The dog came bounding back, and seeing his master in a predicament, and hearing the horse groan, barked till the evening hills echoed the sound, which was deep in proportion to his magnitude.

—That's telling them, Elton, came down the hall to her from below, —Jew liberal press... and she was up to get the door closed, back to shy an uncovered breast from the abrupt gaze of Orson Welles enveloped in a riding cloak, fur collared, and steel clasped, with stern features and a heavy brow; his eyes and gathered eyebrows looked ireful and thwarted now demanding to know where she'd come from, just below? do you mean that house with the battlements? pointing to Thornfield Hall, on which the moon cast a hoary gleam, bringing it out distinct and pale from the woods, that, by contrast with the western sky, now seemed one mass of shadow, demanding Whose house is it? Mister Rochester's. Do you know Mister Rochester? No, I have never seen him. Can you tell me where he is? I cannot...

—Liz? She'd pulled up the sheet, working a fingertip along the ridge of her cheekbone from the jar of cream opened on the table as the music swelled lifting him to his saddle, where he reached down demanding his whip. The door slammed open —Liz! Now what in the hell! A touch of a spurred heel made the horse first start and rear, and then bound away; the dog rushed in his traces: all three vanished. He'd turned down the sound, waving the newspaper there in the grey light, —look at it! How could... he came down on the bed, —you just did this? while we were sitting there?

She looked, no more help than the sound she made.

—It's it's, don't need a kid in the house it's like having a kid in the house! Like having a, sitting right there you were sitting right there in front of me with that God damn blue pen look what you did!

—Oh Paul, I didn't mean...

—How the hell could you do it! I've got to file these things Liz I've got to send a copy to Ude! How the hell can I send him a, look at it, shaggy blue feathers these little dots on his shirt make him look like a God damn bird?

—I was only trying to...

—To what, make him look like a, just because he's about four feet tall you had to put these shaggy feathers sticking out off the back of his bald head make him look like some squat little God damn duck?

—Paul I was only, I mean that's how I remembered where I wrote down that phone number because he looked like the, because he reminded me of that picture of a...

—What, of what, a duck? God damn good picture of him Liz I gave it to them myself, gave it to the newspapers myself look at it, turned it into a cartoon look at it. Give him some dignity whole God damn point of getting it in the paper this is serious Liz! Thirty forty million of them out there with a dollar in their pocket this is serious, can't you get that? Try to get him in the paper give him a little dignity? People drowning out there good honest believing people and you turn it into a cartoon?

She drew the sheet closer. He'd turned away, sitting hunched on the foot of the bed there, shoulders fallen, absorbed in the pantomime of a brand-wise woman ministering to a groggy victim of lower back pain through its smug conclusion before he was up again, crumpling Reverend Ude's sullied profile into a wad, —God damn it Liz. Try to get

52

something going here I don't even know who's trying to call
me, one call I get one call and you write it down in a bird
book, can't find it can't find the mail at least you're bringing
the mail in, you got over that didn't you? Told yourself you
could open the mailbox and you finally did it, can't you do
that with the rest of this? Tell yourself we're not up here
running a cartoon show? He flung the paper wad at the
shadow of the wastebasket, —I went to file this before I looked
at it I can't even find the God damn file. Liz?

—Oh...?

—Last time I had it... he was down untying a shoe,
—last thing I put in it was that McCandless clipping when
was that, Sunday's paper? Can't find a God damn wait, I'll
get it, might be... he reached the phone, —Who...? Never
heard of her no, wrong number... He straightened up
thrusting off his shoes, caught a hand on the dresser's corner
tripping out of his trousers, finally bared feet planted wide
fighting a shirt button, a hand down to scratch, dangling
there silhouetted in tumid portent against the moon ascend-
ing in solemn march; her orb seeming to look up as she left
the hill tops, from behind which she had come, far and far-
ther below her, and aspired to the zenith, midnight dark, in
its fathomless depth and measureless distance: and for those
trembling stars that followed her course.

—Paul?

He got the phone again. —What...? Look I just told you,
there's no Irene here you've got the wrong God damn number! He came down heavily beside her.

—That might be his wife, it might have been for his...

—Whose wife.

—Mister McCandless, maybe she's Irene Mc...

—She's got a long wait.

—Oh I meant to tell you... she came up on an elbow,
—this morn...

—Misprision of treason, he could get twenty years.

—Paul?

—Meant to tell you I talked to Grissom this morning, got my appeal set up for Monday... His arm came under her shoulders, —stop making my whole God damn VA check over every month for alimony we can see some daylight.

—Paul do you think I could, maybe I could go away for a few days?

His hand closed on her breast. —Where.

—Just, somewhere I...

—Too much going on here Liz, you know that... his hand laboured her breast, —just get things off the ground we can take a week someplace.

—No I meant, I meant just me.

—But, but what do you mean just you, look all this going on you've got to be here. Just get this Ude deal on the tracks and there's three or four calls that should come tomorrow, you've got to be here for the phone... He drew her back, drew her glance from the scar gone livid from ribs to groin with the flat fall of his legs toward the screen where a warm glow suffused the lower steps of the oak staircase, issuing from the great dining room, whose two leaved door stood open, and showed a genial fire in the grate, glancing on marble hearth and brass fire irons, and revealing draperies and polished furniture in the most pleasant radiance, intruded upon by the tumescent rise in his hand. —Did you call that doctor Liz? that appointment for your insurance claim? His hand came down to smooth her knees apart, his leg came over. —Liz?

—Yes I, I'll call them tomorrow...

—Look you've got to call him, get in there for this examination so I can get my companion suit going... His fingers drew tight, separated, fretted in systematic search and seizure as her knee fell away, —get these disability benefits back I'll have a little cash, Grissom wants a thousand dollars retainer plus disbursements against sixty percent of the settlement to handle it... he eased over her, eased down where his hand intervened, —asking half a million all depends on your airline suit... his hand withdrew to close on her knee

—show the, show the shape you've been in since the crash
I've, how I've been deprived of, does that hurt?

—No my, my knee not so... she breathed sharply,
—how it, bruises... His head dropped there, left her face
ashen over his shoulder in the light playing up the glistening
strain of his back from the screen where a demoniac laugh,
low, suppressed, and deep, came uttered it seemed at the
very keyhole of the chamber door. As she gazed, the unnat-
ural sound was reiterated, and she knew it came from behind
the panels. As though her first impulse was to rise, and her
next to cry out, something gurgled and moaned, and steps
retreated up the gallery toward the third story staircase. The
door came open under her trembling hand and there was a
candle burning just outside, left on the matting in the gallery where the air was quite dim, as if filled with smoke.
Something creaked: it was a door ajar and the smoke rushed
from it in a cloud. Within the chamber tongues of flame
darted round the bed: the curtains were on fire: the very
sheets were kindling. In the midst of blaze and vapour Orson Welles lay stretched motionless, in a deep sleep.

—I, I have to breathe she whispered, freed an arm to reach
the box of tissues and he was up, bumping furniture, tripping over a shoe, gone down the dark hall, and she listened
for some noise, but heard nothing. It seemed a very long
time elapsed, and then she heard his unshod feet tread the
matting, and he snapped the screen into darkness.

—Oh honestly, please I've asked you not to smoke in the
bedroom.

—Just, fine just looking for something to put it out in...
He found a saucer, drew heavily there at the window where
branches caught on the rising wind outside dashed the
streetlight's gleams on the pane before him. He rubbed a
thumb there. —Liz...? as though he could see his smudged
thumb clear, —did she wash the windows? Woman who came
in to clean, did you tell her...

—There wasn't time. Now will you please put that out!

—What did she do all day? He drew again quickly before

he crushed it in the saucer, —twenty five dollars what did she...

—It was thirty dollars and she was here for a half day. She cleaned.

—Thought they said twenty five look, when she comes next week tell her to do the windows, start right off with the windows... He came down heavily out of reach, —thirty dollars, start looking for somebody who speaks English can answer the God damn phone, Haitians you don't know what the hell you're in for. We used to get their blood over there, medical corps got it cheap they were so God damn poor they're selling their blood never knew what you were getting. God damn medic I told him you better be good and God damn sure where that bottle of plasma up on that hook came from before you get that God damn needle any closer.

She half rose, snapping the sheet square, pulling up the cover. —You'll have to remember to leave me thirty dollars for her next week.

—Most of the time didn't make any God damn difference... he turned, taking blanket and sheet with him. —Casualties coming in from the combat zones, they were mainly spades anyhow.

—And a dollar carfare... she snapped back a share of the cover. —It's fifty cents each way.

Lids closed against the streetlight's gleams scattered on the wall, the empty mirror, it scarcely mattered: the chase continued on what passed for sleep taking with it what passed for time till finally, eyes fallen wide again crowded with movement still as the breathing beside her, she came off the edge of the bed and brought the room and her own face back to ashen life down a winding walk, bordered with laurels and terminating in a giant horse chestnut, circled at the base by a seat, leading down to the fence. She drew the blanket close against a sudden burst of rain at the window spattering the streetlight out there over its panes and her eyes dimmed, to come wide again with the lashing rain: what had befallen the night? Everything was in shadow; and what ailed the chestnut tree? it writhed and groaned, while wind roared in the laurel walk, near and deep as the thunder crashed, fierce and frequent as the lightning gleamed striking the great horse chestnut at the bottom of the garden and splitting half of it away.

The river lay obscured by mist that had hung heavy since morning, casting the slow climb of the mailman up the black tributary of the road as the drift of a figure being poled on water, drawn on a steady current along the leaf sodden bank toward the step standing forth there like a landing where she'd burst out earlier, as though by chance, to intercept him before he reached the box; where now, back to working the damp wads of paper towel on the glass in the alcove, her frown reduced to a distant shade the halt measure of the old man out there on the corner with his flattened dustpan. Rain, two days of it, had brought leaves down everywhere, even a torn branch afloat on the dark current rising under the window where her motions abruptly stopped, her frown broken wide on the raincoat wilted figure looming so close he was looking right up into her face. She caught breath and her balance, barely down from the stool when the knock came at the door. Opened to a hand's breadth, she saw the frayed cuffs of the raincoat, stayed the door with her foot. —Yes? what...

—Mrs Booth?

—Is, are you Mister Stumpp?

He just looked at her. His face appeared drained, so did the hand he held out to her, drained of colour that might once have been a heavy tan. —My name is McCandless, he said, his tone dull as his eyes on her, —you're Mrs Booth?

—Oh! Oh yes come in... but her foot held the door till it pushed gently against her, —I didn't...

—I won't disturb you, he came in looking past her, looking over the room and the things in the room the way he'd just looked at her, looked her over getting her in place, getting things located. —I just came for some papers, I won't disturb you.

—No I'm glad you, to finally meet you, we've wondered...

—Came up last week I couldn't get in there, he was past her for the kitchen, —new lock on the door I couldn't get in.

—Yes I know it yes, we had to have the plumber in to...

—I heard about it.

—I mean if we'd known where to reach you, if you'd just called before you...

—Never mind, just a damned nuisance.

—Yes well it's, I mean it's been rather a nuisance for us too Mister McCandless, if you'd left an address, a phone number some way to reach you, she came on behind him. —That card you sent about the furnace we didn't even know what country you were in, how could we send you a new key. I can't even let you in now, the plumber...

—I've got one... had it out in fact, rattling the padlock.

—Yes well, well good you must have called the agent, if we'd known where to reach you, things like this happen people call you we don't know where to...

—Who.

—Called you? I don't know. The IRS. I don't know who else. People call and hang up. I start to say they can leave a message if we hear from you and they hang up. You have some awfully rude friends.

—They may not all be friends, Mrs Booth... he'd slid the door open, paused there looking in. —You're welcome to have the phone taken out you know, came over his shoulder, —the agent said you wanted it left in till you could make your own arrangements, it hardly matters to me. I can call now and have it discon...

—Oh no that's not what I, I mean you're welcome to leave it yes I really don't mind answering it at all, if we just knew where to reach you, where to tell them to reach you these rude calls and people coming to the door just so rude I couldn't... she broke off, talking to his back hunched there in the doorway lighting a cigarette cupped as though in a wind, as though ducked away from some bleak promontory, from the deck of a ship. What people at the door, he wanted to know.

—Just, well there was just one but he wasn't nice at all, he wouldn't even tell me his whole name I mean, just his first one I can't remember it. Just these hard little round eyes he had on a speckled jacket and kind of yellow...

—What did he want? came back through the open door.

—To talk to you, he just said he wanted to talk to you, she said into the room where books rose from the floor heaped against a fluted column to a whorl of walnut, the leg of something, a buffet, a sideboard, she stood still looking round her as though for something to do, to explain her presence here in the kitchen, her own kitchen, her own house, stood there emptyhanded looking at the telephone until it rang. —Yes? Yes it is... Oh... her voice fell, she turned her back on the empty doorway, —for an appointment with Doctor Terranova, yes... No it's in connection with, with my... she got by the end of the table, got as far as the cord would reach —with the plane crash yes but not, I mean not my lawsuit my husband's... her voice gone still lower, —his companion suit for loss of, of my services due to my injur... what? No, no of my, of marital services due to my... What, now? or when it happened... and near a whisper —my age now is, I'm thirty three, I... no I said thir... No I can't now, I can't give you a whole history now you'll have to... no you'll have to call later.

Smoke settling in still layers barred the doorway. A light had gone on in there, and the sound of movement, a chair, or a drawer pulled open. She found her morning's coffee cup and rinsed it at the sink. Out over the terrace the mist lay featureless as the day itself come into being and left adrift with no better than the clock to dispense its passage, to turn her abrupt as her glance to it back for the front door streaking the glass panels with her damp towel wads against the shade out there poling along with his broom paused every third step, every second one, gazing ahead, getting his bearings.

When finally she heard it again she started at the loudness of her own voice, —Hello...? rising with conviction at each word, —no I'm terribly sorry Senator, Paul's not here... talking at the phone, past it to the open doorway —I think he plans to be in Washington very soon, he's had to make a trip south something suddenly came up in connection with, pardon...? gathering aplomb and even cordial condescension, —that's terribly kind but I honestly can't say, we do want to get down to Montego Bay for a few days with friends if Paul can possibly take the time but you know how busy he's been with the... and abruptly the open doorway was gone, the door pushed closed, slammed in fact, —it's nothing no, I can't talk to you now, I'll be... her voice fallen, —well call later then, call later...

Silenced, the vexation in her voice surfaced in her hands

back streaking While the bonnet is trimming, the face grows old, on the glass of the sampler; culling the morning's mail for Doctor Yount, Doctor Kissinger, Dan-Ray Adjusters, Inc. crumpled and tossed; B & G Storage, The American Cancer Society and The National Rifle Association aside unopened; a flood of glossy pages from Christian Recovery for America's People, the community college flyer's offerings unfurled in mini-courses on Stress Management, Success Through Assertiveness, Reflexology, Shiatsu, Hypnocybernetics and The Creative You; Gold Coast Florists torn open: Floral arrangement $260? Mounting to her eyes, her vexation seized wherever she turned them to be seized in turn by the unwavering leer of the Masai warrior on the magazine cover displayed, along with Town & Country and a National Geographic, on the coffee table, and she picked up the bird book for refuge in godwits and curlews, sandpipers, snipe, the repose they conjured as quickly gone with another turn of the page and she was up and through the kitchen, tapping on the white door —Mister McCandless?

It rolled back sharply as though he'd been waiting there. —I just remembered... she stood clutching the book, a finger tucked in its pages witnessing her urgency, —the man I said came to the door for you? Lester. His name was Lester... She got a brief nod for that, a murmur of dismissal but she stood looking past him there square in the doorway to bookshelves filled floor to ceiling through the planes of tobacco smoke, papers in stacks, in rolls, shadeless lamps, leather cases, filing cabinets pulled open, —are you a writer? she blurted.

—I'm a geologist, Mrs Booth.

—Oh. Because there are so many books aren't there, and papers and, and look! You have a piano! Isn't it? under all these things, I saw the corner of it I thought it was a buffet or something, a marvelous old sideboard we had one all the drawers done in velvet where we kept the silver but it's a spinet isn't it, couldn't it go in the alcove? in the living room there in the alcove...? It needed work he told her, the sounding board was warped. —Oh. Because it would be so sweet there in the alcove, maybe we could get it fixed couldn't we...? Why, did she play? —Well yes but, I mean not for a long time, those little Haydn pieces and things like that but not, I mean nothing modern, I mean I never got to Debussy or even...

He'd try to look into it he said, turning away, —now I know you're busy please don't let me keep you.

—No that's all right. I mean I've just been cleaning the windows in there, they're so fogged with smoke. You smoke a lot don't you... Too much he agreed, tapping tobacco from a glazed envelope into a paper. —Like that window right over your table there, she nodded past him, —you can hardly see through it.

—I don't especially want to see through it Mrs Booth. Now please don't let me...

—Wait I'll get you an ashtray... and she was back that quick with a saucer, —if you need anything else... He stood over the still commotion of papers spread on the table there, motionless till he reached for the ashtray he'd been using. —I just meant if you want a cup of tea or anything... and she stumbled, turning for the door, tumbling the books stacked against the piano, —oh, I'm sorry, I'll...

—It's all right Mrs Booth please! just leave them!

—Well all right but... she straightened up, —if you need anything... and she got through the door to pause in the kitchen, again in the living room and she was up the stairs running a bath, turned off as abruptly as she'd turned it on, and down the hall past empty bedrooms loosening her blouse, bringing the television screen to life with animated mischief in the lower intestine. She turned it off. Digging under scarves, blouses, lingerie in the top drawer she brought out a manila folder riffling the score or so of hand written pages, crossings out, marginal exclamations, meticulous inserts, brave arrows shearing through whole paragraphs of soured inspiration on to the last of them abandoned at what it might all have been like if her father and mother had never met, if her father had married a schoolteacher, or a chorus girl, instead of the daughter of a stayed Grosse Pointe family, or if her mother, lying silent even now in the cold embrace of a distant nursing home, had met a young writer who...

She was up for the moment it took to find a pen and draw it firmly through young writer who, take up rapidly with man somewhat older, a man with another life already behind him, another woman, even a wife somewhere... his still, sinewed hands and his... hard, irregular features bearing the memory of distant suns, the cool, grey calm of his eyes belying... belying? She found the dictionary under the telephone book, sought for bely and could not find it.

—Mrs Booth?

—Oh! She was up, —yes? His voice came up the stairs to her, sorry for the bother but might he use the telephone? —Yes, yes do! and she caught her eyes in the mirror gone wide with listening, gathered in a frown as all that reached her were yelps from the road below where the boys, when she came to look down, straggled up the hill broadcast flinging something one to another, a shoe of the smallest of them coming on well behind where the mist stayed the day as she'd left it. Then as though listened for herself she reached the telephone and raised it silently, there was only the dial tone, and she placed it as carefully back, exchanging a glance with the mirror which she recovered in arch detail down the hall, bent so close over the bathroom basin that her eyes' dark circles deepened until hidden under daubs of a cream lightener, the fullness of a lip modified, eyelids lined with the faintest of green and the hair punished, drawn, tossed free again before she came down the stairs. He was standing over the kitchen table leafing through the bird book where she'd left it, his apologies revived without a look up, he had to wait for his call to go through he said, something wrong with the circuits.

—Oh. When that happens I just keep dialing, they...

—This is out of the country.

—Oh. Oh well sit down then, in the living room? I mean I was just going to make tea... Was there a drink? and yes, scotch would be fine, leafing past plovers, willets, yellowlegs greater and lesser, had anyone been in that room? he asked her abruptly, besides the plumber? —Well no, no. I mean it's been locked, how could we... Not her no, he didn't mean her, but anyone else? the man who showed up at the door, did he come in? —No, he stayed at the door. He put his foot in the door.

—You said he just wanted to see me? didn't ask any questions?

She turned with an empty glass, brushed her hair aside, —He asked me if I was your first redhead... but her smile fell flat against his back already turned for the living room. When she came in, ice clinking the glass in one hand, her cup rattling the saucer in the other, she'd done a nice job on the windows he told her, standing there in the alcove, and something about the ivy, that it needed cutting back, almost knocking the glass from her hand as he reached for it. She steadied her cup and sat down, knees drawn tight on the frayed love seat, —and you did find your mail? It was stuck in the door there, one was from Thailand. It had such beautiful stamps that's why I noticed it.

Thailand? He didn't know anyone in Thailand, —never been there... and he settled back in the wing chair as from long habit.

—Oh. Oh and wait yes I meant to ask, is her name Irene? your wife I mean...? His nod came less in affirmation than the failure to deny it. —Because there've been some calls, someone asking for Irene? And all this furniture that's what I wanted to ask you, the agent said she was coming for it, that all of it's hers but they didn't know when. I mean we have things in storage we'd just want to know ahead of time, all these lovely things it looks like she'd just gone for the day, I just don't want anything to happen to it. That little china dog that was on the mantel it's already broken, Madame Socrate when she was cleaning she broke it right in half, I tried to glue it... He glanced up there from the empty fireplace where he'd been staring, it was something of his he told her, raising his glass, never mind it. —Oh. Well of course we'll pay for it but I meant, your wife I mean do you know when she might come for her things? or where we can reach her to ask? Because if we can't reach you, if you're some-place where we can't reach you you might be there for years, you might be gone for twenty years and, I mean...

He'd crossed an ankle over one knee showing a fine shoe, or what had been, well worn, laced with cracks up the instep. —Twenty years, Mrs Booth?

—Yes well no, no I just meant... He was looking straight at her, she caught the edge of what might almost have be-come a smile, rattling the cup on the saucer and she raised it, swallowed, —I mean you travel a lot, your work I mean, you have to travel a lot it must be very interesting work and, and exciting wait I'm sorry, I'll get you an ashtray... He'd flicked ashes at the hearth, and she was back to place a clean saucer before him, beside the magazines. —Places like that, she said.

—It's a very old issue, isn't it... He came forward to crush out his cigarette. This piece on the Masai, had she read it?

—Yes it's, I just finished it yes it's fascinating, I mean we subscribe to it but I get so behind... The ring of the phone brought him half out of the chair but she was up again, —No I'll get it... and then, from the kitchen —Mister, Mis-ter McCandless? were you calling Acapulco? What? Hello...? Oh no it's from Edie, yes no but not now operator. I mean could she call again later?

He'd upset his drink when she came back in, standing there over the wet magazines having trouble righting it, trouble it appeared simply getting the glass squared in his hand. —Oh can I help you? what...

—No! It's, it's all right.

—I'm sorry wait... she came with a towel wad from the windows, —it doesn't matter, they're old... wiping down the red ochred hair, the bared teeth and bared chest of the war-rior. —He's quite frightening isn't he, looking I mean.

—If you're Bantu.

—If I what?

—They steal cattle. I thought you said you'd read it... He'd paced off to the alcove, turned back to the dining room where he stood looking into the empty corner cupboard there, gripping his glass.

—Oh. Yes it's, I mean sometimes I don't read too carefully... and, up looking where he was looking, —we have some lovely china in storage, some old Quimper I mean it's not really china it would look lovely there but I don't know when she might come for it, Irene I mean? your wife? I mean she has such lovely taste everything, you can see her touch everywhere.

—Want to get this porch painted out here, he said abruptly looking out now at the paint peeling on the columns.

—Yes well we never use it but, I mean if you want to do that for us we'd be...

—I wouldn't be doing it for you Mrs Booth, I'd be doing it for the house... He raised his glass for the last drop in it.

—She wanted to take this whole wall out, put in an arch here and glass the whole porch in with all the plants out there, kind of a wintergarden.

—Oh! what a, I mean I've...

—We never did it, he said before he turned away.

—But they're doing marvelously aren't they, the plants I mean I try to keep them watered and...

—That one, up there? I watered it for three months after she was gone before I knew it was plastic.

—But she, for three months? But I thought she'd only been gone for...

—She's been gone for two years Mrs Booth.

The call was for him, —your call to, to Maracaibo is it? the phone unsteady in her hand, and she put it down and came back to the living room, to the alcove windows, as far off as those rooms allowed her, so far she could overhear nothing but —too late... before he came through carrying a soiled manila envelope, pulling on the raincoat, telling her the call wouldn't be charged here, getting the door open.

—But you haven't said where to reach you if anything...

He'd try to call first if he had to come again, pulling the door behind him, sorry to disturb her, and she walked more slowly back to the alcove standing well away. What light the mist had lent substance was failing rapidly down the dark road where the old dog appeared, falling in beside him as he crossed for the sodden bank opposite already losing definition as its leaves lost their colour, and she watched them down together as though they'd followed that dark current down together many times before.

Ashtray, his glass, towel wads and Yount, Kissinger swept up together she came turning on lamps, bent to blow cigarette ash from the table, bent over the trash to bury the doctors deep under bread wrappings, wilted celery, burnt toast, a worn address book she shook free of wet tea leaves before rummaging deeper for a few crumpled envelopes, all of them franked with the insipid postage of her own country, flicking the pages of the address book as she stood. The white cap of the Dewar's bottle had rolled into the sink where she found it, hesitated there with the bottle before she held it under the tap and ran an ounce, two ounces of water into it and then put the cap on, even shaking it a little before she put it back behind the bag of onions.

Up the stairs she paused to run the bath, down the hall undoing her blouse with the worn address book still tight in her hand she'd barely lit the bedroom and slipped off her shoes, barely come down among the papers on the bed bent over the last of them, the cool, grey calm of his eyes belying... her lips moving, when the downstairs toilet flushed.

—Liz? He was already on the stairs. Without pause for the peal of the phone she swept papers and folder together, a stab back for the worn address book and she was standing there selecting a fresh blouse from the bureau's top drawer. —You left the tub running, he came in pulling off his tie, and —why you don't answer the God damn phone, hello...? From where operator...? No, collect call I'm not accepting it no, don't know a God damn soul in Acapulco... he banged it down. —Any calls while I was gone?

—Chick... she stood getting breath slowly, —last night. Somebody called Chick.

—He leave a number?

—He said he didn't have one. He said to tell you he just got out, he'd call you again sometime.

—Nothing from Teakell's office? He had off his jacket, pulling open his shirt —got a car coming for the airport I've got to get down there tonight, flew right over it three hours ago turn right around and go back, have you seen my keys? Liz?

—What.

—I said have you seen my keys look I'm in a hurry, eight a m appointment in Washington they moved up that God damn subpoena I just learned about it, walked out of here without my keys if you weren't here I'd be locked out... He kicked a foot free of his trousers, —walked in just now the front door was open, up here alone I told you to keep it locked you don't know who the hell will walk in, have you seen my keys?

—They're gone Paul. So are mine.

—What do you mean so are mine, they're gone where.

—I found them on the shelf over the bathroom sink and I put them in my purse when I was leaving so they wouldn't get lost and my purse was stolen.

—Your, no come on Liz stolen? He stood over her dressed to the shins where she'd sunk to the corner of the bed, —how the hell could it be stolen, I told you to keep the doors locked didn't I? Walked in just now the front door wide open look, it's here somewhere, take a quick shower while you look for it where did you have it last, think Liz. Think!

—I don't have to think Paul I know. I had it last in the ladies' room at Saks. I hung it on a hook while I was using the toilet, and I looked up and saw a hand reach over the top of the booth and it was gone. By the time I got out there was nobody...

69

—No but, what the hell were you doing in Saks how could...

—I was using the toilet! I wasn't there buying things like any decent woman shopping they closed the account six months ago, I had some time after the doctor he's near Saks and I went into Saks. I looked at all the things I couldn't buy in Saks and then I went to the toilet, do you wonder how I got home do you care? She jammed the bureau drawer closed passing it for the door, —no purse no money no keys nothing, how I got home? how I even got in?

—No but Liz, look...

She did and dropped her eyes. He was standing there in one brown sock brandishing striped shorts clutched in a wad. —The shower's running, when does your car come.

—Half an hour look, got some things to go over come in while I...

—I'll be downstairs.

From the table where he'd dropped it the newspaper assailed her in black letters the size of her fist

TEARFUL MOM: 'PRAY FOR LITTLE WAYNE'

She was still staring at it when he came plunging down the stairs tucking his shirt in. —See that? The Post comes through they really come through, you read it?

—Read what, tearful...

—The story the story, front page story the Post comes through for you they really come through. Liz...? from the kitchen. The refrigerator door banged against the counter. —The mail?

—It's right there... she came in emptyhanded. —Do you want something to eat?

—Get it on the plane... he had the bottle forcing its neck down over a glass —God damn snack flight coming up here you get Squirt and a cookie, is this all? He scattered the mail with one hand, had the phone up in the other. —Got to make some calls. Liz?

—I'm right here.

—Said you saw the doctor, what did he come up with. Hello...? Hey, is old Elton there? This here's Paul... Talked to Grissom he said these pretrial hearings are coming up any day now, get this doctor in there with the bad news or you're dropped from the case and mine goes down the drain with it, I tell you Grissom wants a thousand dollars retainer? Hello...? Holding on here for Elton yes, lose the case and the thousand goes with it just like the last one, you beat that? How he could lose that appeal? She's out there living openly with this guy right out in the open, he tells Grissom he won't marry her because I'm paying her more alimony than he could if he married her and things didn't work out tells Grissom that right to his face, bastard makes light boxes couldn't pay her a dime so I pay for his light boxes, God damn judge gets up there and hello...? No when did he leave... No no don't bother, I'll see him down there. I'll be talking to you. God damn disability check in one pocket and out the other, where was I.

—Buying light boxes.

—Look Liz this is serious, clear up these little things before I go down there may sit around a week waiting to be called, I tell you Adolph said Sneddiger's offering me legal counsel? Bastards trying to set me up all running scared with these God damn leaks going on, hello? Calling Mister McFardle, this is... Jim McFardle yes this is Paul Booth calling, trying to tie the can to your old man's corpse they want to bury me with it, get him under the Logan Act there goes the whole God damn estate, two million in lump sum retirement benefits, three hundred thousand accumulated vacation pay, two hundred more in the stock bonus plan and an option on another five hundred thousand shares at twenty percent below the market, life insurance, Bedford, Longview every God damn thing in sight, I tell you Adolph's selling Longview? Knows God damn well I've been trying to raise the investment for this media center down there if your pal Orsini comes through in time we may still nail down an option and get the, hello? Hello? who... Left for the day? Well look, let me talk to his sec... what? You mean everybody's left for the day? Well who do you... you're the what...? No well why did you answer the, never mind... I said never mind! God damn cleaning woman picks up the phone so I pay for the call, way they do things down there Senator's out of town so his whole staff's pulled out by what time is it, car coming for me any minute look what did he say.

—Who Paul.

—The doctor, said you saw the doctor I've been trying for five minutes to find out what happened when you saw the doctor.

—I waited for forty minutes until his nurse took me in and left me naked on a table with my knees pulled up under my chin and a paper sheet over everything but my ass, twenty minutes later he came in behind me and said how do you do Mrs Booth to my shivering ass and then he put a finger...

—No now wait Liz, you... He put his glass down, —what the hell are you talking like that for you don't...

—I wanted to see if you heard me.

—I heard you! He got the glass again, —no God damn reason to talk to me like some wiseass DI what did he say.

—He wants me to have some more tests, he's sending me to...

—Look Liz can't keep stringing it out. I just told you this crash suit comes up the doctor's not in there with all your bad news my companion suit goes out the window, half a million right out the window did you tell him to get his report in fast?

—You don't tell somebody like this what to do Paul, you don't...

—Why don't you! Works for the God damn insurance company doesn't he?

—He does not work for the God damn insurance company, no. The insurance company's doctor is Doctor Terranova, I'm seeing him next week. This is a specialist Jack Orsini sent me to for my...

—Wait did Orsini call me? or his lawyer? Said he was looking into this investment I lined him up for, little cash he wants to lie low for a while did I tell you he just billed the estate forty thousand dollars? Tried to squeeze out that hundred thousand for his foundation when Adolph said no dice he bills him forty for your father instead, professional services rendered last two years of his life? The bottle came down sharply on the rim of the glass, —professional services finally sends the old man right over the side so Adolph just bills it to the estate, forty thousand scribbles a check like he scribbles checks to Yale covering his ass every time he turns around, did he call?

—Adolph?

—Orsini Liz, you don't listen! He wrenched the ice tray, —just asked you if he'd...

—He didn't call no. I told you who called. Chick called. Orsini's still away, I think he's with Edie she said they might go to Acapulco from Mont...

—Now well Christ! The ice tray came down with a crash. —Sitting right here you were sitting up there phone ringing when I came in why the hell didn't you tell me! Told you I've been waiting to hear from him, I pick up the God damn phone you heard me turn down a call from Acapulco why didn't you wait, where you...

—I'm going in to sit down. When is your car coming.

—Be here any minute what time is it, he came on without turning for the clock, picking up ice cubes, sweeping up the mail —Liz...? Shiatsu, Reflexology and The Creative You joined The American Cancer Society in the trash, —this all the mail? Halt by the abrupt blank of the locked door, —those letters for McCandless they were stuck in the door here, what happened to them.

—He came for them.

—What do you mean who came for them.

—Mister McCandless... She was sitting in the wing chair turning pages of Natural History.

—But he, you mean he was here?

—He, yes he came for some things in his room he, and he couldn't get in... she smoothed a tremor through Warriors with their girlfriends and mothers participating in song and dance, —the new lock, he was quite upset.

—Why didn't you tell him the plumber gave the keys to...

—I wasn't here Paul. I went into New York for the doctor, I think I mentioned it.

—Fine great and you lost your purse at Saks how do you know he was here, walks right in I told you to keep the doors locked didn't I?

—It's his house Paul. I'm sure he has a key.

—Walks right in nobody here look I don't like it Liz, a criminal the man's a criminal, yesterday's paper didn't I show you? did I? Up for sentencing next week for felony he grabbed a plea, brought it down from misprision of treason to misprision of a felony he could still get ten years, know what he was doing? No nickel and dime pickpocket he was in there peddling these infrared nightscopes on the wrong side of the fence, kind of guy you want walking in the front door?

She looked up. —Was he, was there a picture of him?

—Picture of him testifying with a bag over his head, still trying to nail his buddies probably why he was trying to get into his room there, pick up the evidence turn them in get off with two years it's not kid stuff Liz. You alone here somebody like that don't know what the hell can happen, get the locks changed keep them locked I don't want him in here.

—It's in the lease Paul that's ridiculous, he has a right to get into that room he's got to get into the house to get in there he could have us put out, we haven't even paid this month's...

—Rent look maybe I won't, maybe I won't. Hold back on it see what happens look, he goes up for two years ten years we don't go down to the bank here and put it in his account how the hell does he know? Up there on the rock pile what the hell can he do? Misprision of treason Liz that's what they had him for he's a God damn traitor, expect me to pay off a God damn traitor?

—Paul honestly, we're not even sure he's the...

—Goes around with a paper bag over his head and these phone calls? Mail from these African countries that weren't there a week ago where you walk down Main Street and some spade cuts your throat for the hell of it? It's not kid stuff Liz how do you know what's in that room, walks right in the house nobody home how do you even know he was here?

—I didn't say nobody was home Paul, I said I wasn't. Madame Socrate he knows Madame Socrate that's where we got her, when I got home she said he'd been here he, she said he was fâché when he couldn't get into the...

—Fashay look got to do something about her Liz, that kind of money can't even answer the phone? She do the windows? He got to the nearest of them, ran the wet streak of a thumb down it —so God damn gloomy out there you can't tell the wait, car coming must be my car where's my bag.

—By the door where you left it.

Lights climbed the alcove windows, glowed past the one where he stood and a black car made the slow turn under the streetlight. —Night like this probably ran off the road somewhere... he turned with the letters he'd been flourishing as though they'd just appeared in his hand, —stuff at B & G Storage say they'll auction it off if the bill's not paid. Liz? Stuff we've got stored at...

—I heard you. What do you think they'll get for your stones.

—Not just stones look don't start that, stuff of yours there from Bedford eighty ninety thousand dollars there they want nine hundred ten dollars, God damn ransom nine hundred and wait, Liz? Just remembered look, have you got any cash? Running short all I've got's this check on the Pee Dee

Citizens Bank not even sure it's good, she spells hundred h u n e r d sat through the whole funeral eating Cheez Doodles, Liz? that fifty I left you?

—You left me money for Madame Socrate.

—Fine great fifty dollars get the God damn windows washed can't even tell the difference, what...

—Well you wanted them cleaned and she, and they're cleaned! People work hard that's what you pay them for, their work that's all they have to sell so you pay them for it or they, or you do it yourself if you can't tell the difference why didn't you do them yourself!

—No now wait Liz, look...

—No you look! Nine hundred dollars your boxes of stones in a tomb there they might as well be in a tomb you look, the other one the other bill in your hand flowers two hundred and sixty dollars? What flowers where, somebody spends half the day on these windows and you're spending two hundred sixty dollars for a floral arrangement?

—What the hell's got into you Liz... He came down slowly on the frayed love seat, brought a shined and tasseled imitation of elegance up to patient rest on his knee, —did you look at it? He opened the bill and then held it out to her, his face as true as his footwear —see who it was sent to? Cettie Teakell?

—I, no I...

—Didn't have time to tell you, I sent them out in your name I didn't have time to tell you... and he watched her, kind as a cheap new shoe, watched her catch breath, catch the trimmed fullness of her lip still tighter, —just thought you'd want her to know that you...

—No Paul I'm sorry she said, her breath gone again, her eyes coming up but unable, they seemed unable to rise past the shoe cocked over his knee till it went down as he gained his feet, regained all she'd lost there.

—Just you get ahead of me sometimes Liz, he tossed a match across her at the fireplace, —jump to conclusions. Trying to get things together here look, getting things lined up everything's just about ready to fall in place so God damn many pressures why I don't try to tell you everything I don't want to upset you. Try to give you the big picture you take one corner of it and run, jump like I said you jump to some conclusion the whole God damn thing falls to pieces like these flowers, I send these flowers you jump to some conclusion we end up arguing about flowers, see what I mean?

—Paul I'm, I said I was sorry I'm not arguing I just didn't...

—Didn't think Liz, you didn't think. Look. Certain things maybe you can't see quite as clear as I can. Maybe you don't want to. Maybe it's just because you don't want to, I can understand that Liz. I can understand that. But it shows through anyhow, kind of a whole negative way of looking at things I get the feeling sometimes you're not quite with me, not backing me up I've got to have the feeling you're behind me Liz. See what I mean? He'd gained his stride, newel to alcove, back to the newel post punctuated by abrupt puffs of smoke, looking out the front door —incidentally. Next time you get a chance to talk to Edie, see her picture all over the papers with Victor Sweet you ought to tell her to slow down Liz. Making a God damn fool of herself, Sweet stands as much chance for that nomination as Uncle Remus, he gets it he's got as much chance to win as the tar baby. You see Teakell out there with his Food for Africa program he's got the whole third world by the short hair Sweet couldn't carry Lenox Avenue, why the hell old man Grimes doesn't step in there and put the brakes on her himself, you follow me? He trailed smoke to the alcove windows, —see here? She didn't even get in the corners. Fifty dollars to clean the windows she can't even do the corners, problem's not just Edie Liz it's where Sweet's getting his real backing, tied in with all these peace groups it's got to be coming from the outside you know what that means. Tar Edie with the same God damn brush while we've got Ude here all over the front page with his Africa missions where he can deliver the votes you follow me? story right here in the paper? You mean you didn't read it?

—Well not, no I...

—Just gave it to you why do you think I gave it to you, told you they put their best feature writer on it didn't I? Thought you read it while I was in the shower this is what I mean Liz, feeling I get sometimes you're not right in there with me where the hell do you think I've been for two days, look... in a flush of newsprint —whole God damn page listen. The innocent boyhood dreams of Wayne Fickert, which once took shape like the white, billowy clouds floating against the brilliant heavens smiling down on the sparkling blue waters of the Pee Dee river, will never come to pass for the boy who dreamed them. At ten o'clock this morning, little Wayne was buried here on the sunny, flower strewn bank of the river he loved, in a ceremony which the Reverend Elton Ude, the dynamic leader of Christian Recovery for America's People, called the opening salvo in God's eternal war against the forces of superstition and ignorance throughout the world and elsewhere, and the recovery of the Christian values represented by the simple, God fearing folk gathered there before him in the bank who, on, should be on the bank not in the bank, a crowd estimated by an official spokesman at, must mean me, at just over six thousand, who have made America what it is today see how she gets the whole flavour of the thing in there? Liz?

—What.

—See what I mean, best writer they've got listen. Known to his many followers as a devoted student of the Bible, Reverend Ude highlighted his river theme with words from the book of Exodus. And it shall come to pass that thou shalt take of the water of the river and pour it upon the dry land, and the water which thou takest out of the river shall become blood upon the dry land. Citing the drought conditions now prevailing in Africa, he identified that dark continent as the dry land named in the prophecy where millions of souls are waiting to be harvested in the name of the Lord. We all know, he continued with the homespun eloquence that has won him his devoted radio following and a nationwide weekly television audience as well, that the day foretold in First Thessalonians is at hand, the day when the Lord himself shall descend from heaven with a shout, and the dead in Christ shall rise first, and then we which are alive and remain shall be caught up together in the clouds, to meet the Lord in the air, and those who are not saved are doomed to be cast down into the burning lake which is the eternal dwelling place of Satan. Shall we abandon these millions of souls to an eternity without Christ? No friends, under a...

—Paul...?

—a heavy anointing from the Holy Spirit our Africa missions are crying out for your prayers and your support, and I'd just like to see them all saved and washed in the blood of Jesus Christ Liz what is it!

—I just thought, I mean maybe you can read that on the plane if you...

—Reading it right now Liz, first chance I've had to really read the God damn thing he's already broadcast it, taped it for television problem is we're going different directions here, brings me in as media consultant he needs some clear hard headed thinking to get things on the tracks, I think we're hitting them for this new media center and he's up there spouting about building a where was I, here. Recalling the day Wayne Fickert made his decision for Christ, Reverend Ude saw this fine youth going forth one day from the Christian Recovery Bible Mission School to take the Lord's word to these very farthest reaches of the world, and his despair when little Wayne was snatched away. Heavy of heart, Reverend Ude confided to his listeners, he had come on that sad evening to this very spot, seeking the Lord's will. And suddenly, he said, I heard the voice of the Lord speaking to me. He told me that from this very spot where we're gathered here together, the spirit of little Wayne would one day go forth in this legion of fine Christian educated men and women to carry the words of his holy gospel to the ends of the world. For in his infinite wisdom and mercy he had taken up little Wayne in a pure unblemished state, uncorrupted by the filth that abounds in our libraries and motion picture houses, the atheist doctrine of evolution that has transformed our classrooms into altars of secular humanism, and the slaughter of a million and a half innocent unborn children in our abortion hospitals throughout the land.

—Paul I just thought, if you...

—Thought what, listen. I stood here weeping, with...

—Before your car comes, if you want something to eat I can...

—Get something on the plane here, just get me some ice, how my own mortal weakness had left me open for the wiles of the great deceiver Satan in doubting the Lord's purpose. For it was not little Wayne, the mortal boy, but the purity of his spirit that the Lord has chosen to lead us forward in his holy name. And as his will came down upon me, trembling, I suddenly heard the voice of the profit Isaiah, wherein The carpenter stretcheth out his rule; he marketh it out with a line; he fitteth it with planes, and he marketh it out with the compass, and maketh it after the figure of a man, according to the beauty of a man; that it may remain in the house. And as I pondered the meaning of these words from on high, what had been a day of mourning burst before me as a day of glory! For did not they ask, when Jesus came unto Nazareth, Is not this the carpenter's son? He who builded this great edifice of refuge for the weak, for the weary, for the seekers after his absolute truth in their days of adversity and persecution, as we are gathered here today before the onslaught of secular humanism, builded with his simple carpenter's tools from the humble materials closest to his hand his father's house, wherein are many mansions? And as the clouds of evening broke I saw before me, here where you all are standing right now on the banks of our beloved river, the buildings rise, the dormitories, the sunny classrooms, the green ballfields of the Wayne Fickert Bible College, sending forth to our missions even unto darkest Africa Full Gospel Christian men and women for this last chance the Lord has provided us for the harvest of souls in his name

Liz? To make this miracle come true, can you hear me?

—I'm getting your ice.

—A little water in it, to sit down prayerfully with your pen and checkbook Liz? God damn glass has a chip on the rim get me another one, for the Lord's purpose cannot be accomplished without your loving support. Concluding his spirited call to action as the television cameras rolled closer, Reverend Ude pledged to send absolutely free, in return for donations for purchase of the land, a bottle of water from the Pee Dee, which he saw as one day taking its place beside the Galilee. Closing his appeal with words from Revelation, And he showed me a pure river of water of life, and let him that is athirst come, and whosoever will, let him take the water of life freely, Reverend Ude now turned to introduce the vivacious dark haired woman who had been seen weeping silently throughout the ceremony as Mrs Billye Fickert, the boy's mother. Clearly overcome by the proceedings, Mrs Fickert could only express her tearful gratitude that her son had been baptized and entered the waiting arms of the Lord in a state of grace. Drawing again upon Exodus, Reverend Ude quoted, The Lord is my strength and song and he is become my salvation, calling upon the deep baritone voice of war veteran Pearly Gates, who came forward in his wheelchair to lead the singing of Down By The River with new lyrics composed especially for the occasion by Reverend Ude himself. After the minute of silent prayer that followed, the faces of the throng gathered before him, many of them still aglow with the memory of tears in the brilliant sunshine, were raised by Reverend Ude's voice, now calm and serene, saying that he had sought for some sign of the Lord's blessing upon their endeavour. Pointing to a lone bluebonnet blowing bravely on the parched, barren bank of the river flowing brilliantly before them, That there, he said in a hushed tone, is for little Wayne. Liz you still out there? Just wanted some ice in it...

She came in to set the glass down before him. —I put in more whisky too, I thought...

—Good yes, almost done listen. Following the formal cer-
emonies, Reverend Ude ambled among the throng in the
neighborly manner that has gained him so many devoted
adherents, comparing the quantities of fried chicken being
shared and enjoyed on all sides to the miracle of the loaves
and fishes. Among the day's most active participants was
Pearly Gates, his deep inspiring baritone voice well known
to Reverend Ude's radio listeners everywhere, the Good
Conduct medal gleaming on his broad chest as his motorized
wheelchair, a recent gift of the Christian Recovery Bible
Mission School, whisked him deftly among the assembled
mourners with a cheerful word of faith and hope for young
and old alike. Unable to attend the services was the boy's
father, Earl Fickert, who currently resides in Mississippi where
he is engaged in the automobile business, really gets the whole
picture across doesn't she?

—Doesn't who...

—This writer Liz, right here. Doris Chin. Best they've
got, ends up, listening? Elsewhere, in a sombre footnote to
the day's activities, a light rain fell on an unmarked plot in
the county cemetery where, in a silence marred only by the
shovels of three inmates from the county jail, the remains
of an elderly drifter, his name known only to his maker Liz
what are you doing, wandering around the God damn room
I'm trying to read something to you.

—Nothing... she turned from the window —I just thought,
I mean if your car...

—All right you read it, here... He was up thrusting the
page at her, —foot of the column right there at the end,
want to see what it sounds like then you read it. He got by
her to push open the door under the stairs, —go ahead I can
hear you...

She sat down to it. —Three people were killed and fourteen injured here late this evening when a school bus went
out of control and plunged into a ravine on route one eleven,
according to state police. The passengers, all students at the
nearby Christian Recovery Bible Mission School, owners of

82

the bus, were among the last of a crowd estimated by authorities at over five hundred who had attended prayer services following the funeral of...

—What the hell is that! The toilet seat banged down behind him —here give me it, where is it...

—Here, right where you...

—Well Christ. He pulled up his belt, —didn't see it there, tucked it down in the corner where you don't even see it, look. Says he couldn't be reached for comment, preparing for a speaking engagement in Texas Reverend Ude was in seclusion seeking spiritual guidance, according to a spokesman... The paper went down in a heap, —see him get out of this one, just got their indoor plumbing paid for now he'll have the whole God damn state highway safety commission in there on these broken down school buses... He'd seized the empty glass and sat down, —all the pieces falling into place suddenly the whole God damn what are you doing!

—Just, I thought I'd get you another drink.

—Drink all you think's I want a drink! He wrenched the glass down hard on the coffee table. —Get something to, thought you're getting me something to eat I better get something to eat, food they give you on these God damn planes where you going...

—There's some chicken, some cold chicken if you want it with, I'll get it... She was already in the kitchen, —Paul? It's somebody calling about the flights from LaGuardia, it's the weather they canceled your flight, they... what? hello...? Paul? They want to know if you want a place on a helicopter from LaGuardia to Newark, Paul...? He was drumming his fingers on the chair arm. —Do you...

—I heard you!

—Do you want them to hold...

—I said no! his voice gone hoarse, hand suddenly gripping tight to the arm as though it were the chair itself lurching abruptly, dropping away from under him, the tendons standing out hard under the bursting course of the veins —can't, can't do that... sinking back, raising both hands in the air, looking up at them as the veins subsided, and they came down and he reached out to seize something, anything, Natural History magazine staring fixed at its cover. —Looks like my God damn crew chief. Liz...? He dropped it face down, reached for Town & Country —where'd these magazines come from? turning it about for the address label, —bring magazines home from the doctor's waiting room why the hell do you take Town & Country? why don't you bring home Time and Newsweek? Read about something real not a lot of, this the doctor you just saw? Kissinger?

—I can't hear you Paul, I'll be in in a minute.

—This your famous Doctor Kissinger? What are you seeing him for he's a proctologist, got asthma why the hell are you seeing a proctologist.

—Paul? Do you want mayonnaise?

—Why do I want mayonnaise! He had his glass in one hand, swept up the newspaper with the other coming through to the kitchen —picture in the paper here he, what are you doing.

—I just sliced this chicken, do you...

—Told you I'd eat on the plane look, this the same Kissinger? Picture here on his way to operate on some sheikh what are you seeing him for.

—He's a consultant Paul, the one I tried to see last week Jack Orsini sent me to, he's supposed to be the best diagnost...

—Here it is look, picture of him with the Ogodai Shah and his wife Christ take a look at her, Empress Shajar looks like a high class belly dancer, ugly old bastard isn't he? Says Kissinger's in there to do a colostomy on him probably bill him for a cool million, what's he charging you?

—I don't...

—Probably had his bill in the mail before you got out the door, did you sign an insurance form? Get this insurance straightened out Liz, got to get this God damn medical insurance straightened out before we, that the door? My car look, I'll try to call you from... he broke off. He just stood

there. She was into the room behind him before he managed
—You don't even bother to knock?

—Hey, Bibb... came past him without a glance, without a
word for him into the brief flurry of her embrace.

—What a beautiful suit she said, stepping back her arm's
length. It was a glen plaid, cut long at the vent. —Paul...
her hand still on the sleeve, her other out as though she'd
just introduced them —Paul's just going to the airport, we
thought it was his car.

—You look good Bibbs.

—Told you let's try to keep this God damn door locked
Liz... he was over forcing it closed, swollen with dampness
against the doorframe, looking out where the streetlight
glinted on a dark car pulled up still against the hedge beyond
the corner. He stood there tapping a foot, his back to their
voices in the kitchen till a shock of laughter, her laughter
brought him round —Liz? his voice sharp as his step —look,
if McFardle calls in the morning tell him to tell the
senator...

—With a B, and a U...

—Paul I'm sorry, what is it?

—Nothing! He was over filling his drink, —finish your
jokes.

—No it's nothing, he was just telling me about Sheila
running down the aisle at Saint Bartholomew's in a sweater
with a big letter B on it shouting today is Buddha's birthday,
let's hear it for Buddha, with a...

—B? and a U? The bottleneck came pressed down hard on
the glass, —says he's a God damn Buddhist can't even spell
it? It's crap anyway that story, I saw it in the paper. What's
he doing here, the usual? stops in to piss on the floor and
borrow some money?

—Give you good karma, Paul. Doing you a favour, ask
you for ten bucks I give you the chance to do a kind deed,
earn yourself a little good karma man you're going to
need it.

—See that Liz? doing me a favour? Like fixing my car he

God damn near got me killed look Billy, take your karma and shove it. He raised the glass and brought it down, as he did so following down the draped ease of glen plaid lounged before him. —What's the new suit. A little good karma for Adolph? squeeze some more money out of Adolph?

—Oh, man... the glen plaid shifted wearily. —What is it with him anyhow, Bibb? Her hand lay still across her forehead sheltering her eyes, and did not move. —Look man... the folds shifted again, —I didn't get a fucking nickel out of Adolph. What I got out of Adolph is you trying to take over Longview, turn it into some media center for your redneck evangelist.

—You see that Liz? see that? Same thing, jump to conclusions same God damn thing look, they're selling Longview to get it off the books before this lawsuit comes up, ever hear of it? Twenty three stockholders' suits consolidated into one thirty four million dollar suit against VCR and your old man's estate ever hear of it? Grimes Sneddiger all your old man's buddies signed up with these Belgians moving in on VCR, they'll sit up there and perjure themselves blind before they'll hand over thirty four million to these God damn stockholders. How the hell did they think we did business there anyhow.

—You tell them, Paul. You carried the bag.

—There. See that Liz? Who was out doing the work while he was smashing up cars and screwing anything with legs, walks in here in a four hundred dollar suit and wants to borrow ten dollars reminds me, wait. Anything in the till there Liz I just need carfare get out to the airport, take this check down to the bank in the morning see if they'll cash it.

—Well I, I'm not sure Paul I...

—How much is it Bibb?

—It's a hundred dollars but it's a little bank somewhere down in the...

—Not a God damn thing wrong with it probably just take it a few more days to clear than...

—Give you seventy five for it, Paul.

—What?

—I'll give you seventy five bucks for it.

—What do you mean sev, it's a hundred dollars a check for a hundred dollars what do you mean seventy five.

—Cash. I mean look at it man, the Pee Dee Citizens Bank? And I mean look at that signature, Billye Fickert? Who's that, some moonshiner you picked up?

—Billy please, if you can really cash it couldn't you just...

—No come on Bibb, I mean Paul's the smart operator isn't he? Knows all about discounting commercial paper doesn't he? A roll of bills had surfaced from somewhere deep in the folds of grey, come up tight in a fist on the table —moving into the big time here, he's got a friend at the Pee Dee Cit...

—Shut him up Liz look, something important before my car comes, I think I hear it. If I get a call on this book advance, didn't get a chance to talk to you about it an advance on a book this publisher's interested in, just tell him you think I'm thinking in terms of twenty thousand leave a little room to move in, there's the car I'll try to...

—But what about your flight? She was up, —will they take you to...

—I'll get there.

—Make it eighty Paul... He had the roll of bills tight in his hand, —I mean look at this big favour you're doing me taking it. You're giving me this chance to do this good deed man, I mean look at this great fucking karma you're giving me.

—God damn it Liz will you, look Billy take your God damn karma and shove it, shave your head give you a red blanket stand you out on Tu Do street with a God damn bowl you ever seen a monk barbecue? Know one God damn thing about karma you'll come back as...

—Billy give it to him! Cash it all of it! just, just give it to him! And two fifties came casually from the heart of the roll of bills tossed on the table where she swept them up, coming after him to the door. —And Paul? She pressed the bills in his hand there —I didn't, those flowers to Cettie I didn't thank you...

—Keep the door locked.

—And Paul...? But he was already pulling it tight behind him against the burst of headlights, the car door slammed and she watched the red glows down the darkness before she turned. —Why do you do that? She was still at the door, her back against the door. —Why do you have to do things like that.

—Like what. I mean he didn't even sign it, grabs the money and runs he didn't even endorse it, what good is it... He crumpled the check into a wad and tossed it at the trash. —You need any cash?

—No. Just if, that twenty you borrowed, if...

—Here... he thrust a thumb into the roll of bills and dropped one on the table without looking at it. —Where's he going anyhow. He runs out of here didn't even have carfare, I mean he's crazy Bibbs. He's crazy.

—Washington, she said, and pushed the plate to him, —do you want this chicken?

—And like what was all that when I called you earlier, I'm teddibly sorry senator I mean you sounded like Edie's old Aunt Lea. We do want to get down to Montego Bay but Paul's so teddibly busy and then he stamps in here with if Mcsomebody calls tell the senator some kind of bullshit, what's all that.

—It was nothing she said, sitting down —just, nothing.

—Then you hung up. I mean he's getting you as crazy as he is, you think he's going to take you to Montego Bay? He couldn't take you to Atlantic City, I mean this last minute bullshit about some book advance. He's going to write a book? He can't do anything Bibb he's never finished a fucking thing, his big resort deal they pulled right out from under him? Then all you hear about's this big movie he's going to make about Marco Polo with some more of your money and when the money's gone you never heard about it again. I mean how can you live with this bullshit.

—It's just, I don't know. Something happens...

—I mean that's what I'm saying, not a fucking thing happens! He walks in the door and...

—No I mean it's, nothing happens till he walks in the door, I don't know what it is, as long as something's unfinished you feel alive it's as though, I mean maybe it's just being afraid nothing will happen...

—How can anything happen! That's why he's got you locked up here, he's scared shitless some old friend will find you he's scared something will happen, he can't finish anything because he's scared shitless of finishing anything why don't you pack up. Pack a bag and get out of here Bibbs, listen. I'm going to California I'll wait for you. Tonight, pack a bag and I'll wait for you.

—I, I can't.

—Why not why can't you. Leave him a note tell him you just have to clear some of this bullshit out of your head, this broken down house the whole wet gloomy everything dying out there in the sun, get a look at it. Why can't you.

—Because I, it wouldn't be fair...

—Fair? Oh man, to him? I mean when was he ever fucking fair to anybody, this same bullshit Bibbs it's this same bullshit. He married you for money and makes you feel guilty for having it so he blows it, the worse things get the more he piles on the guilt he's got your mind so bent nothing happens till he comes in the door? I mean who else comes in the fucking door.

She was staring at the benign face of Benjamin Franklin on the bill there on the table before her as though to catch his eye. —No one, she said, —no one.

—You know Bibbs? He was standing there leaning against the doorframe, —like I've always wondered. I mean how you'd always find somebody that's just not as good as you are? I mean like that Arnold? and that guy from Florida that's going to be this great actor and the old man threw him out of the house? I mean it goes way back, like playing

doctor with that little prick Bobbie Steyner they said only
had one ball? where he got you down in the boathouse and
tried to get your pants down?

—No, no Billy honestly...

—No I mean no shit Bibbs. These real inferior types I
mean this real instinct, like you were always this beautiful
girl with red hair and this real pale white skin and these
great high cheekbones and this whole like, like something
vulnerable where they want to get in there to protect you
and waste you all at the same time? and like they're the only
ones you'd ever let in? where he's pulling your pants down
and you still think you've got the upper hand? Like I mean
it goes all the way back where you practiced on me when I
was like three, when you put that little yellow fucking doll's
dress on me in that toy crib and you were the mommy or
you wouldn't play with me? No I mean don't laugh Bibbs...
But she wasn't, it was a sound choked off somewhere between that and loss —where if I didn't answer when you
called me Jennifer you wouldn't even talk to me? He'd turned
away looking into the living room, cracking his knuckles behind him, filling the doorway.

—But it was, Billy don't you see it was how it all started,
because you were the only...

—Man I know how it fucking started! I mean that time at
the table when I threw some applesauce and the old man
grabbed me and put my plate on the floor in the corner, if
you want to behave like a dog you can eat like a dog does, I
mean I was his dog till he got his own fucking dogs. I mean
you don't ever fucking forget that. All his big crazy ideas
where he's this advisor to presidents, this master of corpo-
rate strategy, master of this far flung mining empire master
of bullshit all he ever did was push people around and let
somebody else pick up the pieces. He bullied anybody that
got near him like he bullied us, like he bullied mother like
he bullied you till you'd do anything to get out, so you did
what you always did. You find this inferior person, you know

90

he's fucking inferior and you've married the same thing you tried to get away from. Like why do you think the old man took Paul on in the first place, because he'd found somebody just as fucking inferior as he was, the only difference the old man was smart and like I don't mean intelligent, I mean there's a big fucking difference. Like where Paul first showed up talking about he's this big wounded hero with...

—Billy why, why! and he doesn't talk about it, he's never talked about it he won't even...

—Then who talked about it, I mean who told the old man how he's sleeping in this Bachelor Officer Quarters when these VC sappers break in there and blow him up with a mortar round, you think he made that up? and like where he's got this Bronze Star with clusters going into combat with these real bright ribbons sewed on his camouflage jacket and his fucking one gold bar it's supposed to be dulled and he wouldn't dull it? Like he's going to show them, I mean he's got this platoon they're under strength like two thirds of them black from Detroit and Cleveland I mean they don't give shit for being a hero but he's going to show them. He sets himself up this perfect target and he's setting up the whole fucking platoon I mean it's the old man Bibbs, where he always had to be the big deal at the expense of everybody under him. I mean did you ever tell him what Paul told you his own father said when he went in? his fucking own father? that he was God damn lucky he was going in as an officer because he wasn't good enough to be an enlisted man? From a pocket somewhere he came up with a crushed cigarette and stood there lighting it, spitting out smoke —I mean how Paul could ever have told you that, how he could even have told you...

—What are you going to do in California, she said finally.

—Man like if I had anything to do why would I go to California. I mean come on Bibbs pack up. We'll be there in the morning.

—I can't. I can't, it's not just Paul it's, things I have to do, doctors, these lawsuits about the plane crash I have to see their doctor before the...

—You've seen him Bibb you've seen him fifty times I mean you're in there with ninety other people, how's that going to change the lawsuit.

—Not just mine it's Paul's too he, it doesn't matter no I don't want to talk about it. I just can't go.

—Paul! That's what I mean everything comes back to fucking Paul, you mean his lawsuit? this bullshit about half a million dollars for loss of these fucking services he's trying to go through with it? Oh man... and he reached abruptly across for the blank pad by the phone, seized the pen with it —I mean he's the one that's wiping you out Bibb not some old plane crash, look... Figures mounted the paper, —half a million dollars, if he had a hundred dollar a night call girl that's five thousand nights every night, that's thirteen years screwing every fucking night you think any court's going to listen to that bullshit? He thrust the pad away, cracking the knuckles of one hand in the other, looking at her. She didn't look up, didn't move, and he got up suddenly. —I went out to that place, he said, his voice fallen, —yesterday, out to Hopewell.

—But what, she looked up sharp —what...

—Nothing. I just went. He'd turned away, —all these spaced out old cruds they had them around this long table making nut cups for Halloween, I mean it was like nursery school at the wrong fucking end of the line. She just lies there, this tube in her nose she didn't even know I was there. There's this big sign somebody put by her bed You are in Hopewell, New Jersey. I mean she must wake up sometimes and ask them where she fucking is. I've got to go, Bibbs... he'd come round and put a hand on her shoulder. —You sure? All he got was the shake of her head coming up from her shoulders but she came with him, came as far as the door where she seized his wrist.

—Could you stay?

—Have to be at Newark by ten... That was all; and she

stood with all her weight against the door motionless in the sudden glare of headlights, until they swept an arc across the windows and were gone.

In that house more frequently now she would find herself paused to listen, as she did passing back to the kitchen, though for what it was never clear. Once there, she turned on the radio which promptly informed her that traffic was being detoured in the vicinity of the BQE because of an overturned tractor trailer truck and she turned it off and picked up the hundred dollar bill, and then she came round to find the crumpled check on the floor and smooth it carefully against the refrigerator door before she put them both under the napkins and placemats in the drawer. Lights went out behind her, **TEARFUL MOM** wailed mute from the coffee table where Town & Country lay menaced by the Masai in a glint from the streetlight.

In the tub she examined a fading bruise on the inside of her knee. In the bedroom, she brought the television screen to life with two men struggling on the top of a speeding train until one hurled the other off as it crossed a trestle and she watched, wrapped in a towel, for the satisfaction of the flailing figure dashed on the rocks below before she pulled open the bureau's top drawer as the train sped on.

Two, then a third palm size page fell free of the worn address book, a meticulous chaos of initials and numbers, crossings out, writings in, arrows spanning continents, bridging oceans, MHG Golf Links New D tlx 314573TZUPIN; Bill R, Mtdi and numbers crossed out for BA and new numbers; for funding GPRASH Luanda and numbers; Jenny Dpnt Crcl and numbers; SOLANT and numbers crossed out; Seiko and numbers, IC, more numbers; she restored them haphazard and dropped it into the folder spread open on the bed where she came down to the last page taking her pencil straight to a man somewhat older and drawing it through another life, writing in other lives; through another woman for other women; through somewhere, for a wife hidden now in Marrakech, biting the nub of the eraser over his still, sinewed hands when the phone brought her upright.

—Yes hello...? No, no he's not here who is it, if he calls I can... Well yes he was here briefly Mrs Fickert, but he had to turn right around and... pardon? Well he, well yes of course he's married. I mean I'm his wife. Do you... hello?

The train sped toward her and she caught the towel together at her breast up fetching Webster's New Collegiate Dictionary, and it roared right over her as though she'd gone down on her back there between the tracks. Opened to the Ds now, licking her fingertip past dogtrot, dive, her finger ran down dishevel, dishpan hands till it reached disinterested, where the precisely incorrect definition she sought was confirmed in a citation from a pundit for the Times, she drew a line through indifferent and wrote it in, worrying at calm with faint prods of the pencil point: the cool, disinterested calm of his eyes belying? She hatched calm in a cuneate enclosure, licking her finger paging back to the Cs for cunning, past cut-rate, curt, running down from cuneiform and held, abruptly, at cunnilingus. She was reading it slowly, finger back to her lips, pp. of lingere, more at LICK, when the phone rang again.

—Yes? she cleared her throat —yes? hello... She came back on the pillows staring at a woman rudely her junior and blonde at that emerging refreshed from the shower. —No I'm not but, but wait. Wait, hello...? She, whoever you are, I mean you don't need to keep trying to call her here she, you see she's been gone for two years...

The woman on the screen caressed a chaste limb with something from a bottle, turning to look straight at her, and where she came forward now to run her finger with a resolute tremor on to stop sharp at cunning her eye leaped it to cunt. And as though there'd been no interruption, no two years fallen away in Zaire, Maracaibo, Marrakech, —Places like that... BA, Mtdi, Thailand? —never been there... she lay back on the bed as though she'd never left it, —all these lovely things it looks like she'd just gone for the day... the damp warmth of the towel turned chill and fallen away, feet curled in on the bed in the frolic of the streetlight through the trees, her nipples drawn up hard and a hand passing down her breast and out to the knee flexed up for its reach to touch the bruise there, gliding down slowly on a hard edge of nails to the rising fall where its warmth lingered with the close warmth of breath in the suspense of her knees fallen wide broken, shuddering, by the shock of her own voice.

—Yes hello! Oh... oh I'm... she caught breath, —I'm sorry Mister Mullins I didn't recognize your voice... She cleared her throat, —no, no I haven't seen Sheila since... I know yes of course you do, I know she's not well but... No he was here, Billy was here a little while ago but he... with him? No, no she wasn't no, he... He didn't know I mean I don't know no, where he was going he didn't... If I hear yes of course I will, yes...

Knees drawn up she pulled the towel round her bared shoulders and a shiver sent breath through her, staring at that page till she seized the pencil to draw it heavily through his still, sinewed hands, hard irregular features, the cool disinterested calm of his eyes and a bare moment's pause bearing down with the pencil on his hands, disjointed, rust spotted, his crumbled features dulled and worn as the bill collector he might have been mistaken for, the desolate loss in his eyes belying, belying... The towel went to the floor in a heap and she was up naked, legs planted wide broached by scissors wielded murderously on the screen where she dug past it for the rag of a book its cover gone, the first twenty odd pages gone in fact, so that it opened full on the line she sought, coming down with the pencil on belying, a sense that he was still a part of all that he could have been.

h er anxious morning greeting in the bathroom mirror
was not returned: the glass was steamed over, and she tram-
pled a clump of brown socks, a sodden towel getting to her
bath, coming from it back down the hall for an exchange in
the mirror over the bureau gone from bleak to critical as her
eyes met there and fell to her breasts, to the open drawer
idly turning up sweaters, blouses, pulling things on without
a second look, finally drawn to the stairs and down by the
smell of burnt toast.

—Liz?

—You came in so late last night I didn't...

—Look I don't believe this... He was sitting at the kitchen table in shorts and black socks, papers spread out in the blue haze from the toaster. —Montego Bay collect, thirty nine minutes. Fifty one dollars and eighty five cents.

—Oh. Oh that, must have been Edie...

—Look I know it must have been Edie. I just want to know why she called collect. I just want to know why in hell you'd accept a collect call from Montego Bay.

—Well I didn't realize it Paul the operator said it was Edie calling and I just, I so wanted to talk to her...

—She's trying to run through two million dollars from her dead aunt and she has to call collect?

—Well she, I don't know maybe she didn't have any change and...

—Change! Fifty one dollars and eighty five cents change?

—I don't, why it's always money... She poured scorched coffee, standing there at the sink looking out at a lawn chair overturned in the drift of discoloured leaves on the terrace, —why it just always has to be money...

—Because it always is money! See this? Comes in the same God damn mail, invitation to a gala she's giving for Victor Sweet.

—Oh! she turned, —could we...

—Donation two hundred dollars. I mean ever since I've known you Liz, every God damn invitation we've ever had from your rich friends has donation hidden down here in the corner, two hundred dollars five hundred don't they ever give free parties like other people? Just buy some whisky have some friends in give a party?

—Well of course Paul they, I mean these are benefits they don't, we don't have to go.

—Go? a benefit for Victor Sweet, go? told you where he gets his backing didn't I? Walk in there's half the KGB to meet you, told you where he takes his orders didn't I? Run him against Teakell they think they'll have a mouthpiece out on the Senate floor pushing disarmament, part of their whole God damn peace offensive tell you something else Liz, I heard

97

he's got a prison record. Want your flaky friends giving galas for jailbirds with a tax writeoff helping the blacks without getting their hands dirty same thing Liz, your brother and his greasy Buddhists same God damn thing. Show contempt for Victor Sweet by giving him money and contempt for the money by giving it to Victor Sweet, he couldn't pour piss out of a boot if you wrote the instructions on the heel. Look at Mister Jheejheeboy, look at her Burmese, money like that's supposed to mean you can buy the best, best food, best cars, friends, lawyers brokers all these God damn doctors but the money attracts the worst so that's what they buy, they buy the worst and the worst scare off the best because you're not leaving money to the kids that's not what happens. You don't leave the money to the kids you leave the kids to the money, two or three generations everybody's crazy.

—Everybody who, Paul.

—Look at any of this big old money, you'll see a nut or two at the dinner table won't you? They take away Uncle William's striped trousers think that will keep him in the hospital, last he was seen running up Second Avenue in nothing but his underpants? Ten years ago the cops would have picked him right up, now everybody thinks he's just out jogging don't even turn around take a look at your father, Billy in there pissing on the floor if that isn't...

—You left me out, didn't you?

—Didn't say that Liz I didn't say that, didn't say you're crazy, have to admit it's God damn strange though don't you, five years ago you read in the paper somebody put a rattlesnake in somebody's mailbox you're still afraid to open one? just getting things lined up here with Senator Teakell now you want me to show up at a benefit for Victor Sweet?

—I didn't say that Paul. She'd turned back to the window, her eyes raised now to a sodden streamer of toilet paper blown high in the limbs of the mulberry tree. —Just, my friends I just wish you'd leave them out of your...

—Oh come on Liz, it's Edie's gala isn't it? She gets up there in a five thousand dollar gown, all the lights on nobody home and they drop their...

—I'm not talking about Edie just Edie I'm talking about Cettie! I'm talking about Reverend Ude showing up at that hospital in Texas with those hideous flowers the day her father came down to see her and all the...

—No now look Liz. Jump to conclusions we don't have to drag through that again, coincidence they both happened to...

—That those newspaper photographers just happened to be there? that your Doris Chin just happened to be there to tell us how he gently took Senator Teakell's arm at the bedside and drew him down in prayer honestly!

—Same thing Liz same God damn thing, jump to conclusions if you hadn't called that florist and...

—I didn't call them they called me! They called about the bill for a six foot cross made of white carnations they'd sent her, when I said I couldn't imagine such a thing they told me it went with a card from Reverend Ude's deepest something in the bowels of Christ it was sickening, the whole thing it was perfectly sickening.

—Look I said I was sorry they didn't come from you, must have got the orders mixed up they...

—Well thank God they didn't. Telling me you'd sent her flowers in my name, that ghastly thing it looked like a funeral why did you tell me that. Lining things up with Senator Teakell why didn't you just tell me that's what you were doing instead of, of using her just using her, lying there half dead you never thought of me did you, that I might really want to see her. Your Reverend Ude walking in out of nowhere to wash her in the blood of Jesus it didn't occur to you that I might really want to go down there and, just see her...

—Oh come on Liz what harm was there, here. Pour me some coffee, what time is it. Got your watch on?

—It was in my purse. Look at the clock, she said without doing so, looking instead at the cat out there crouched in the leaves.

—Look I looked at the clock Liz it says five twenty three,

you think it's five twenty three in the morning? Electricity must have gone off last night... and his sudden turn in the chair twisted the livid scar coursing up from the drab plaid of his shorts, set sculptural muscles bolting through his shoulders, down his arm for so simple a thing as snapping on the radio which promptly invited him, invited them both in fact, to deposit money in the Emigrant Savings Bank. —Got her under so much sedation she doesn't know what's going on anyhow... he was tapping a pencil on the pile of bills in front of him, —so what harm was there. I told you Ude was out there on a speaking tour didn't I? Had a divine call to go in and pray for her happened to be the same day her father showed up from Washington, whole thing just a coincidence it said that right there in the paper didn't it? Ude gets his message of faith and prayer in papers all over the God damn country, says divine providence brought them together in the shadow of the valley of look, just because you don't believe in faith and...

—Oh stop it Paul stop it! Honestly.

—What. Honestly what.

—Don't believe in faith and...

—What I just said isn't it? Problem look, problem Liz you don't try and see the big picture he came on scattering bills, envelopes, mailing pieces in thrilling colour, flushing the blank side of a letter opening Dear Friend of the Bowhead Whale —look. He had a blunt pencil, —here's Teakell... and a smudged circle appeared and shot forth an arrow. —Got his own constituency here... a blob took roughly kidney shape, —Senate committees and the big voice for Administration policy up here... something vaguely phallic, —and his whole big third world Food for Africa program over here... and an arrow shot to distant coastlines shaped up abruptly in a deformed footprint. —Now here's Ude... a cross this time, releasing an arrow —same God damn constituency... and it penetrated the blob —but look. He gets his whole satellite television operation in operation... and the cross, gone abruptly from Latin to Calvary with steps added for emphasis, radiated jagged streaks, the blob erupted —he's all over the God damn country, constituency goes from way up here to all his blacks down here... a smudge unconnected to anything, —you think they can't mark their X on a ballot? think Teakell plans to spend his life in the Senate? Taking his big stand in this third world confrontation going over there right now on a fact finding tour and here's Ude's missions right on the spot... and an arrow leaped from the true cross to strike the distant coastline, spewing aggressive miniatures into the deformity that rose to accommodate them in splayfoot proportions when the phone rang. —Hello? who, God damn it wait... he rescued the page —get a paper towel... but she'd already torn off a length, setting his cup upright where the phone's cord had caught it, sopping up coffee from the scattered bills, notes, invitations to send off for 20-Pc. Bath Towel Sets with Free Digital Quartz Watch, to buy books, buy wrench sets, save seals, sell dinnerware, borrow money, booklets threatening tribulation, apocalypse, inviting eternity in florid colour —hey there, Bobbie Joe? Just going to call you. Just finishing up a breakfast meeting here with my staff, thought I'd fill you in on the big picture. Now what we... not the movie no, not talking about the movie yet I'm talking about mapping out our media strategy for the next big push got a pencil handy...? Better not try that no, little too complicated you better get a pencil I'll hold on, Liz can you clean up this God damn mess? These right here, these brochures got to take them with me... he thrust forth Tribulation, the Christian Battle Map, Guide to Eternity, Harvest Time for —get me some more coffee? seen my cigarettes?

—I'll have to make it, there's not...

—Thinks I'm calling him about a movie, big movie they want to make call it The Wayne Fickert Story get the kid's mother in there as the, hello? got the pencil? Good, now here's the big picture, we... not the movie I just told you not the movie look, talking about keying our overall media strategy to your daddy's next big appearance. Got him on the front page we want to keep him on the front page, that's the whole... I said his next big appearance, crusade out there just kicked things off we've got California wrapped up, taped, broadcast, headlights purple ribbons the whole package, what he... what...? No well that's just what I'm saying Bobbie Joe now just listen here. What your daddy wants now, he wants a platform that's going to give his image real dignity, He wants... well I know he has but we want to show them a real serious issue he can sink his teeth into, that's... the what...? No wait, that's... Look that's not what I... No now look here Bobbie Joe, I know they's eight hundred million Catholics out there he considers a field ripe for harvest but let's not jump the God, jump the gun here. I'm talking about education, school education. Now here's this big southwest regional educators' conference where they've got him up there giving the keynote address? You've got prominent educators coming in from all over Texas, Kansas, Mississippi, Oklahoma Arkansas the whole backbone of American education? Now what we... no wait a minute, don't want to get into that no, break a few school bus windows that's not what I'm talking about, look. He's just announced he's founding the Wayne Fickert Bible College now that's the... call it the what? When did he promise you that, he... No but that's way back when you were just a little old boy, he goes and changes it now to the Bobbie Joe Ude Bible College you'll have these media people in there twisting things around now what he's talking about up there, he's talking about these high education standards. That's what he's got Wayne Fickert Bible College dedicated to. Now he takes that real good idea of yours where the men students will all wear jackets and ties? Starts right off there talking about these high academic standards and the... what? That's a, c, a, d e m i c you got that? What...? Well go find a piece of paper then I'll hold on, Liz? Can you stop all this messing here and go get me a shirt?

—Do you want the...

—Just a shirt any God damn shirt, stand here freezing to death while he looks for a piece of paper, gets a pencil it doesn't occur to him he'll need something to hello? All set now...? Not every word no, just giving you a list of talking points for your daddy to go over for this speech here. First he's talking about this desperate need for academic excellence? how it's being threatened throughout the land by these same forces threatening the Constitution? that's the... what? That's capital c, o, n look Bobbie Joe, is your sister there...? She just wet her what? No, no I mean Betty Joe, your big sister Bet... locked up in the what? but who... Caught holding hands with a boy now that don't sound so... Oh. Oh, well now she's bound to meet a real nice white boy one of these days don't you fret, now you got a dictionary there anywhere...? Well I know it's a real big word but you'll just have to do the best you can till your daddy sends out for a dic... Well he can't just not allow a dictionary in the house because it's got swear words in it, now let's get... all right, just do the best you can, hear? How the US Constitution protects religious freedom, that's the right to enforce prayers in the schools you got that? Next thing he talks about academic freedom. Now that's where they feel real strong, teaching these science courses where these same forces trying to destroy the Constitution are trying to stop them teaching science like they're trying to stop free speech, pushing his television show off the air, twisting the ratings lying with statistics the whole... of the what...? No well now I'd just go a little easy on that Satan the father of lies for right now Bobbie Joe. This audience of real good Americans they already know that, he wants to talk to them more about how these liberal media people are trying to squeeze him so he can't get up there and preach against sin, can't support his Africa missions, trying to keep his Bible College from sending out these fine well educated Christian men and women for... to where...? I know that Bobbie Joe but we're not talking about Jaypan now, a great harvest field that's been long neglected I know he's got a real heavy anointing to get in there and save them but this audience isn't coming to hear about Jaypan, hundred million of them all bunched up in those little islands they've got enough Buddhism and Shintoism to keep them busy besides, they don't vote he can harvest them later, let's just take one continent at a time here. Now Christianity's an American religion, that's what he's talking about isn't it? the only bulwark there is against the spread of the evil empire? That's what he's... well now wait, I'd go easy on the... Well now look, I think this audience is pretty well harvested already or they wouldn't be sitting there, they come out of the hall and he has you outside there selling the Little Wayne lapel pin, the t shirts with the smartly designed Little Wayne logo and your record albums Pearly Gates singing Elton Ude's Christmas Favorites you're going to get the liberal media twisting the whole God, whole thing into a carni... Who, Pearly Gates? What kind of a parade... Well your daddy he can just bring that in talking about the constitutional right to bear arms but I'd just go real easy on this Bobbie Joe. See I know your daddy's got Pearly Gates all fired up about how angry Satan is over all the souls you all have rescued but this audience now, they're all educators. Now that means you've got a nice white audience out there they might just not take to it, he better just stay with the singing hold on a minute... cupping the phone against his groin, —this the only shirt you could find?

—You said just to bring you any...

—White one right out there on the chair, never mind I'll get it myself hello? Look, now one more thing. You tell your daddy make sure he's got a flag up there on the platform when he... No now listen here, his picture on the front page all over the country they's going to be yankees seeing it too, it better just be the regular American flag, and you tell him when he's done his speech he just doesn't need to give any press conference, all they'll... Look I know they's all friends there Bobbie Joe but you get somebody infiltrating from the liberal media they'll twist things around to beat all get out, like they did when your daddy said he was a Zionist? that that's the Holy Land where you'll have Jesus' Second Coming but he won't show up till all the Jews there are born again? where they had him saying that the only thing that keeps the Jews Jews is being hated by everybody else? Who do you think runs this liberal media, now look. When he's done his speech he just wants to get down there and circulate with these prominent educators, you hear? Get their names and addresses everybody registered for this conference and get your Bible students down there working on your mailing lists that's the... Well then get some of them off the night shift at the bottling plant, somebody gets his Pee Dee water a week late's not going to kill him now one more thing. Your daddy tell you there's somebody supposed to meet me later there at National Airport? Little gift shop right there at the... no problem I'll have on a red tie, little gift shop right there at the head of the ramp you make sure he's there, hear? Got to hurry now, I... you bet. We'll... You bet Bobbie Joe, you... you bet. Liz? What time is it.

—I told you, I don't...

—Turn on the God damn radio won't even tell you what time it is, do it myself... and he had the phone again, —look. One more thing, waiting to hear from somebody named Slotko he's a partner in a big time Washington law firm most prestigious in the country, triple A gilt edge you don't get near him without the right credentials I've got him working on your old man's VCR stock option, make sure if he calls that you, wait... pressing the phone close, dropping it, —got to hurry.

—What time is it? She'd already reached up for the clock.

—Late I've got to get dressed and look, can you mop this up here? this pile here got to take it with me...

The radio warned her that five million Americans had diabetes and didn't know it and that she might be one of them and she got over to turn it off, to tear another length of paper towel, to look in the refrigerator for yogurt she'd brought in the day before and could not find it, and she'd just made tea when he was down again buttoning a white shirt, jamming it into his trousers. —Any coffee?

—No, I'd just made a cup of tea but...

—Better than nothing, he reached past her for it —look

where did I put the, you find my cigarettes?

—I haven't seen them Paul.

—Try to keep track of anything here can't even, what was I talking about.

—Well you wanted me to make...

—Not talking about making coffee Liz, something important before I went upstairs something important.

—You wanted me to make sure to wait for a call from some Washington lawyer named...

—Slotko, see? if you'd just listen? Write it down so you won't forget it... he found the blunt pencil, —not just some Washington lawyer Liz he's the best you can get, top contacts inside the Administration I gave him a few pointers on the estate picking up your old man's stock option before they get VCR in court, twenty percent below market the price keeps slipping where all these God damn leaks are coming from, maybe just plain disinformation from the other side trying to knock the bottom out from under this confrontation building up over there part of their big peace offensive putting the blinders on these woolly minded Victor Sweets calling for disarmament? speech I showed you last week he's right in there doing their work for them?

—Well he, I think all he said was we should keep an open mind about...

—Keep an open mind your brains will fall out look, where is it... and he found the page he'd rescued dry, —Belgian syndicate up here maybe it's them driving the price down to buy in cheap. They've got Grimes in their pocket, here's Grimes he's got Teakell in his pocket why he's going on this fact finding trip, why they had him up on the Senate floor with that front page speech about these strategic mineral reserves over there, protecting vital US interests... smoothing the page flat, smudging the pencil strokes nearer that beleaguered coastline, —why Teakell stepped in and got me a dismissal on these hearings. Scared I'd get up there and testify it was common company practice, pay them off to do business over there or you don't do business at all... and a scrawled loop, infinity open ended? or a fish —Grimes and the whole God damn VCR board calling the shots from the start. Elections coming up this Administration needs a big win any God damn place they can get one, build up grass roots support's why Teakell's people need Ude's mailing list, his missions out there harvesting souls for the Lord... a sudden cluster of ciphers, —Teakell right back here harvesting votes... and a horde of v's appeared launching an arrow, another arrow —Grimes to Teakell, Teakell to Ude, Ude to the point everything goes both ways... more arrows, —everything to everything else... and a hail of arrows darkened the page like the skies that day over Crécy. —Liz?

—Oh? She turned from making pale tea with the leaves still wet in the strainer, staring out to the disconsolate garland high in the limbs of the mulberry tree, down the fence where the wild grape's few blemished leaves still clung to the tangle of curl and tendril and the rest of them gone to earth in scraps so withered brown they'd no more claim left to identity than torn scraps of a grocery bag, on down where the Virginia creeper lingering flushed a deeper red and bittersweet paled yellow toward the sparse heights of the wild cherry caught in the glance of morning sun in hesitating shades of yellows, even pinks as though, as though suddenly arrested in its inconspicuous departure, as though —Paul?

—You follow me? Fit the God damn...

—I want to go down and see Cettie.

—all the pieces together and, see what?

—Cettie. I want to go down to that hospital and see her.

—But you, I told you Liz, just told you they've got her sedated she wouldn't know you were there, lawyers came in to get a deposition from her suing the car company she couldn't even...

—That's not what I'm talking about!

—Plenty of time to see her later when she can...

—Later? She stood there, looking out where she'd been looking. —You'll have to leave me money for Madame Socrate.

He sat back, gazing at the scribbled mess in front of him as though silenced by admiration. —Been thinking about that Liz, washes windows you can't tell the difference she can't even answer the God damn phone, probably illiterate somebody calls her in French she couldn't even write it down if they did, just thinking we can do without her for a while and look. If this writer, this Doris Chin if she calls this afternoon just tell her I'll be gone two or three days, four at the outside tell her...

—I won't be here Paul.

—What do you, be where wait get this will you? He pushed the phone toward her —if it's that Bobbie Joe again tell him I just left, tell him...

—Hello...? Yes well he's, who is it... cupping the phone at her breast. —It's a Sergeant Urich.

—Never heard of, wait it might be the VA give me it, might be about my pension hello...? What...? No, twenty fifth, I was in the twenty fifth infantry what's the... platoon leader look, what's it about who... look, I... No look I, medical, eighty percent look how the hell did they get hold of my record, who... No well look now look I'm, I can't just told you I can't just too God damn busy I'm, got to be out of town be out of, out of the country just too God damn busy no I'm, goodbye no, goodbye... He held the phone tight for a moment, and then hung it up. —Liz?

—Who was it, what...

—You find my cigarettes?

—No, no I told I...

—Look in my jacket in there? would you? just look in my jacket?

She came back emptyhanded. —They're not...

—God damn cup... it shook, and he steadied his hand without spilling it, putting it down again —got a chip in it, right on the rim where you drink look, if you get a call. If you get a, if you get a call from this, from this what's his name you just wrote it down didn't you? Call from Washington, this...

—Mister Slotko.

—Call from Washington this Mister Slotko, just let me finish will you? Look in the mail, big time law firm probably turn it into a ten page letter ten dollars a word all you want's yes or no, picking up this option all you want's a yes or no supposed to call this afternoon, if he...

—I won't be here Paul. I have a doctor's appointment.

—Doctor, God damn it Liz I mean look... he swept the bills into a wet heap, —doctor, doctor doctor add these up you could buy your own God damn doctor, medical insurance looks the other way if you're not in the hospital couldn't you just go to one? Spend a week in one get things all straightened out?

—I wish I could.

—Get one doctor sends you to another doctor, split their fees and send you to...

—This is the airline insurance company's doctor, Paul. This is the examination you've been telling me to...

—All right go, go, he runs into any problems tell him to call me, headaches, dizziness nausea I can fill him in what time is it, thought you just set the clock.

—Will you just leave me the money for Madame Socrate before you forget it?

—All right! He was up digging deep in a pocket, —always getting in one step ahead of me... carefully peeling off a ten, another, fives —just try and learn some patience...

—And a dollar for her carfare?

—Here! God damn nickel and diming you call fifty one dollars small change like your God damn brother, he gives me seventy five dollars for a hundred dollar check should have told her to stop payment on it.

—Shall I suggest that when she calls?

He stopped half through the door. —When who calls.

—Tearful Mom. Or do you plan to see her later yourself.

—See? Same God damn thing don't drag that up again, he came back bunching jacket and tie, rummaging the pockets —think I gave her this phone number? Probably got it from Bobbie Joe before we sent her off to the fat farm shaped her up for Ude's big crusade, up there on nationwide television she's bringing in donations faster than they can count them already thinks she's a movie star don't drag that up again... jamming papers together on the table, rescuing one from the floor —God damn near forgot this... brandishing the page of scribbles, —Liz?

—I'm right here.

—I know you're right here! What do you think I, look. Notes I made I thought maybe you'll help us out on this mailing piece, got nothing to do here this afternoon just sit down and run it off? Started it myself but it just doesn't have that woman's touch yet, leave you these notes you can work something up all we want's a simple, honest letter Sally Joe Ude's writing to all these Chris...

—Who's Sally Joe, his wife?

—Hasn't got a wife Liz, she ran off with a feed salesman last year this Sally Joe she's his mother, she...

—Well can't she write it? Is she so old she can't write?

—Didn't say she was old Liz she's hardly in her forties, now...

—But how can she be his...

—Because she was fourteen when she got married, way they do things down there now will you stop interrupting? She's just not too God damn great with the written word, now...

—I shouldn't have asked.

—Right. Now what we want, just take a minute to run through it with you here opens with dear friend in Christ, Jesus, Christian mother she says I'm writing to you personally because I'm real worried about my son Elton, don't you get too literary like saying I'm extremely concerned scare them right up the wall, just this honest sincere Chris...

—Paul, I don't think...

—Don't have to, right. Now she says she had a letter from this other dear Christian mother out there saying Elton looked

110

sick on the television and is he all right, how the first thing any good Christian mother wants to do is take care of her son so that's why Sally Joe's writing this letter, to say she just can't keep quiet anymore about what's going on. Elton's not sick she says, reason he looks so God damn ragged on television is the persecution he's getting from these forces trying to stop him delivering God's word, all these lies in the liberal press take any God damn thing he says and twist it around like this great harvest in Mozambique? I show you that?

—No, but it hardly sounds...

—Talking about his Voice of Salvation radio and this great harvest they're reaping in Mozambique, press picks it up and says what harvest, it hasn't rained there in three years everybody starving, going blind, pellagra cholera they know God damn well he's not talking about a plate of beans, talking about harvesting souls for the Lord twist around whatever he says, smear stories like that his mission's running deficits of eighty thousand a day that's why Sally Joe's writing this personal letter. Wakes up there in bed at night that's what I mean Liz, this woman's touch, wakes up and hears poor Elton creeping around the prayer room seeking God two or three million dollars in debt now what she wants, what she wants, Liz?

—I think I can guess.

—Right, just a little prayerful gift maybe ten or twenty bucks help get this God damn money pressure off Elton out there trying to save the country or he may just crack up.

—Paul honestly, it's all...

—Just be patient Liz? think you can just be patient for a minute? Getting to the God damn point here what she's talking about it's America, pray for America pray for Brother Ude all the same God damn thing, send in your prayerful tax deductible gift because if Elton cracks up that's accomplishing Satan's purpose whole God damn country go down the drain. Last chance that's what he's talking about, how deep this country's sunk in sin's why God's chosen Elton to broadcast this last warning's what these forces are trying to wipe out here, don't pull up our socks and bring in the Holy Spirit God damn fast the whole future of our great nation may depend on Elton's not cracking up, just pray for him send along this little gift and the Lord will use it to stop these satanic forces trying to see what she's saying Liz?

—It's a very nice letter, Paul. Maybe if you take out the...

—Nice? you think so?

—The letter from the dear Christian mother asking about Elton's health yes, it's a very nice touch. You might want to take out the God damns but otherwise it's quite, after all you say you're getting an advance on writing a book and this should be good prac...

—Didn't say I'm writing a book by a woman did I? He pulled the tie under his collar, joined it for the knot —still doesn't quite have that kind of warm sincere woman's touch though look, look Liz. Told me once you'd started a novel didn't you? long time ago?

—That was a long time ago.

—Write a novel you make up these different characters? put them in these situations getting rich, getting divorced, getting laid where they're talking to each other you pretend you're these characters so they sound real? Same God damn thing Liz, sit down for ten minutes pretend you're this good loving Christian mother Sally Joe writing a nice letter to...

—Paul honestly! I, no, no why don't you get Doris Chin she, with her lone bluebonnet blowing on the flower strewn banks of the Pee...

—One God damn time I ask you to do something? can't support me can't back me up? He pulled the dark plaid knot tight at his throat, —can't sit down for ten minutes write a nice letter like any good Chris...

—Because I'm not a good faithful illiterate Christian mother because I'm not Sally Joe! She'd turned her back to the window, her hands tight behind her on the edge of the sink. —Is that the tie you're wearing?

—Is, what the hell does it look like! Can't do this one

112

little God damn thing, can't back me up can't support me stand there making fun of Sally Joe now you're making fun of my clothes?

—It's just your tie, Paul.

—What the hell's wrong with my tie!

She picked up her cup of pale tea. —Someone you're supposed to meet at the airport? the little gift shop at the head of the ramp? and you'll have on a red necktie?

—Just, God damn it... he came down heavily in the chair pulling away the knot at his throat, —always one step ahead of me... and he sat there slumped, staring at the arrows and crosses, the gang of ciphers, horde of v's, arrows and smudges. —Try to get the whole God damn thing together here there's always somebody in there waiting to cut you down, depend on them to come through you look around and they're not there. That movie I started and the big star playing Marco Polo OD'd on drugs? this whole big media conference center idea I had for Longview it was mine Liz, whole God damn idea was mine what happens. Your pal Jack Orsini all lined up with the investment, Ude still hung up on his broadcast licensing so Orsini pulls back and Adolph sells Longview right out from under us and the whole God damn, why I'm just asking for a little patience Liz all I'm asking, back me up a little that's all.

She emptied her cup into the sink and stood there running water into it. Outside, the movement of the cat on the leaves was almost imperceptible and below, the yellows and pinks of wild cherry were already gone with the lost glance of the sun; still she looked.

—Try to, try to get all the God damn pieces together, he came on to her back, —wring a dollar out of Ude down there he's already got one hell of a mess building up with the IRS, county health board ready to close him down says his new indoor plumbing's dumping raw sewage into the Pee Dee and they're going over that school bus wreck with a fine tooth comb, next thing somebody comes out of the woodwork with a court order to dig up that old bum he baptized says it's her brother, now they want to get Pearly Gates up there. Whole God damn hall full of white schoolteachers they want to get Gates up there in his, get Gates up there...

He was sitting with his shoulders fallen, staring at his hands, when she turned with —I think it's getting late Paul, if you...

—Look did Chick call? He looked up, —he ever call back?

—Well he, no, no not since he called to say he'd just got out, that's all he said. I mean I didn't know who he was or...

—He was my RTO. Chick was my RTO... He'd gone back to staring at his hands, one over the other there on the table as though to hold it still —whole God damn, call you up like that out of nowhere we want a real showing from the Lightning Division, come down to that God damn wailing wall see all your old buddies even get you a wheelchair, ride down Constitution Avenue in a God damn wheelchair... and his hand broke away to seize one of the sodden pamphlets opened to display a figure suspended by the wooden limitations of the artist's intentions headlong against black over a firescape of torment —get Gates up there, comes back both legs smashed no parade he'll have his own God damn parade. You get Bobbie Joe, you get Ude up there Reverend Ude under his powerful anointing by the Holy Spirit already insulted the Jews now he's ready to take on the Catholics, he's got Gates fired up with how Satan's mad as hell over all these souls they're harvesting for the Lord do any God damn thing he can to get their crusade going against the forces of the Antichrist Ude says God's promised to give him an army, valiant soldiers of the cross marching on to war, they get this hall full of white schoolteachers? wheel in this big spade in combat gear? You'll see them climbing right up the God damn walls where's the, got to get going I thought you'd set the clock... His chair banged the wall and he came up sweeping the booklets together, —take these with me thought I'd turned on the radio, find out what the hell time it is where you going.

—I was just going up to get your red necktie.

—I've got it Liz! Right there in my God damn bag now don't, try to show a little God damn patience... He stood shaking his shoulders into his jacket, tearing away the dark knot at his throat and jamming it into a pocket, wadding up the papers piecemeal in a turn for the living room where he opened his bag and jammed them in —and look... He got a foot up on the edge of the coffee table pulling the lace tight with a sharp tug for emphasis, and it snapped —God damn it! and he was down on the edge of the chair with the shoe off, hands trembling in his effort to rethread it and when he got it back on and knotted he sat there, and then he suddenly reached out to seize the magazine of Natural History. —I have to look at this God damn face every time I sit down? crushing it up in his hand —God damn smartass grin I still see it at night listen, if that, listen Liz if that same, if that Sergeant Urich if he calls again hang up just, hang up. Bands, flags, Drucker and his bag of ears just hang up they, fall in behind because they shut us out, eighty percent disability says they can provide a wheelchair? sit there in the rain see these weeping mothers running their fingers over a name nobody can pronounce? He twisted the magazine hard in both hands thrusting it at her, —just get this God damn thing out of the house?

—Don't you want to take a coat? she came after him.

He had the front door open but he stood there, looking out, looking up, —little bastards look at that, not even Halloween till tonight but they couldn't wait... Toilet paper hung in disconsolate streamers from the telephone lines, arched and drooped in the bared maple branches reaching over the windows of the frame garage beyond the fence palings where shaving cream spelled fuck. —Look keep the doors locked, did this last night Christ knows what you're in for tonight... and the weight of his hand fell away from her shoulder, —Liz? just try and be patient? and he pulled the door hard enough for the snap of the lock to startle her less with threats locked out than herself locked in, to leave her steadying a hand on the newel before she turned back for the kitchen where the radio, muttering to itself all this time, took this opportune silence to tell her that three men whose boat had capsized in Long Island Sound had been saved in a thrilling rescue operation by the Coast Guard and she snapped it off, her eyes drawn in a kind of perplexity there emptying the cup of tea he'd left cold on the table and putting it aside unrinsed in the first of what became, as the morning fell away, a progress through the house of chores abandoned, dry wisps of lingerie in the bathroom basin and damp towels and socks as far as the floor in the hall, the vacuum cleaner dragged out and left and even paper towels and the spray bottle to the head of the stairs where she caught the bannister, turned back for the bathroom and quietly threw up.

She woke abruptly to a black rage of crows in the heights of those limbs rising over the road below and lay still, the rise and fall of her breath a bare echo of the light and shadow stirred through the bedroom by winds flurrying the limbs out there till she turned sharply for the phone and dialed slowly for the time, up handling herself with the same fragile care to search the mirror, search the world outside from the commotion in the trees on down the road to the straggle of boys faces streaked with blacking and this one, that one in an oversize hat, sharing kicks and punches up the hill where in one anxious glimpse the mailman turned the corner and was gone.

Through the festoons drifting gently from the wires and branches a crow dropped like shot, and another, stabbing at a squirrel crushed on the road there, vaunting black wings and taking to them as a car bore down, as a boy rushed the road right down to the mailbox in the whirl of yellowed rust spotted leaves, shouts and laughter behind the fence palings, pieces of pumpkin flung through the air and the crows came back all fierce alarm, stabbing and tearing, bridling at movement anywhere till finally, when she came out to the mailbox, stillness enveloped her reaching it at arm's length and pulling it open. It looked empty; but then there came sounds of hoarded laughter behind the fence palings and she was standing there holding the page, staring at the picture of a blonde bared to the margin, a full tumid penis squeezed stiff in her hand and pink as the tip of her tongue drawing the beading at its engorged head off in a fine thread. For that moment the blonde's eyes, turned to her in forthright complicity, held her in their steady stare; then her tremble was lost in a turn to be plainly seen crumpling it, going back in and dropping it crumpled on the kitchen table.

It was still there when she came back down the stairs, differently dressed now, eyeliner streaked on her lids and the colour unevenly matched on her paled cheeks, there was still a quaver in her hand when she reached for the phone, in her voice when she said —Who, hello...? She swallowed and cleared her throat, her free hand moving to smooth the picture out flat on the table before her —I'm sorry, who... oh... The voice burst at her from the phone and she held it away, staring down close at the picture as though something, some detail, might have changed in her absence, as though what was promised there in minutes, or moments, might have come in a sudden burst on the wet lips as the voice broke from the phone in a pitch of invective, in a harried staccato, broke off in a wail and she held it close enough to say —I'm sorry Mister Mullins, I don't know what to... and she held it away again bursting with spleen, her own fingertip smoothing the still fingers hoarding the roothairs of the inflexible surge before her with polished nails, tracing the delicate vein engorged up the curve of its glistening rise to the crown cleft fierce with colour where that glint of beading led off in its fine thread to the still tongue, mouth opened without appetite and the mascaraed eyes unwavering on hers without a gleam of hope or even expectation, —I don't know I can't tell you! I haven't seen Billy I don't know where he is! I'm sorry... she crushed the picture up in her hand, —I can't now no, no there's someone at the door... Someone hunched down, peering in —Wait! She had it crushed in a step for the trash taking Natural History's crumpled Masai with it, —wait... she caught breath coming through, seizing

117

the knob tight, and then —oh... getting it open, —Mister McCandless I'm sorry, I, come in...

But he paused where she'd faltered, caught the newel with her hand. —Something wrong? I didn't mean to alarm you.

—No I'm, please, please go right in and, and whatever you...

—No, no here, sit down. He had her arm, had her hand in fact firm in one of his —I didn't mean to alarm you.

—It wasn't that... but she let him lead her to the edge of the frayed love seat, her hand in a sharp tremor as his escaped it. —It's the, just the mess out there, Halloween out there...

—Like the whole damned world isn't it... he was pulling off the battered raincoat, —kids with nothing to do.

—No there's, there's a meanness...

—No no no, no it's plain stupidity Mrs Booth. There's much more stupidity than there is malice in the world... Something in a paper bag protruding from the raincoat pocket banged the coffee table as he passed and he caught it up more carefully, and then from the kitchen, —Mrs Booth? I didn't know you had children?

She turned sharply. —What? He was sorting keys from a pocket when she came in, standing there over the blobs and crosses, lightning strokes, hails of arrows —oh, oh that that's just, nothing... She sat down, at her elbow the eyes stared from the paper bag holes on the ragged shred of newsprint —do, do you? She edged it under the damp heap of bills, —have children I mean? He didn't have children, no, he told her, over thrusting a key in the padlock, shaking it loose. —Oh and wait, wait I'm glad I remembered. Have you got another key? to the house here? He nodded, why, had she lost hers? both of them? —No they were stolen, I mean my purse was stolen with both of them in it I know it sounds silly but...

—It doesn't sound silly. Where.

—Was it stolen? At Saks, in the ladies' room at Saks, I'd

been... When, he wanted to know. —Last week, about a week ago I'd been... And what else was in it, credit cards? a driver's license? anything with this address? —I don't know, I'm not sure I mean there wasn't much money and my card at Saks wasn't, it had expired anyway and there was nothing you'd, anything like a license. I've never had a license. I mean I don't even know how to drive.

He was having difficulty getting a key free of the ring, twisting it awkwardly, finally getting it off with a wince, —here... handing it to her, —incidentally, that man who showed up here looking for me? Has he been back?

—Oh he, no. No that rude one no, I mean not that I know of and I've hardly not been here, Paul wants the house kept locked so I've been here whenever he's away not that I wouldn't anyhow, she came on as though a pause would lose him through the door he'd slid open, —be here I mean. Paul's gone now he'll be gone for two or three days and you'll probably leave before I come back, I mean I have to leave in a few minutes I have an appointment this afternoon but it's not like, it's not really going somewhere... He'd gathered up the wadded raincoat, turning for the door, hadn't he over-heard her on the phone mention Montego Bay? —Oh did you? And she was up pursuing this parting pleasantry of his round the end of the table with —when you were here last yes I, maybe I did but we've had to postpone it. We have friends there who, people who Paul's awfully fond of but he's been so busy, he travels so much now but it's all just business, places like down south and Texas and Washington I mean no place you'd ever really want to go to... She'd come as far as the door where he stood just inside, examin-ing the room as though for some detail in its disarray that might have changed since he'd left it. —They all just expect everything to get done then it's always Paul that has to do it, he's the one that has all the ideas he depends on people then he looks around and they're just not there that's why they depend on him so much, he...

—Yes while I think of it he said, his back to her standing there making a cigarette, —would it be convenient to give me a check for the rent?

—Yes I, that's what I was just going to say... she recovered the cautious step she'd taken into the room where the books lay cascaded from her last retreat there, —I mean that's why Paul forgets things here sometimes, when he left this morning he forgot to give me the rent check to deposit I mean if we mailed it to you, if we mailed you the rent then I'd know I mean I do the mail but if we still don't even know where you live?

—I wish you would then, he said, found a pencil somewhere and tore the corner from a discarded calendar, just temporary, he was staying at a friend's place while he got things cleared up.

—Oh... she read the scrap he'd handed her, her voice fallen, —it's not a real address is it, I mean it's just a box number it's not where you're staying with somebody who, you mean probably staying with somebody you've met since you, since she left I mean, I didn't mean...

He'd finally turned facing her through a gasp of smoke, sunk back against the table length litter of papers, books, folders, dirty saucers, a coffee cup, a shadeless lamp. —It's simply a man I've known for a number of years, he said, —nobody there, he's out of the country. Now I don't want to keep you, you said you had an appointment and I've got a good many things here to...

—Yes I didn't mean to pry, it's just... she backed off to the door, —I mean I don't blame you, living alone here for two whole years with everything like, everything just waiting like the silk flowers in there when you come down the stairs wait, oh wait I just thought of something before you start what you're doing wait, I'll get it... and she left him reaching down a thumbprinted glass from a bookshelf, pulling the bottle from the paper bag in the raincoat pocket and pouring a level ounce. He'd emptied the glass, made another cigarette and lit it at the sound of her down the stairs, the lines of her lips more clearly drawn now and those on her lids at less hazardous odds she came into the kitchen holding out the worn address book. —It was in the trash, it looked important I thought...

—Do you go through my trash?

She'd stopped short, across the table where he seized it from her —I didn't mean, I thought maybe you'd thrown it away by mistake it looked...

—It's, all right he muttered, standing twisting the thing in his hands as though he might have said more before he turned for the trash to drop it in, and then he paused, bent over, reaching down into the trash after it —here, you don't mind if I rescue this?

—No wait don't not that no I, wait... She caught the corner of the table, flushed, —oh... getting breath, —oh. He'd straightened up with the Natural History magazine.

—I thought you'd thrown it out.

—No that's all right yes, yes for that story about, on the cover? you said they steal cattle? And her sudden urgency seemed to weigh everything on his response, the Masai and their cattle raids, as though right now in this kitchen, clinging to the table corner, nothing else mattered.

—Well, well yes, he said —they, it's their ancient belief that all the cattle in the world belong to them. When they raid other tribes they're just taking back what was stolen from them long ago, a good serviceable fiction isn't it ... He held the magazine out to her —you might want to read it? It's not what I want anyhow, there's a piece here on the Piltdown fraud I can just tear it out and...

—That's all right no, no keep the whole thing please. I, I just wish I could stay and talk to you, do you know what time it is? The clock stopped last night and I...

—It's two twenty, he said consulting no more than her hands seizing one in the other, following her haste through to where her coat lay flung over the newel.

—I won't be back till after dark, I mean it gets dark so early now but if you need anything, if your work keeps you

121

here I mean there's food in the refrigerator if you, if you get hungry before you go... She reached for the coat but he already had it, holding it up for her —because I won't get home till it's dark and that, Halloween out there, if they did that last night... she'd turned, a hand back to hold her hair up away from the sudden glint of perspiration beading the white of her neck where he settled the collar, —what they'll do tonight... All she'd get tonight would be the little ones in costume he told her, getting the door open on the blown leaves, the disconsolate streamers, the shaving cream exhortation across the black stream of the road where he watched her hesitant step down as one into the chill of unfamiliar waters, watched her down past the carrion crow raising scarcely a flutter before he pressed the door closed for the snap of the lock.

Then he stood there, his gaze foreshortened to the stitched silence of the sampler's When we've matched our buttons... and when he did turn it was to walk over to the alcove and stand there looking out; to pause over the cyclamen, flick its silk petals for dust; to stand running a hand over the rosewood curve of a dining room chair looking over the plants, looking out past them to the unraked lawn, pressing a loose moulding into place with his foot each step, coming through to the kitchen, retracing steps leading him back through the sliding door to stand, where he could approach them close enough, reading the titles of books, taking one down to blow it off and replace it or simply run a finger down the spine, before he got over to light another cigarette and spread another folder on the litter before him. There he turned papers, removed one, dropped another crumpled into the Wise Potato Chips Hoppin' With Flavor! carton at his feet, folded, tore, made another cigarette put down beside one still smouldering in the yellowed dip of marble at his elbow shattering its still blue curl of smoke with an abrupt exhalation of grey to stare at a page, at a diagram, a map detail, a torn shred of newspaper already yellowed and he was up again, staring out through the clouded pane at the halting drift of the old celebrant out there, broom and flattened dustpan going on before, his wavering course to the dented repository ahead broken by doubtful pauses, getting his bearings, gaping aloft at faith stretched fine in the toilet paper celebration over-head. Inside there he poured another ounce of the whisky and went back to the kitchen, to the dining room, stopping to square the table and draw the chairs up even around it, putting his hands on things, till finally his steps took him mounting the stairs themselves and down the hall to the open bedroom to stand in its doorway looking, simply look-ing at the empty bed there. He'd come back up the hall, past sodden mounds of towels, socks, a long glimpse in at the white frill there in the bathroom basin when something, a movement no more than the flutter of a bird's wing, caught his eye through the glass at the foot of the stairs and he stepped back. Then the sound, no more than the sharp rustle of a branch, and the door came open, went closed again on the figure abruptly inside, one small hand on the newel like something alighted there. —Lester?

—What are you doing here.

—You didn't know? It's my house... He came out on the stairs, —you should have told me you were coming, saved you some trouble... and down them, —you could have been up on a morals charge.

—What are you talking about.

—The ladies' room at Saks.

—Still getting it all wrong aren't you, McCandless... and in fact the plastic card he'd sprung the lock with was still in his hand. —Always getting it wrong... and the card went thrust into a pocket of the speckled tweed jacket that seemed, from behind now, to draw the narrow shoulders even more close as he stood by the coffee table looking about. —Inter-esting old house, you know what you've got here? the head cocked this way, that, —it's a classic piece of Hudson river carpenter gothic, you know that?

—I know that, Lester.

—All designed from the outside, that tower there, the roof peaks, they drew a picture of it and squeezed the rooms in later... darting now along the line of the ceiling moulding to the crumbled plaster finial where it met the alcove's arch, —you've got a roof leak there... as though he'd come to give an appraisal, come up to buy the place, —have it fixed before it gets worse. You getting into the redhead?

—You should have asked her.

From the alcove back to the chimneypiece and down, his steps followed his glance through to the kitchen as the phone rang and he stood there at the table studying the smudges, crosses, hails of arrows till it stopped ringing. —She got kids?

—You should have asked her.

And at the sliding door now, —I thought you were neater than this, McCandless. What was this, the garage? He stepped in over the cascaded books, a carton marked glass, fluttered a hand up to stir the still planes of smoke. —I thought you were going to quit those cigarettes... He turned half perched on the edge of an open filing cabinet. —You see these white doors from the outside, it still looks like a garage. Who did all the work in here, put in all these bookshelves, you? But all that came back was a puff of smoke, a hand reaching past him for the thumbprinted glass. —You know that's the worst thing you can do at your age? the cigarettes and the whisky? They work together, kill the circulation. Lose a couple of toes and you'll see what I mean.

—How about a couple of thumbs.

—Maybe you got it backwards. Maybe that never really happened, McCandless. Maybe what really happened was what happened in your rotten novel... The boots dangled bump, bumping against the metal file. —I didn't hear about it for a month. I didn't hear about it till I was back in Nairobi. Maybe it was just bar talk.

—No no no, don't try that on me no, you knew damned well I was still there when you pulled out. You knew they had Seiko.

—Seiko was theirs. He knew what was coming... Bump, bump, —trouble with you McCandless, you'd always blame somebody else wouldn't you. What do you know about the redhead.

—They rented the house, they got it through an agent that's all. Is that what you want to know? what you came all the way up here for? Worried about my health, chat about architecture is that what you...

—Just taking an interest... One of the boots thrust out to flick open a manila folder heaped on the floor. —You rented them the house, what are you doing here.

—Cleaning things up. I came up here to get things cleaned up what about you. What in hell are you doing here.

—What things.

—All of it. Everything.

—Quite a job. At your age that's quite a job isn't it... Pages spilled from the manila folder with a stab of his boot. —What's this.

—Read it. Take it with you and read it.

—I don't want to read it. I don't need to read it... He bent over the file drawer to push aside a folder, another, —maybe I can help you. Clean all this up you'll need some help won't you, he brought up papers in a handful, caught one from dropping with the rest —here's your accident policy with Bai Sim Casualty, Burundi, convenient offices everywhere. Loss of life five thousand dollars, taken out by Lendro Mining that's not very flattering is it.

—One trip, that was one trip across the...

—Now wait, wait. Loss of both hands, both feet, both eyes, a hand or a foot and an eye you still pick up the five thousand. That's not bad is it. Nothing here about thumbs though... He'd glanced up at the tobacco spilling from the ends of a paper being drawn into a new cigarette, —or toes, it's got to be the whole hand or foot. Loss means actual severance through or above wrist or ankle joints for hands or feet, maybe you'll have better luck next time... and he let it fall with a new handful of envelopes, ticket folders, a prescription —didn't know you needed glasses, I never saw you with glasses here, you better hang on to this... He held out a bank note, —ever get back over there you may need it. What are these.

—They're comic books. Take them with you and read them.

—I don't want to read them.

—No take them, take them. They're good clean fun, one there on God creating the universe and there's a really juicy one on the wages of sin take them along, hand them out on the subway.

—And don't start that again.

—I start it? Good God Lester you're the missionary, you're that skinny kid in the cheap black suit, the black tie and that cheap white shirt you washed out every night in the...

—Who are you working for, McCandless. He waved away a fresh cloud of smoke coming down from the file, turning up folders stacked on the floor with the point of a boot. —You've got some job here, you know that? he came on, unrolling a map far enough for a glimpse of familiar coastline to let it go with a snap, picking up a notebook to riffle blank pages, dropping it to hold up a glossy square of colour. —What's this.

—What does it look like.

—It looks like an infrared scanning. I know what it looks like. Where. Where was it. He stood there kicking at a heap of magazines, Geotimes, Journal of Geophysical Research, Science, —we lost track of you there for a while, you were out in Texas? Oklahoma? I saw your name in the paper didn't I?

—How in hell do I know what you saw in the paper.

—Testifying as the big expert witness? the big authority on the age of the earth? One of those trials over teaching science in the schools, you were the big...

—Genesis, teaching laundered Genesis in the schools where do you think those damned comic books came from. Try to teach them real science they'll run you out of town, tell them the earth's more than ten thousand years old they'll lynch you, the same damned smug stup...

—You wrote this? He'd straightened up with a magazine crushed open in the heap. —What did you find up there.

—Up where.

—The Gregory Rift, it's about the Gregory Rift.

—I know what it's about, that's my name on it isn't it? Take it, take and read it.

—I don't want to read it. Were you up there for Klinger?

—I wasn't up there for anybody.

—What did you find up there.

—Same thing the Leakeys found up there fifty years ago, those fossil remains they dug out of the volcanic ash on Lake Rudolf read it, take it and read it.

—You ought to stick to this, McCandless. You ought to stick to writing science, you know that? The magazine went tossed to the floor, —your fiction is really rotten, you know that? He'd kicked aside a cobwebbed roll of canvas, the black on white, or was it white on black roll of a hide, getting over to run down a row of books in the bookshelf, Plate Tectonics, Second Gondwana Symposium, Continents Adrift, —Runciman's History of the Crusades volume two, where's one and three. Greek Tragedy? Travels in Arabia Deserta? And here's your man with the grasshoppers isn't it... he pulled the Selected Poetry down and blew dust from it, —you've got everything mixed up here. It's like the inside of your head, you know that? and he thrust it back unopened. —four drinks and you'd start on the grasshoppers making merry in the...

—No no no, no it's the little people Lester, *The little people making merry like grasshoppers In spots of sunlight, hardly thinking Backward but never forward, and if they somehow Take hold upon...*

—Look. You've got a Bible here.

—*Foolishly reduplicating Folly in thirty-year periods; they eat and laugh too, Groan against labors, wars and...*

127

—What's the Bible doing here. It's in here upside down. What's it doing upside down.

—Maybe it tripped over Doughty, read it. Take it with you and...

—I've read it. He pulled it out to right it, —it's got no business here, you know that? You've got no business with the Bible.

—Always get it right don't you, came through a fresh billow of smoke. —That hat has no business on the bed, these chickens have no business in the parlour like you having business with...

—Don't start all that.

—You were what, thirteen? when you were ordained? Signed up for two years over there in your cheap suit when you were twenty? Up there in the Luwero Triangle restoring the Ten Tribes of Israel, firing up the Bagandas for the Second Coming someplace in Missouri with your moronic angel and the golden plates he'd hidden in a...

—I said don't start that! We, we've heard it we've heard it before, the same harangues, the same raving, ranting...

—No no no, no it's history Lester, five hundred years of it, your Portuguese sailing into Mombasa plundering the whole east coast, ivory, copper, silver, the gold mines spreading the true faith right up the Zambezi valley slave trading all the way? the whole damned nightmare sanctified by a Papal Bull good God, isn't that what you'd call having business with the Bible? So damned busy picking through my books find that one, Christianizing the Bakongo kingdom in the fifteenth century read it, take it and read it it's up there on the next shelf, baptizing Nzinga dressing him up in European clothes teaching him manners till he finally figures out they're selling his whole damned population to the plantations in Brazil and they...

—You ever think what your lungs look like inside, Mc-Candless? Look at this. Will you look at this? He'd turned reaching through the drift of smoke to snap on the shadeless lamp rearing from the litter at the end of the table, coming away dangling a black length of cobweb —just touch it, feel it, that's what they'd feel like, that's what they look like... The thing stuck to his fingers and he bent down for the short sleeve of the zebra hide's foreleg wiping his hands on it. —I thought some doctor told you you were at the end of the line, that's what we thought happened when we lost track of you but you always know better don't you, you're always smarter than everybody else they're all just grasshoppers, aren't they, like this... as though it were what he'd been looking for, bringing down a book in a yellow jacket —it even looks cheap, even the title, even this name you made up you wrote it under.

—It's a name isn't it? Look in the phone book. It's just not mine.

—You make money on it?

—That's not why I wrote it.

—That's not what I asked you. It's rotten you know that? He'd cracked the spine, spreading its pages —picking his nose, listen to this. Picking his nose in the back seat of the mud spattered Mercedes, Slyke hunched down in the darkness watching them carry the body back to that's me isn't it. Slyke, that's supposed to be me? You never saw me pick my nose here, here's the only good thing in it up at the top of this chapter, where it says the fool is more dangerous than the rogue because the rogue at least takes a rest sometimes, the fool never, you know why it's good? Because you didn't write it, why didn't you write it.

—Because Anatole France wrote it before you were born, says it right there doesn't it?

—You never saw me pick my nose. It's disgusting, you know that McCandless? Why did you want to give him a name like Slyke. Why did you write it.

—I was bored.

—You were always bored. You were bored the first time I met you, you thought I wouldn't read it? You've got

Cruikshank in here as this character Riddle, you thought he and Solant and the rest of them wouldn't know who wrote it?

—You think I even thought they'd read it? got better things to do haven't they? Forging passports, tapping tele...

—You think it didn't show up in his briefings? They read everything down there, funny papers everything even trash like this. Maybe they thought you're trying to get back at them.

—You think I'd waste the...

—Maybe they think you're where these leaks are coming from.

—What leaks.

—Maybe they...

—I said what leaks. Can you come out straight with it just once?

—I never lied to you, McCandless.

—Enough damned times you just didn't tell me the truth.

—That's a different thing.

—A different thing? Like freezing my bank account, who's got the IRS in there freezing my bank account.

—There's a very fine line, you remember that? There's a very fine line between the truth and what really happens, you remember who told me that? He'd put down the book and stood there turning up papers in the glare of the lamp. —You remember that? We used to talk, didn't we.

—One damned time you finally got it right, every, ev, ev...

—That's a great cough. Better than the last time I heard it, you been practicing? Think it's trying to tell you something?

—Why don't you tell me something. Not the truth, not from you no, no I'll settle for what really happened, why they're after me all of a sudden for unreported income that year, you knew about it you handed it to me. Cruikshank was your COS in Matidi he knew about it, he had to, now suddenly nobody knows about it but the IRS.

130

—Then what are you worried about, what do you...

—Not worried I'm just damned fed up! You're still working for Cruikshank?

—I'm still working for Cruikshank. I just told you, I'd never...

—Never lie to me no, then just tell me what in the hell you...

—What are you worried about. There's no record you were ever employed is there? They'll deny any classified operation you know that, that's agency policy. Anybody knows that, read it in the papers.

—In the papers, read it in the papers like this ringer they've got showing up in court with a bag over his head?

—Like him.

—Who is he.

—Ask them. Ask Cruikshank.

—I'm asking you. I'm asking you Lester, break in here when you think nobody's home with this nonsense about the redhead, am I getting into the redhead as though we're still sitting there in the Muthaiga Club before they set you up with that thin lipped Somali, before Cruikshank and his...

—That's a different thing. That's a different thing, Mc-Candless. We never got that much from you anyhow... He stood turning up slabs of colour, pinks and blues, unlabeled diagrams, —nothing we weren't already getting someplace else till you went to work for Klinger... and he held up a map detail to shake the dust from it, spread it flat on the file. —Is this his site?

—I don't know what it is.

—Don't tell me what you don't know. Just tell me what you do know. Klinger was trying to round up investment when he pulled you out of that broken down Tabora Middle School wasn't he? or had they already fired you. He sent you out with your little hammer and magnifier to see if that site he'd cornered was worth further exploration and you came back and told him what you'd found. When he showed up with his exploration permits he had what he said was your mapping, he had the remote sensing and these infrared scannings, high resolution photographs down to eighty square metres all over the whole seven thousand acres lining up claims with that mission boy down in the Chamber of Mines. You both knew there was a claim running into the mission's land, they'd already developed two shafts running right up to the edge of it. They made Klinger an offer he thought was too low so he was running around to Lendro, Pythian Mining, South Africa Metal Combine, all of them with these reports on the ore body he'd found out there on the mission land trying to raise the ante. What about it.

—What about it.

—These reports. What did you know about his reports.

—I knew you and Cruikshank were seeing every damned one of them. I knew you were paying somebody off to get copies of everything he came up with.

—How good was it.

—You saw it all. Ask Klinger.

—Ask Klinger.

—Well ask him! I didn't work up his proposals he did, I never saw them.

—What did you find.

—I told you. Ask Klinger.

—What's the last time you saw him.

—I never saw him again and look Lester, put the top back on that box and put it back where you got it. Whatever you're after it's not in there.

—Is this Irene?

—That's Irene. Put it back.

—Pretty. You never told me she was that young... the snapshot dropped back in the box and he stood there fitting the top on. —They found Klinger in one of those alleys back of the Intercontinental with two holes in his head.

—Is that it? You think I know who killed Klinger? Is that what all this is?

—Nobody cares who killed Klinger... He reached the box over to an unsteady heap spilling from an armchair behind

132

him, —could have been anybody. He was getting his hands on that slut that worked the New Stanley, we figured it was that Afrikaner she said was her husband. They were both gone the next day. It's like Dachau in here, you know that? He struck out to shatter the tranquil column of blue smoke rising between them, —will you put it out? You're not even smoking it, look at it. It's just lying there smoking. You're making me smoke it too, you know that?

—Why don't you just stop breathing then, go out and get some fresh air, let yourself out like you let yourself in.

—When's the redhead due back.

—I don't know.

He'd settled back on the metal file, watching the bottle come up to lose a level ounce into the dirty glass, reaching suddenly for the smoking cigarette to stamp it out on the yellowed marble. —Go ahead and kill yourself with these things, you don't have to kill us both do you? The boot heels had taken up bump, bumping against the side of the file. —What do you know about the redhead's husband.

—He's behind two months' rent, that's what I know about him.

—You ran a credit check on him didn't you? when they rented your house here?

—I didn't run anything. They gave the agent a bad check for a month's rent they made good a week later and that was it.

—You don't look out for yourself very well do you. You never did... He leaned down to crumple together a handful of loose pages from the folder on the floor. —The IRS down on you, you're probably short of cash, he came on dropping one page and going on to the next, the next, —you always were... and without looking up —I'll give you two thousand dollars for the work you did for Klinger.

—Still the big spenders.

—Cash. It's here isn't it? in this mess here someplace?

—Maybe you're looking at it.

—I'm not looking at it! I'm looking at a lot of, this how

you make your living now? writing for the schoolbooks?

—How I made one.

—It's better than your rotten fiction, you should have stayed with it.

—Stayed with it? What do you think that trial in Smackover was all about.

—No I'm serious, McCandless. I'm serious, don't start on your Smackover. Two thousand cash. Look at your shoes, you...

—Think I made it up? like the name on that book there? You think ignorance isn't dead serious? Red dirt, rolling hills, a rail line, trickle of a stream and a town grows up there, great trees meeting overhead down the main street and some civilized person names the place Chemin-couvert. A generation or two of ignorance settles in and you've got Smackover, a hundred years of it and you've got a trial like that one, defending the Bible against the powers of darkness they're doing more to degrade it taking every damned word in it literally than any militant atheist could ever hope to. Foolishness bound in the heart of a child but the rod of correction shall drive it out so they whale the daylights out of their kids with sticks. And they shall take up serpents so they get liquored up and see how many rattlesnakes they can get into a burlap bag, talk about homo habilis in East Africa two million years ago, homo sapiens homo anything they know what a homo is don't they? the men of Sodom telling Lot to bring out his two visiting angels for a little buggery? back in Deuteronomy breaking down the houses of the sodomites? an abomination in Leviticus? these vile affections in Saint Paul burning in their lust to one another? Cutting a little close to the bone here, Lester? Talking about having business with the greatest work ever produced by western man and that's what you...

—I'm talking about the work you did for Klinger. I'm talking about what you found on Klinger's site out there McCandless, not your little grandstand play in Smackover they cleaned that up in Tennessee sixty years ago, all your ranting about Genesis and evolution the whole...

—Cleared it up? and evolution disappeared from their textbooks for a whole generation going around like they'd all had lobotomies no no no, stupidity's a damned hard habit to break, something right here I just saw it... Papers, clippings, ashes spilled right and left in the table's litter, —damn! The bottle almost went over, —little taste of life in Georgia it's right here someplace...

—Your own mapping, diagrams, field notes all of it, two thous...

—Here, here read this while you're waiting... a pamphlet in ominous black, —the Survival Handbook, it's a little literature from Smackover, tells people like me what to do when people like you are snatched up to meet the Lord in Second Thessalonians for your space age picnic in the clouds while the rest of us are...

—Always get it wrong, don't you. It's First Thessalonians, four, seventeen and I'm not sitting here waiting for a little taste of Georgia, I'm waiting for you to...

—No no here it is, here it is listen. You think that circus in Tennessee straightened things out? Here's a judge in Georgia right now, listen to him. This monkey mythology of Darwin is the cause of abortions, permissiveness, promiscuity, pills, prophylactics, perversions, pregnancies, pornotherapy, pollution, poisoning, and proliferation of crimes of all types what happened to pederasty, penis envy, peeping Toms, you think he's got business with the Bible? those bums in Samuel that pisseth against the wall by the morning light? that gang sitting on the wall in Isaiah drinking their own...

—Two thousand.

—their own piss and eating...

—Cash, two thousand cash... he tapped his breast pocket. —What are you making another of those things for, I just put that one out.

—That's why I'm making another one. You're still a little dense aren't you Lester, it's pretty damned obvious isn't it? You put that one out so I make another one, perfectly logical sequence isn't it? like Paleozoic, Mesozoic, Cenozoic? All the facts staring you square in the face like they stared at those primates out there proclaiming the truth? choking on Genesis? A very fine line good God, I was wrong wasn't I, it's an abyss, it's the...

—Well what did you want! What did you expect out there, a handful of simple people brought up to believe in the...

—It's not a handful! You call half the country a handful? Almost half the damned people in this country, more than forty percent of them believe man was created eight or ten thousand years ago pretty much as he is today? they believe that? Two versions right there in the first two pages, have your choice. You get the animals first and then man around the sixth day, male and female created he them, or you get man from the dust and then the animals show up lined up like kids at summer camp to get their names and finally Miss America made from a spare rib. God dividing the light from the darkness, the water from the waters and making the firmament why not Pan Koo? why not China? The sleeping giant waking up in the dark smashes the void to make heaven and earth, his breath...

—His breath the winds, his voice the thunder, his sweat the rain and dew, one eye the sun and the other the moon and his fleas men and women I've heard it, I've heard it all McCandless I've heard it from you, you think I came up here to listen to it again? You think you're back in one of these broken down schools where you can rave and rant like this? bully and browbeat everybody in sight because that's what you do. Because you're smarter than anybody else aren't you, like this hero you've got in this rotten novel, this Frank Kinkead... He had the book in the yellow jacket again tossing over its pages five, twenty at a time, —he never picks his nose does he, he's too good for that isn't he. He's supposed to be you isn't he.

—Not supposed to be anybody, what do you think a novel...

—This part here? where he's proceeding on a sea of doubt?

That's pretty bad, proceeding on a sea of doubt that's pretty bad, you know that? And that part where he's trying to give his life a course of inevitability? where he wants to rescue his life from chance and deliver it to destiny? I wouldn't believe that, if I didn't know you I wouldn't believe anybody would talk like that, going around full of outrage because nobody's as smart as he is like those primates you were straightening out in Smackover, you know something? The preponderant IQ in America's around a hundred, you know that? you're going to tell them about Aegyptopithecus sitting around up in the Sahara eating fruit thirty million years ago? you're going to tell them they all come down from Australopithecus ten million years ago when they can't even pronounce Chemin-couvert? He waved off a fresh burst of smoke, —you ever wonder why people pull out on you? That part in here where this Frank Kinkead is telling Slyke he thinks his wife is going to pull out on him that's Irene, isn't it. You changed her name to Gwen but it's really Irene isn't it, it's you sitting there in the New Stanley bar talking about people who live as though life was reversible, about taking responsibility for the consequences of our own acts the same ranting, raving... the book snapped closed. —I'll give you five thousand dollars for the work you did for Klinger.

—Why waste your money. You know what he told them.

—We know what he told them. We want to know what you told him. He was a promoter trying to hustle up some heavy investment, you think he's going to say there's nothing on that mission site but thornbush?

—Why don't you go out there yourself, Lester... the glass came down empty, faltering in blind search for a place to rest. —Go out and look for yourself, you've got the mapping, you've got those high resolution photographs that's more than I had. All you need's the pocket magnifier and a hammer, they're right there under those papers take them, this old tent you've been stepping on take it with a broken down truck and a couple of boys from the mission and go look for yourself.

—It's all right here. Why should I go out there, it's all right here isn't it? can you find anything in this mess? You've saved every piece of trash you've ever come across... He caught the 36-1 lb. Crisco carton closer with the heel of a boot, —you know what's going on out there now? You can't get near that border. There isn't any border. There's nothing between the mission station and the Limpopo but the African National Congress running loose with Kalashnikovs and Katyusha rockets, a little PLO, Cubans, KGB posing as sanitary engineers and every trash mercenary you want, French, Portuguese, East Germans, Mossad agents, a little SWAPO spilling in and these South African Z Squads and the MRM keeping things destabilized till it's time for the showdown, go out there now you'll get your legs blown off before you walk ten feet. You saw what happened when they just picked you up for questioning, what you said happened. What you said happened McCandless, this time you wouldn't have to make it up. This time they'd make those Danakil up in the Afar who'll cut off your dingus for a prize for their girlfriends look like hell's kindergarten, don't you know what's going on out there?

—I don't know what's going on out there no, and I don't...

—All waiting for somebody to step in and draw the line, it's as good a place as any. You don't read the papers? Take your dirty tent and a couple of mission boys out in a broken down truck like those two that strayed off the mission station for water, they were lucky to get off with their throats cut, you didn't see that?

—I didn't see that, I don't read the papers and I don't give one damn what's going on out there, what I'm trying to tell you Lester. I'm through with it, I've been around the ring twice and I'm not going round again isn't that clear?

—Then what good's this work you did for Klinger. What good is it to you, it's just part of this trash heap you're cleaning up isn't it? His boot rummaged the open carton turning up scraps of pages, torn envelopes, nondescript landscapes, —timetable for the Benguela railway what good is that to you, it's no good even when you're standing there in Kolwezi hoping for a train. Here's your contract with the Euthanasia Society when the time comes you can't make your own decisions you haven't signed it, what good is it. Five thousand cash. Five thousand for your timetable and the rest of this rubbish or five thousand for your field notes, diagrams, original mapping all of it, what's the difference. You don't give one damn what's going on out there what's the difference to you? Here... he was back digging in the file drawer for a dented yellow tin of —State Express, when did you open it, ten years ago? and came up with a passport perforated CANCELED flicking its pages stamped in blues, greens, reds, ovals and triangles, stayed by the photograph. —You looked better then, didn't you. Like this Frank Kinkead, that's what he's supposed to look like isn't it, this cool unwavering glance where he says from now on he's going to live deliberately? He's like you isn't he, he expects everybody else to behave like he would in their situation. If they were you they wouldn't be in their situation in the first place... He waved off a grey billow of expired smoke, —but he's too good to pick his nose isn't he, he's too busy rescuing his destiny from chance isn't he.

—You saw how it ends.

—I know how it ends. It doesn't end it just falls to pieces, it's mean and empty like everybody in it is that why you wrote it?

—I told you why I wrote it, it's just an afterthought why are you so damned put out by it. This novel's just a footnote, a postscript, look for happy endings I come out mixed up with people like you and Klinger.

—Five thousand. He tossed the canceled passport into the open carton, —you're going to need it... and his boot thrust out to tip the shoe crossed over a knee there, —see that? See where there's no hair growing till way above your ankle there? That's what I told you, that's the whisky and the cigarettes working on you together that's your circulation failing, that's when your toes turn green. Either smoke your cigarettes or drink your whisky that would mean you'd decided to, that you wanted it, but both of them together you know what that is McCandless? That's a character flaw, that shows an inferior character you know that? Talk about your lobotomies, when you used to say I'd rather have a bottle in front of me than a frontal lobotomy where'd you get that, that's somebody else too isn't it because you've got one, the figures on lung cancer right in front of you like the facts staring those primates square in the face out there choking on Genesis and you say it's just a statistical parallel and light another. Five thousand. You're going to need it just for hospital bills... and his boot, gone back to fretting the carton, brought him down for a handful of scraps, snapshots, repetitive landscapes, uncomposed glimpses of dips, outcroppings, —is this it? He held one out, —Klinger's site? They all look the same.

—If you don't know what you're looking for.

—I know what I'm looking for. It's in this mess someplace if you, is that it? Everything you got up for Klinger you've sold it, you've already sold it.

—Fine, I sold it. If that gets you out of here I've sold it.

—I don't believe you. Who, who did you sell it to. I don't believe you, McCandless. He threw down the crumpled snapshots shaking free the torn half of an envelope, —what was in it. Eyes of addressee only what was in it... and he was down digging a hand in the carton, —where's the rest of it. You might have some classified material in this mess you know that? You might have walked off with some classified material... he straightened up emptyhanded. —They could clean this place out, get a court order and come in here with a truck they could clean you right out, you think that's something to grin about? Go ahead, pour another drink, you ever seen the FBI on a rampage? Tear out your bookcases rip up your floors you think they wouldn't do it?

—You think they'd waste the time? you think they'd even...

—I'll tell you who'll waste the time. I'll tell you who'll

waste more time than you've left alive McCandless. That's somebody who thinks there's a leak and brings the pressure down from the top, and won't stop till they find it. Maybe three or four agencies running down sources and none of them knows what the other ones are after. They don't know who else is after what they're after. They're so jealous they won't share the time of day. They don't know if the other side's in there too, they don't even know who's on the other side and every one of them thinks the other ones have been penetrated so they penetrate each other. They're afraid they're being fed disinformation so they put out a little disinformation of their own, the only thing they know is if somebody says he's got what they're after and they haven't got it, if the other side says they've got it and pulls out the rug there's no way to prove they haven't. What did they pay you. That work you did for Klinger, you just said you sold it who did you sell it to. What did they pay you.

—I thought you didn't believe me.

—I don't... He came down stiff on the heels of the boots, picking short steps past the roll of the tent, the heaped magazines, back scanning the rows of books. —Maybe they'd turned Klinger. Maybe they thought we'd doubled him so they dropped him in that alley. They'd turned Seiko... he was pushing books aside on the shelf, peering in at the wall behind them. —Seiko brought you in, you knew that... He reached in tapping the wall there, pushed more books aside and tapped again. —You're not that important, you know that? Just a piece in the puzzle, a little piece in the big puzzle... He stood picking paint from a moulding with his thumbnail, —how much are you holding out for, ten?

—If it's not that imp...

—Ten thousand dollars, did you hear me? Because we don't like surprises. Because Cruikshank thinks there might be something to that story about the strike you made thirty years ago when you first went out there, that strike up above the Limpopo when nobody would believe you, when the...

—Then why should he believe me now. That bloodless

bastard why should he trust me now any more than I trust him. He's still trying to recolonize the whole continent? take it back a hundred years when Europe cut it up like a pie and they all took a piece?

—I said cash, McCandless. Ten thousand cash you don't have to trust anybody, sitting here in this mess pretending you don't know what's going on over there? Look at it, it's a nightmare, twenty years of independence and the whole continent's a nightmare, they've wiped out everything it took a hundred years to put together. Everything's gone backwards, more than a million of them killed by their own governments, the rest can't even feed themselves. Ninety five percent of those countries used to grow their own food now every one of them imports it, seven or eight hundred different languages they can't even talk to each other, one in a hundred of them's a refugee, sleeping sickness, river blindness, starvation, madness, anywhere you go there's madness, people going staring mad is that any better? is that what you want?

—Good God no Lester, far be it from me. Better off with your missionaries back there in good old King Leopold's Congo, the Belgians using them for pistol practice, chopping off their hands, stringing them on fences, burning their...

—Will you stop it? It's just your, you know what it is? It's cheap. It's like your book there it's cheap, it's the same cheap, condescending, twisting things around like this having business with the Bible and all the rest of your cheap...

—Nothing cheap about it Lester, a trillion dollars' worth of weaponry and your evangelicals in there warming things up with don't fool yourselves thinking I come to send peace on earth, I come not to send peace but a sword. Holy, Holy, Holy! Merciful and Mighty! Sing them a few bars of that? The Son of God goes forth to war A kingly crown to gain; His blood red banner streams afar...

—Whose evangelicals do you want then! Whose fundamentalists do you want, talk about your little taste of Georgia how about a little taste of Islam? You think your Georgia

142

judge there sounds any different from an ayatollah? You talk about chopping off hands, you want them sitting you out there in a public square with the Moslem Brotherhood piling in shouting Allah Akbar while they, where's your insurance policy, actual severance through or above the wrist and you run in to collect your five thousand from Bai Sim convenient offices everywhere? Whose jihad do you want, McCandless! They've been at it for a thousand years, they've been at it since ten ninety when Hasan brought his cutthroats out of Qum, cut your throat and they're guaranteed a seat in paradise. Talk about having business with the Bible how about having business with the Koran, if you think...

—That's a generous offer, how about having business with neither damned one of them. I don't quite follow what you're trying to...

—You could end up on the wrong side, you know that? You know that, McCandless?

—I'll tell you one thing I know. I'll tell you...

—Because maybe they turned you. Maybe people think they turned you. It's the same thing.

—I'll tell you one thing, people don't think. You're up there picking through my books why don't you look for the...

—Don't, no don't start that again, look for the second book of the Republic take it with you and read it, it's good clean fun we've been over all that, don't...

—No no no, no it's the Crito, Lester. Where it doesn't matter what the many think because they can't make you wise or a fool, it's Crito you're looking for, right up there next to the encyclopae...

—It's not what I'm looking for! I'm not talking about what the many think, I'm not talking about what I think, I'm talking about what Cruikshank thinks. If you won't take ten thousand for this work you did for Klinger he thinks you've been turned, you've already handed it over, you've been sold out for nothing... He'd come sharply away from the bookcases, back toward the table, tripping on a heap of magazines, catching balance to give them a kick, —I'll tell you

143

what I think. If that work you did for Klinger is here in this mess someplace you couldn't find it if you wanted to. You came up here to clean it up and you can't clean it up, you know why McCandless? You can't clean it up because you're part of it. You've got no more money than what's in your pocket, you haven't even got carfare to Luanda where they might take you in... He'd come close enough, waving away the smoke, to reach down for —your thousand shilling note here, get back to Kampala this will get you a bed for the night if they don't put out your eyes and leave you in a ditch first. Here. Here's your Survival Handbook just in case you miss our picnic in the clouds and if anybody's going to miss it you are. Keep handy for future reference says it right on the cover, you're going to need it. Here's your timetable, all it was good for was so you'd know how late the trains were, now they've all run off the tracks and you're left sitting here with the timetable smoking your, wait, wait don't make another one here, smoke one of these... he'd seized the tin of State Express, —talk about stupidity and you sit here smoking yourself to death here, smoke all of them... he shook them loose over the table there, —smoke them all they're as dead and dried up as you are, your Frank Kinkead raving about scratching the surface of reason and there's this void right under it aching to believe anything absurd, where he wants to give out free chess sets like they give out free Bibles for endless cheap entertainment, anything to fill the emptiness any invention to make them part of some grand design anything, the more absurd the better, magic, drugs, psychedelics, Pan Koo and the Tibetans' prayer wheels, the assumption of the Virgin and the three secrets of Fatima, Moroni's golden tablets or just God, God, God... Suddenly he had the bottle by the throat —here, have a drink. Where's your euthanasia contract sign it, I'll witness it for when you're physically or mentally disabled and can't make your own decisions maybe it's here, maybe the time's here have two drinks, have five... he thrust the upended bottle's neck into the glass, —have twenty...

144

—What in hell are you doing!

The bottle was wrenched away and he backed off, holding his hand down to look at it like something alien, stroking his smarting wrist at the joint with a healing care looking for something to wipe away the splash of whisky, the smell of it, —sixteen, McCandless. That's the last offer. That's their limit, I didn't set it they did, that's what I'm authorized... he stood wiping his hand on the back of his trousers, —cash. Any currency you want, anyplace you want it delivered and a one way ticket to get there, if you want a cover we'll provide you a cover, show up in Kinshasa selling snowshoes and we'll provide it. Sixteen thousand.

—What's this one way ticket, your wicked fleeing where no man pursueth? you think I'm on the run?

—It's when, McCandless. When... He was back far from reach scraping a moulding, down tapping the wainscotting, —when no man pursueth, Proverbs twenty eight, but the...

—And the righteous are bold as a lion is that it? You break in here picking through papers, tapping the walls what do you...

—It's but, McCandless, but the righteous are bold as a lion Proverbs twenty eight, one. He tapped, tapped again, straightened up —You know what this was in here? This was the kitchen, you know that? You've got this wainscotting all the way around and listen... he tapped, —now listen over here. You hear the difference? This is the flue. This little cement slab this is where the stove was and this is the flue for that extra chimney. You've got an extra chimney out there that doesn't go anyplace, I couldn't figure it out. This was the kitchen, your kitchen in there was the dining room and your dining room was the family parlour. It's too bad you never had kids, you know that? He'd turned backed against the dictionary stand there just inside the sliding door, —you could have bullied them with all your great ideas like you bully everybody else... he flicked over a page of Webster's second, tossed over a sheaf of them where a card stiff with invitation and the subscript Hope you and Irene can

145

come lay inserted in the cleft, —you know that? I said we used to talk, we never did. You used to talk. You talked and I listened, Helen Keller in the woods when the tree falls and all the rest of your, the truth and what really happens you know something? They didn't recruit me McCandless, Cruikshank didn't recruit me. You did. You know that? He tossed over pages, paused appearing to study a colour plate display Orders of Knighthood and of Merit in garish contrivances of crosses and ribbons. —Just leave this whole mess behind you and you're out there with sixteen thousand walking around money. We don't have much time.

—I heard you.

He heaved the book closed. —You ever think of putting smoke detectors in here? You could have a real fire, you know that? Books, papers, nothing but paper, your beams have been drying out for ninety years. You ought to think of your tenants McCandless, you ought to put in smoke detectors. You ought to think of the redhead. Anything you've got squirreled away here would be gone in a minute with the rest of your trash, anybody who was after it wouldn't have it but they'd know nobody else would show up with it and pull out the rug. You think fires start by themselves? He pulled the jacket tight, turned through the door for the kitchen, buttoning it. —You'll thank me someday, you know that?

—I'll thank you right now Lester, came on behind him, into the kitchen, —I'll thank you for leaving.

—Get smoke detectors in there now they'd go off before you could put them up. What was that about the ladies' room at Saks.

—She had her purse stolen. It had her keys in it.

—Could have been anybody... He'd stopped there standing over the table, arms drawn close as wings, studying that page of crosses, smudges, hails of arrows as the light came on. —You know one good thing in that rotten book of yours? He turned the page to one side, to the other, —that scene where this Frank Kinkead is out on deck setting up this steamer chair on that night passage down from Mogadishu? where he gets his thumbs caught in the hinges when he comes down in it and his own weight's got him trapped there yelling for help, he's out there all night and nobody goes by but the black boy who sees him twisting around yelling and just thinks he's drunk. Maybe that's what happened... He had the page upside down, brought it back as he'd had it. —Maybe that's what really happened.

—Maybe Methuselah lived nine hundred years. Here, I'll let you out.

—Wait, you know what this is? He thrust the page over, —it's Cressy. I just figured it out. It's the battle of Cressy, look. Here's Edward the Third up here, and here... the long smudge under his thumb —the rear center in reserve, the Black Prince on his right and Northampton on his left and the archers, two wings of English archers eleven thousand of them, look. The battle order's drawn up between Wadicourt and Cressy this is Cressy here, it ought to be further up... he got the pencil by the phone, a circled X —here's Cressy here, and here's the French. Here's Estrées down here it ought to be further over... a circled + —here's the French attack look, these long arrows from Estrées under Philip of Valois, he's this big cross here and all these little crosses coming up here twelve thousand men at arms, six thousand crossbows and all these draftees, these little v's? These irregular columns coming up from Abbeville it ought to go like this, the road went like this... a heavy parabola —and here, here's the thunderstorm, this big lightning streak? The storm that delayed the first attack when the crossbows went in and the English longbows cut them down on both flanks, their own cavalry rode down on them from behind... the horde of ciphers —by midnight the French army wiped itself out look at them, sixteen attacks and the archers cut them down every time they came in, I wish I'd seen that. That was the beginning of firepower... he emphasized a smudge and stood off from it. —I wish I'd seen that.

—Always get it right don't you, Lester.

—Sixteen thousand, McCandless. Here's a phone number... he scribbled in a space just east of Estrées. —You don't
have much time.

—I'll let you out. It's Halloween out there too.

—What do you...

—What you came for isn't it? trick or treat? I'll let
you out.

—You know something, McCandless?

—I said I'll let you out!

But even with the light gone on there under the sampler
by the door, and the door pulled open, —you see that now?
this was the front parlour? for guests? They probably kept
the blinds drawn so the sun wouldn't fade the carpets. Those
drapes, those silk flowers all of it, she's got nice taste hasn't
she, the redhead. She'll walk out on you too, you know that?
How old was that Jeannie, the one you had down in the
Bureau of Mines she lived on DuPont Circle. They always
do, don't they? And even there in the open gape of the doorway on the dark outside he'd caught a hand loath on the
doorframe, looking down the road where figures, three, four
of them came blown in white sheets up the hill toward the
broken patch of streetlight. —You know the rottenest thing
you did in that book? Making Slyke a Mormon. You didn't
need to do that. It wouldn't have changed the story any.
You want to know something, McCandless? God loves you
whether you like it or not, you know that? The wind up
from the river brought the straggling figures closer, close
enough for the headlights of a car rounding the corner to
freeze them catching at masks as it passed. —They want a
haunted house, they've found it... and then, out on the
crumbled brick where the wind in the festooned branches
scattered the light on the black of the road, on the fence
palings opposite and the exhortation melted down the windows of the white frame garage beyond, —lucky thing for
the redhead they didn't hang you up by your dingus.

When the headlights flashed on, the four had already gained
the step pushing the smallest of them forward, white skull

mask askew and a hand up to raise it on eyes absorbed with greed for the coin from the depth of a pocket, and the black car moved sweeping its lights across the front of the house as the door closed against it.

Past the ringing phone in the kitchen he stopped for a rag from the cupboard, wiping his hands on it back in the sudden stillness of the room, wiping off the bottle and raising the quavering lip of the glass to pour back half an ounce for the good ounce that spilled and wiping that up, sitting down, taking a sip, picking up the scattered cigarettes one by one back into the tin and lighting the last one before he swept papers, bills, folders from the open file drawer into the carton. Here and there he paused to set something aside, to study a page, or a picture, crumpled with the rest till the carton was full and he carried it in to the hearth, down digging for matches, heaping the empty grate, pulling the wing chair closer as the blaze came up, sitting there with the notebook unopened on his lap. Headlights glowed at the windows, passed the alcove and were gone. The wind had risen out there, throwing the leafless branches dancing in black silhouette, setting up the creak of a beam in the dark somewhere up past the head of the stairs. He came forward to stir the fire with the edge of the notebook, an old school looking sort of thing in crudely chiaroscuroed covers, Compositions lettered on the front, Name left blank, he banked it against the flames and got up pulling off the jacket he'd had on all this time, walked into the kitchen and looked in the refrigerator, into the dining room and looked at the plants, filled a clean glass to water a wilting member of the jewelweed family, moving more slowly till now he was back staring at the books in the bookshelves, taking one down, and another, running through them to stop at pages checked in the margins, to stare at those passages perplexed as though someone else must have marked them, must have found some stinging revelation in this inconsequential line, or that one, jamming them back till he came on one with a narrow orange spine as if it were what he'd been after all this time. He came out with it, and the glass, and a sheaf of cobwebbed papers from under the table, brought it all out to the fire in the living room which he stirred into life with a stick from the copper tub by the fireplace where he stood for a minute looking into the flames. Then he walked straight into the kitchen and opened the refrigerator, took a pot out and raised the lid on some chance kind of stew sporting wrinkled peas, greying peaks of potato, and put it on the stove; went on to pull closed the sliding door, the light still on in there; stopped to come down abruptly and dig in the trash for the worn address book. Round the end of the kitchen table he turned on the radio which eagerly informed him that a group of handicapped mountainclimbers had carried an American flag and a bag of jellybeans to the summit of Mount Rainier before he could bend to turn the dial, slowly, bringing in the full chord of a cello.

Back to the fire, he threw in the canceled passport, the worn address book, added crumpled papers, crumpled snapshots where repetitive landscapes, glimpses of dips, outcroppings, curled and turned black, added a split piece of ash from the copper tub and sat back in the wing chair making a fresh cigarette, the glass at his elbow, opening the slight book's paper covers to page 207 where it was marked with a slip of paper, a list in an open and generous hand, milk, paper towels, Tampax, tulip bulbs, which he crumpled and tossed into the flames before he took up there, *I distrusted romance. See, though, how I yielded to it.*

A man, I suppose, fights only when he hopes, when he has a vision of order, when he feels strongly there is some connexion between the earth on which he walks and himself. But there was my vision of a disorder which it was beyond any one man to put right. There was my sense of wrongness, beginning with the stillness of that morning of return... while from the kitchen, the chords of Bach's D major concerto heaved into the room around him and settled like furniture.

150

$\mathcal{S}$he lay back on the bed as though she'd never left it, the damp sheet turned chill and fallen away, feet curled close in the frolic of sunlight through the trees outside and her nipples drawn up hard with a hand passing down her breast, out to the knee flexing up for its reach, gliding down slowly on a hard edge of nails to the rising fall and the warmth of breath lingering in the villous suspense of her legs fallen wide broken, abruptly, by the sound of her own voice. —It's an amazing thing to be alive, isn't it... catching the hand back to sequester the white of her breast —I mean, when you think of all the people who are dead? And then, sharply

151

up on an elbow —was that true, what you said last night? about having malaria? But whatever his answer might have been was lost in the muffle of her breast where his lips came up opened, and his tongue —wait... She held his face away, fretting his profile there under the eye with a fingertip —just, hold still...

—What are you, ow!

—No it's just, hold still it's just a little blackhead... bent closer, eyes creased in clinical concentration, a sharp thrust of her nail and —there. Did that hurt?

—Just didn't expect it, what...

—Wait there's another one... but he had her wrist in a turn that sank her back on the pillow, his hand gathering her breasts closer again and his lips —wasn't that a strange dream? She held his face pressed against her, —but they always are aren't they, when they're about death, I mean when they're about somebody dying and you don't even know who it is? Her fingers brushed the forehead, the hard cheekbone, the hard line of the jaw's fixed appetite there at her breast, —when he used to read out loud to me and I thought all the books were about him, and he wasn't really reading to me at all. Huckleberry Finn, The Call of the Wild, those stories by Kipling and that book about the Indian, the last Indian? He was just turning the pages and telling the story the way he wanted to. About himself. They were always about him... and the touch of her fingers went harder, hard as the lineaments they traced —it must have been about him, that dream. Don't you think so?

—You told me last night he was pushed off a train. I asked you when your father died and you said he was in a train accident, he was pushed off a train. Maybe that was a dream too.

—No but isn't it strange? I mean how you always want to tell your dream to somebody in every exact detail? and they couldn't care less? He didn't want to tell his, he said, and no, they weren't bad, they weren't complicated, they were just dull, they were about this house, a lot of them, finding the porch caved in, or a whole side of it missing, finding somebody he'd never seen before in the living room painting the walls orange, his hand now slipping lower along the swell of her thigh, over the pelvic crest, or they were about things that had happened twenty years ago, nothing he could do anything about, nothing that was any use now, his hand idling further where white gave way in velutinous red, a fingertip seeking refuge in the damp —but did you ever think? She was up on that elbow again, turned to him so his hand fell still on the white of the sheet, —about light years?

—About what?

—I mean if you could get this tremendously powerful telescope? and then if you could get far enough away out on a star someplace, out on this distant star, and you could watch things on the earth that happened a long time ago really happening? Far enough away, he said, you could see history, Agincourt, Omdurman, Crécy... How far away were they she wanted to know, what were they, stars? constellations? Battles he told her, but she didn't mean battles, she didn't want to see battles, —I mean seeing yourself... Well as far as that goes he said, get a strong enough telescope you could see the back of your own head, you could —That's not what I meant. You make fun of me don't you.

—Certainly not, why would...

—I mean seeing what really happened back when...

—All right, set up a mirror on Alpha Centauri then, you'd sit right here with your telescope watching yourself four, about four and a half years ago is that what you...

—No.

—But I thought...

—Because I don't want to see that! She pulled away, pulled up the sheet, staring up at the ceiling. —But you'd just see the outside though, wouldn't you. You'd just see the mountain you'd see it go down and you'd see all the flames but you wouldn't see inside, you wouldn't see those faces again and the, and you wouldn't hear it, a million miles away you

153

wouldn't hear the screams... What screams, he wanted to —No, no that one's too close, find one further away... and he subsided, looking at the sheet clenched to her throat and the length of her gone under it, recommending Sirius, setting up business on the Dog Star, the brightest of them all, watching what happened eight and a half? nine years ago? —I told you what happened... the sheet clenched firm, —I told you last night no, twenty, twenty five years away when it was all still, when things were still like you thought they were going to be?

—Oh... He gave a gentle tug at the edge of the sheet, she caught it closer.

—Because I could see myself then at Longview, I mean there were always people, he'd have shooting parties, George Humphrey, Dulles, people like that they'd go out in these wagons for birds and, I don't know, foxes? He had Jack Russell terriers, that was when things started to get mixed up, that station wagon with those Jack Russell terriers because we just adored him. When we were little we thought he could do anything and then when we got older, when we started to say things he thought were critical and he sort of drew away and he got those dogs, those hateful little Jack Russell terriers they just adored him, they followed him everywhere they'd do anything to please him and we never could and then Billy, after he was four Billy didn't even try. He'd put some mud on one of my little doll's plates he was pretending to feed one of them, like you pretend with a doll, and it bit him right under the eye and my father came in and, and he picked up the dog. He stood there on the telephone calling the doctor holding the dog, it was all trembling snuggled up under his chin telling the doctor that Billy was teasing it and it bit him, and could he come over and that's when, I mean it was strange. I mean he'd never read to Billy, he never even pretended. It was strange.

Was it? his hand idling its way under the sheet, returning unseen and as though unattended to pause at her breast, perhaps it had more to do with disappointment he said, not of being disappointed but the fear of disappointing someone else, his words unhurried as the straying of his hand, pacing it, of disappointing someone close, of living on the edge of some betrayal that was bound to come along sooner or later, one way or another, his fingertips failing that hard outcropping they sought over the soft unbroken rise under the sheet there and descending a corrugated path to the open plain cradled below, —even the smallest one. Even a gift, like giving the wrong gift and you're telling her you don't know who she is, or you want her to be somebody else. Get it going both ways, that fear of disappointing each other and those inadvertent little betrayals that poison everything else, isn't that it? Isn't that part of it? And his hand now, strayed down from hill to hummock poised there while his voice idled on each as though to recover what had been lost and found and lost again and again —last night, he went on, when they'd talked about letting yourself become the prisoner of someone else's hopes, wasn't that part of it? The weight of his hand sunk deep on the hillock, that whole presumption of taking the responsibility for making someone else happy, the rule of his finger measuring the furrow hidden there —and not just the presumption, the insult, the plain insult of it... he turned thrust hard against the length of her thigh, —the futility of it, even with children...

In a sweep the sheet fell away and she was sitting up cross legged. —I mean have you ever heard? it's really children that choose their parents just so they can get born? He muttered something unforgiving at the knee looming there that abruptly, his hand up to bring it aside —no, no wait. I mean sometimes it's like they'll take anybody isn't it, just bringing some man and woman together who have no other reason to be together at all, or they shouldn't, I mean there's every reason they shouldn't be together maybe they don't even know each other, they probably hardly know each other and they could have done something else, I mean they could just have gone sailing or something but instead they, I mean... her face coloured, looking down —don't make fun of me.

—Why would I want to make...

—I mean because you're so, I'm just always afraid you will.

But he'd rolled over on the evidence, his hand resigned on her knee there where it might have been a shoulder, an elbow, crossing a street, taking her arm in to dinner as though they might just have met, a mere courtesy finding themselves seated together by a host who knew one of them slightly enough to abandon them both to the polite fare exchanged before the soup came in —like this friend of mine, she offered, sitting up pert as though this nakedness still lay hid under some décolletage pierced only in the eye of the beholder, proffering her best friend —when we'd sleep over and whisper about being stolen by the gypsies? and she said she thought she'd been stolen from the gypsies. Because her father, I mean if you ever knew Edie's father... a prospect which seemed to rouse his interest even less than that of knowing Edie and the gypsies, his hand on her knee there as it might have been his hand on her knee under the tablecloth while the wine was being poured —because I thought she knew everything, like she'd say that women had this extra layer of fat that men didn't have, for survival? and we were both just as skinny as boards and were scared we might not, survive I mean. And then she'd talk about living in this previous existence and I believed that too. I mean she was really the one that thought of that telescope, if she got far enough away where she could see herself in this previous existence? As what, he wanted to know, or pretended to, his hand stalling along the course of his recent dry run there against her thigh. —It was always different. And I mean she's the one that told me about all these babies trying to get born... The air would be so thick with them you couldn't breathe he said, good God, when you think of all the people who are dead? —Now you are! and all the polite, the politic, the sheet torn away and with it the flimsy stratagem of the tablecloth —making fun of me, aren't you...

But he'd drawn her down, laid out the length of her beside

156

him —no no no, his voice as calming as the hand along her back, it was all just part of the eternal nonsense, where all the nonsense comes from about resurrection, transmigration, paradise, karma the whole damned lot. —It's all just fear he said, —you think of three quarters of the people in this country actually believing Jesus is alive in heaven? and two thirds of them that he's their ticket to eternal life? fingertips running light as breath down skirting the top of the rift, tracing down its edge, just this panic at the idea of not existing so that joining that same Mormon wife and family in another life and you all come back together on judgment day, coming back with the Great Imam, coming back as the Dalai Lama choosing his parents in some Tibetan dung heap, coming back as anything —a dog, a mosquito, better than not coming back at all, the same panic wherever you look, any lunatic fiction to get through the night and the more farfetched the better, any evasion of the one thing in life that's absolutely inevitable... his fingers searching the edge of the rift and down it, deeper, desperate fictions like the immortal soul and all these damned babies rushing around demanding to get born, or born again, easing the rift wider to the moistened breadth of his hand, —I'd come back as a buzzard Faulkner said once, nothing hates him or wants him or needs him or envies...

—Oh! she pulled away, up on that damned elbow again —have you read Faulkner much?

—A long time ago. If then.

—What?

—Never mind. He'd sat straight up, one foot off to the floor.

—But, I mean don't you like Faulkner?

—I don't like Faulker. I don't dislike Faulkner. He'd got hold of his trousers, —I just don't know why in hell we're talking about Faulkner.

—But why are you, I mean where are you going.

—Cigarette... he had one leg in, —I left things downstairs.

—But no... she caught at his shoulder —I mean, you don't have to right now do you? get up I mean?

—Why not.

—Well because you, I mean because we were talking... her hand running down his arm, down where he'd wilted there before her eyes —and you might not come back.

—As what, a dog? a mosquito? He pulled the trouser leg up sharply, freed his leg for the other one —as a buzzard?

—No that's not what I, I mean I didn't mean to upset you about Faulkner I thought you were talking about Faulkner, and I mean I don't know if I've read Faulkner much either. Except The Heart of Darkness, I think I read that once.

He leaned back, simply looking at her, at the effort clouding the clean planes of her face, blurring the light of her eyes. —That's an excellent thing, he said finally.

—Where the girl's body gets sent home someplace down south right at the start? and the hearse keeps breaking down going to the cemetery? He just looked at her. —Because I mean I still mix things up sometimes. Like the men I heard about on the radio whose boat turned over? and they were saved in this thrilling rescue by postcard? Her hand came straying up his calf still bared there on the bed, over his knee, —do you think that's why people write it? fiction I mean?

—From outrage... he eased his leg closer.

—No or maybe just boredom, I mean I think that's why my father made all those things up, because he was bored, reading to this little girl on his lap he was bored so that's why they were always about him... her hand moved on, paused smoothing hairs in its idle course —because what you just said, about being this captive of somebody else's hopes? and about disappointment? I mean I think people write because things didn't come out the way they're supposed to be.

—Or because we didn't. No... his legs fallen wider for her fingertip twisting in a coil of hair —no, they all want to be writers. They think if something happened to them that it's interesting because it happened to them, hearing about all the money that gets made writing anything cheap, anything sentimental and vulgar whether it's a book or a song and they can't wait to sell out.

—Oh. Do you think that? Her hand had come up now to the fork of his leg, opened, as though to weigh what it found there, —because I mean I don't think so, I don't think they sell out she said, her voice weighing the idea as though for the first time, —I mean these poor people writing all these bad books and these awful songs, and singing them? I think they're doing the best they can... her hand closing there gently. —That's what makes it so sad.

—Yes... he shifted almost stealthily, trying to rid himself of those trousers —you're right aren't you.

—And then when it doesn't work... her grasp closed tighter on the sudden surge, —when they try and it doesn't work...

—Yes that's the, when they, that's worse yes... his thumb tugging down at a beltloop with the haste he'd drawn the trouserleg on —that's the, isn't it that's the worst yes, failing at something that wasn't worth doing in the first place that's the...

—Because you could couldn't you! and her hand was gone. —Write wonderful things I mean, couldn't you. Because your hands... she'd seized the one nearest, —I've watched them. They've done so many things... and she held it up before him.

—Yes, I've seen it he said, sinking back.

—Because haven't you ever wanted to? write I mean? I mean all the places you've been and all the romantic, all the things you talked about last night sitting in front of the fire, about finding gold that first time in Africa when you were so young and they thought you were crazy? and all these places you've been? I mean like Maracaibo they just sound so, they all sound so mysterious and... she broke off, intent examining his hand, splaying its fingers. He'd never been there he told her, that phone call? It was just a job, he'd been looking for work there. —Oh. Because I thought... She'd isolated the thumb, bringing its blackened nail closer, examining it —what happened. What happened... He'd slammed it in a car door he said, three or four years ago, just damned lucky not to lose the nail when the phone rang and she sprawled across the bed for it, —hello...? No it's not no, you've called before I told you she's been gone for two years, I don't even...

—Here give me that! and he had it, —Brian? is that you? What do you... You were just told weren't you? she's been gone for two years? She's not... good, fine, you've been gone for a long time too, I don't... Brian listen, I'm not interested in your trip to Yucatán. I don't want to hear about you living with the Indians. Nothing about you interests... No and I don't want your address to give her when I see her! I don't know where she is can you get that through your head? Just stop calling here, can you get that through your... and he held the dead phone a moment longer before he handed it over, out flat on his back for her hand back from hanging it up to run open down the flat of his belly and back, and back where the surge she'd raised hot in its grasp lay drained at its search, at its seizure dwindling further, —that damned idiot...

—Was that somebody you...

—Nobody! just a, he was just a damned kid who used to, stringy beard and sandals sitting on the floor in there talking about building a houseboat, about Easter Island, about peyote and her eyes just glowed listening to it, that whole superior damned, pour a whisky light a cigarette you're treated like a pariah while he rolls a joint they pass back and forth and she pours the wine no, no he didn't mean any harm but she, neither did she really but I, but jealousy gets you through the night when you wake up alone there. Turn on the light, pour a drink and wander around an empty house at least you've got that, at least you've got somebody you see yourself ripping his beard out, kicking his face in, standing over them both naked in bed with a smoking gun in your hand while she's really probably somewhere alone washing a dish wondering what in hell tomorrow will do no, no that's what jealousy's for. It's like cauterizing a wound, even when it's finally clear there was nothing to it but your own rage it's what's got you through.

—I never knew what it was like she said, —I mean it was always just something in books or the movies because, because I never knew what it would feel like because I never had anybody to be jealous of until, I mean you don't think she'd just come here do you? Right now I mean? just suddenly be down at the front door and just walk in? Because she, because all her lovely things down there, as if as long as it all stays just like she left it she could just walk in and you wouldn't even have missed her... her hand running over his calf where she'd come down pinning his arm with a knee. —You could write about that... fingertips tending his ankle —I mean, you could write about that.

—Could I? *Dance, talk, dress and undress; wise men have pretended The summer insects enviable...*

—What's that about.

—*The breed of the grasshopper shrills, "What does the future Matter, we shall be dead?" Ah, grasshoppers, Death's a fierce meadowlark...*

—Yes that's lovely, I mean did you write it?

—Well I... his head reared to look down his own naked length for hers tumbling its torrent of red at his feet, —not really no, no in fact it's a poem by...

—I mean have you ever seen them mating? Grasshoppers, praying mantises something like that they were so, they were so precise... her fingers tracing along the bone, —you have such lovely ankles don't you, where there's no hair just so clear and smooth till way up here... over his calf, past the knee foraging higher, coming over him taking the upper hand where her fingers rose hoarding the roothairs of the surge filling their encirclement —when I saw them on television once and they were so, just so elegant... her hand in its rise and fall, rise and fall like the leafbroken sunlight climbing her shoulder, falling away as she came down, rising and falling away, her fingertip tracing the vein engorged up that stiffening rise to the crown cleft fierce where the very tip of her tongue came to lead a glint of beading off caught in the sunlight over her shoulder pausing, holding it off as though getting in focus —what's this... and, for the tip of her tongue, the plucking edge of her nail —look, this little place, it's like there was a little scab on the...

—Then that's what it is! Good God I don't know what it is, it's a battle scar, laid out here like one of your grasshoppers pinned on a board what's this, what's that, examine every damned...

—But I didn't mean... and her hand closed tight, its prey swollen the colour of rage, she came up catching balance, reaching out for the phone —Who, hello...? She swallowed and cleared her throat. —Yes who, who... the breath gone out of her, —what...? Well I did! I tried to talk to him but he... Twenty five dollars marked full and final payment yes, that's... No now stop, stop! you, you have no right to call like this and, to call and harass me like this Mister Stumpp, I tried to talk to Doctor Schak about my condition about his nurse about that consultation he wouldn't even listen, he just said my bill why haven't you paid my... Well all right then all right! Tell him that tell him take his fucking bill and she slammed it down, knees drawn up and her face buried there, getting breath.

—Glad I'm not Mister Stumpp.

—It's not funny! She pulled the sheet round her shoulders and a shiver sent breath through her —a, a doctor a stupid doctor... and she got out the iniquities she'd borne at the hands of Doctor Schak and his staff, his —nasty nurse screaming at me when I was right in the middle of a spasm and, and... still having trouble, now, getting breath, her face pressed against her knees, the comprehensive consultation he'd sent to the wrong man the wrong doctor if he'd sent it at all and her records they said they'd sent and they hadn't and this detailed, —what he called this detailed medical history I hardly saw him for five minutes he was leaving for Palm Springs, to play golf in Palm Springs and then this Mister Stumpp, this bill collector Mister Stumpp he's turning it over to Doctor Schak's attorney Mister Lopots if I don't make a deal and send them a hundred dollars I'll hear from Mister Lopots and he'll, it's not funny it's not! And small as her hand was she managed a fist with it and hit him on the shoulder, hit him again with the heel of it.

—No no no, Mister Stumpp? Mister Lo...

—Stop it! She'd gone down with her face in the pillow, both hands drawn in fists —no! for his breath at her shoulder, on the glints of perspiration beading the white of her neck and his hand down her back spreading the rift wide, his weight coming over when that suddenly she turned seizing him with her arms to bring him in, head thrown back and the full swell of her throat rising in the hollowed arch of her jaw surging to meet him with choked bleats of sound for as long as it lasted until he came down, fighting desperate for breath himself, lying still there beside her when he got it and when, minutes later, he slipped off the edge of the bed gathering up trousers, socks, pulling on his shirt he stopped, looking down at her. She lay with her head on her right shoulder, eyes drawn and her mouth hung open with no betrayal of life but the uneven trembling of her lower lip sucked in with each effort at breathing and then falling away spilling the stilled tip of her tongue and he stood there, looking down at her as though she were no one he'd ever seen, as though years and her very identity had fled taking with them any intelligence or the hope of it and surely any beauty, or the claim to it, legs flung wide and her arms loose beside her, her thumbs still crushed into the palms of her hands and as he leaned down to pull the sheet over her, as it sank between her breasts and between her knees lifting again at the tips of her toes, all at once her chest heaved rapidly, her tongue came out licking the perspiration free of her upper lip and the sound in her throat getting breath grew louder, and then with a great sigh she turned on her side and was still, and he stooped to pick up his shoes and hurried from the room.

The sound that waked her was already gone when she listened, the movement no more than the dapple of sun on the wall, on the bed empty beside her, and then again, the bleat of a dove in the branches outside and she was up, her glance at the naked fright in the mirror as startled as the one it gave her back getting past for the hall where she stopped, a bare shiver run through her at the eruption of the toilet flushing below, cowered there against the cold wall until the sounds of a cough, of a chair scraping the floor down there eased her step up the hall where she drew a bath, turning the pallor of her face to every possible angle where her eyes could contain the surfeit of those in the mirror before she took up a comb to fight the damp tangle of her hair.

In the bedroom she rattled drawers opened and closed holding this up to her, that, a veil of a blouse in a printed chiffon she hadn't worn, hadn't seen since this forthright Ragg knit sweater now, country and fall in a light grey flecked with brown though held away it looked, oddly, green enough to pick up her eyes without the urgency of something here in a hard Kelly green from a Christmas long buried and almost unworn, and she'd dressed twice, and drawn her eyes with slow concentration, before she came down the stairs.

Planes of smoke had already settled through the room where he was down on one knee pulling a magazine heap together with twine. —Do you want anything? she said there in the door, —for breakfast I mean? He'd had coffee, he told her without looking up, a cup of it there cold beside the teeming ashtray, pulling the knot tight. —Can I help you?

—Have you got any trash bags?

—I'll look ... but instead she came on into the room, standing over him for a minute, picking things up, putting one aside for something else, —oh look! What is it.

—That? It's called banded malachite.

—Isn't it lovely. The greens in it, I've never seen such

lovely green... she turned the rock face in her hand,
—where did it come from? From Katanga, just copper sul-
fides it wasn't that uncommon, he went on, down again wiping cobwebs from a heap of printer's galleys to add to the
litter on the table when —Oh look! is it real? She unfurled
the stripes up the punctured face, the sparse bristled mane
—did you shoot it?
—Shoot it?
—Well I meant, I mean if they shoot zebras, don't they?
in Africa?
—They shoot zebras... and he sat down, leveling a cigarette paper, tapping the tobacco into it, watching her pick
things up, put things down, a pair of field glasses turned on
him wrong end to, examining him from this distance she'd
put him at intent as she'd been over his hand, his ankle,
tracing up the delicate blue vein with the tip of her tongue
as though he'd fallen into some sort of compact up there
rummaging her bed, her body nook and ravined cranny licensed as she was now to rummage through his life, holding
up a yellow orange rock from the litter, dropping it back for
a glossy square of colour.
—You're not throwing this away?
—Why not.
—But it's pretty. What is it.
—The northern end of the Great Rift, it's a scanning taken
from a satellite. You've got it upside down.
—Oh. She let it go to the floor, —I thought it was art,
and she was turning up pages in a folder of typewritten pages,
—but you wrote all this? did you?
He lit the cigarette he'd made. —You said you had some
trash bags?
—But did you? I mean you said you weren't a writer.
—I'm not a writer Mrs Booth! I'm, now can you, those
trash bags can you...
—Mrs Booth?
—Yes, he was up again, —can you find me those trash...
—I mean honestly, Mrs Booth? She sank down on the

bundled magazines —as if you'd just walked in the door like a, like some bill collector or something you didn't even, no don't pat me, no! She reached out to seize something, anything, dragged up the ragged folds of the zebra hide by the scruff and sat smoothing it, white stripe to black, —I'm not a writer Mrs Booth. I mean it's not even my name my name is Elizabeth, she thrust out at the pages in the folder —and I mean if I'm not Mrs Booth and you're not a writer then what's all that.

He had no jacket on, it was still where he'd dropped it on a chair in the living room and from behind his shoulders appeared to fall, to turn in, to shed substance, standing there watching the morning arrival of the old man out on the corner, broom in one hand and the flattened dustpan in the other as though reporting for duty. —Read it then, he said. —Take it and read it.

Instead, she said simply —You're not throwing it away too?

—Why not! He crumpled a page of it, holding it out —what do you think it is, rich intoxicating prose? poignant insights? exploring the dark passions hidden in the human heart? Rhapsodic, God knows what, towering metaphor? thwarted genius? that little glimpse of the truth you forgot to ask for? It's a chapter for a school textbook that's what it is, a chapter on life forms that appeared in the Paleozoic era half a billion years ago. It's what I did when I made a fresh start here, writing for textbooks, for encyclopaedias that's all it is. All these bookshelves? I built them myself, hadn't seen my books for years they'd been stacked up in boxes, I put up the ceiling and the floor, I laid the whole floor in here, end up staring out the window at that old man out there with his damned recessional toward the garbage can trying to look useful till I, till he finally drove me out of the house.

—But he, that old man? I mean do you know him?

—Know him! A cloud of smoke billowed at the windows, and he leaned down to stamp out the cigarette —every time I'd look up, see him out there every time I looked up pretending he's doing something worth doing look at him, ten dead leaves in his damned dustpan he's still trying to prove he was put here for some purpose? Swing low sweet chariot, staring up there at that string of toilet paper comin for to carry him home good God, you talk about bare ruined choirs? Gaping up there as if he hears their gentle voices calling, that's when I started pouring a drink in the morning.

—No but all this work, I mean I don't see what he has to do with...

—Because it's the same damned thing! here... he dug in another heap, —a high school encyclopaedia entry on Darwin, see all this blue penciling? They cut it from sixteen hundred words to thirty six, evolution theory went from three thousand to a hundred and ten the next edition it won't be there at all. Origins of life get twenty eight, twenty eight mealy mouthed words listen... he had a book, or what was left of one, pages torn from it —here's what they want now, listen. Some people believe that evolution explains the diversity of organisms on earth. Some people do not believe in evolution. These people believe that the various types of organisms were created as they appear. No one knows for sure how the many different kinds of living things came to be. No one knows for sure how many smug illiterate idiots are out there peddling this kind of drivel here's another one, listen to this. Another hypothesis about the creation of the universe with all its life forms is special creation, which gives God the critical role in creation. In some school systems, it is mandated that the evolution and special creation theories be taught side by side. That seems a healthy attitude in view of the tenuous nature of hypothesis. A healthy attitude! He flung it into the carton, —find their biology textbook, you look up geologic eras? fossil remains? Nothing. Paleontology? The word itself it's gone, it's just disappeared. That's when I started pouring a drink and watching the old man out there, watched him trying to pretend there's some damned reason to get up in the morning... He reached for the bottle, but simply stood there resting his hand on it —now, look at him now. See his lips moving when he stops to get his balance? My name is death, the last best friend am I out there with his damned broom justifying an existence that won't turn him loose, how cold your hands are, death. Come warm them at my heart God, how I learned to hate him.

She sat now pursuing black stripe to white, intent as though bent over an embroidery frame. —Wouldn't he be surprised, she said finally. —That you hate him I mean, he doesn't even know it. He'd be amazed...

—Be amazed if I went out there and pushed him under a car to put him out of his misery. I've thought of that.

—I mean that's what those people in the newspapers do isn't it, when they say God told them to do it? She'd brought the face of the hide up flat on her knee, pushing a finger out through a hole where an eye had been —because isn't it strange. I mean when you think that those grasshoppers probably all just know the same thing but I mean with all these people, with all these millions and millions of people everyplace that no one knows what anyone else knows?

—Whatever your grasshoppers know that's one thing, you won't hear it from the females, they're practically silent, it's the males that...

—I'm not talking about grasshoppers! I'm, I mean that's just exactly what I'm not talking about I'm talking about you, about what you know that nobody else knows because that's what writing's about isn't it? I'm not a writer Mrs Booth I mean lots of people can write about all that, about grasshoppers and evolution and fossils I mean the things that only you know that's what I mean.

—Maybe those are the things that you want to get away from. Maybe those are the things that will eat you alive, sitting out there on that star with your powerful telescope watching your father with his Jack Russell terriers, I'll tell you what I'd see if I was there with you. I'd see myself lying under that truck just to get out of the broiling sun, the truck broke down and my boy pulled out, he just slipped away in the night. I told you they all thought I was crazy when they brought me in, when I said there was gold there, well I was. Two or three days out there roasting alive, drinking rusty water from the truck's radiator and I was delirious but I'd sworn to myself if I ever got through it that I'd remember what really happened. That all that kept me from losing my mind was knowing I was losing my mind but that it was there, the gold was there. And when they found it twenty years later it didn't matter anymore, proving I was the one who'd told them, none of it mattered anymore. All that mattered was that I'd come through because I'd sworn to remember what really happened, that I'd never look back and let it become something romantic simply because I was young and a fool but I'd done it. I'd done it and I'd come out alive, and that's the way it's been ever since and maybe that's the hardest thing, harder than being sucked up in the clouds and meeting the Lord on judgment day or coming back with the Great Imam because this fiction's all your own, because you've spent your entire life at it who you are, and who you were when everything was possible, when you said that everything was still the way it was going to be no matter how badly we twist it around first chance we get and then make up a past to account for it, sitting out on the Dog Star didn't you tell me? with your powerful telescope that that's what you'd see? being seduced at somebody's funeral those eight or nine light years away and that you'd be watching what really happened? The phone rang in the kitchen. —And did it?

—It always rings! She started up, wringing the stripes tight —no, whenever we, it always rings...

—Then why do you answer it?

—Because it might have been Paul! She paused there the moment it took for her face to colour, turned for the doorway and through it. —Yes, hello? clearing her throat, —Oh. He said you might call yes, he's not here, he won't be home till tomorrow or maybe Thurs... Yes about the estate, something about a stock option before this big lawsuit? He said he just wants a simple yes or... no I know yes, but... Yes but when you say going off half cocked, I mean I know he gets a little impatient sometimes but he's really just trying to help, he's... All right yes then I'll tell him to call Adolph, not to call you again but call Adolph...

She hung up standing staring down at the phone and then she raised it again, rustling aside papers for one with a number she dialed, and waited, and finally —hello? Yes I'm calling for... am I what? I, no, no I'm not a prayer partner no, I... I'm not calling the Lord's hotline no, all I... to what? No please, I mean I'm just trying to reach my husb... Yes thank you but that's not what I, I'm trying to reach my husb... no not on the Lord's hotline no, I thought... thank you, and she hung it up again standing there staring down at the pile of mail and suddenly reached for it, digging under it for that scrap of newspaper where eyes stared out through holes in the paper bag crushing it up in her hand as she came through the living room to tug the front door open on the still day out there broken only by the stabbing outcry of a crow commanding a height somewhere beyond the refuse of the night, an unhesitant reach for the mailbox and she came in spilling it to the table, Doctor Yount, B & G Storage, Mrs B Fickert (in pencil), Christian Recovery, F X Lopots Attorney at...

—Those trash bags, did you find some?

—What? Oh. Look they didn't even wait! That man who called this morning, that awful Mister Stumpp... paper tore, —he said if I didn't make a deal that I'd hear from Mister Lopots and they'd already mailed it.

—Mister Lopots.

—Well it's not funny! Failure to pay the amount due will result in litigation against you and an increased amount of monies you will have to pay, including interest, court costs, attorney's fees and disburse...

—They're just trying to frighten you, here... he took the letter from her and sat down, —give me the phone.

—Well they are frightening me. Unless payment is made immediately I will have no other choice but to... He'd already dialed. —Wait what are you...

—Mister Lopots? I'm calling on behalf of a Mrs Booth in the matter of Doctor Schak versus Booth, I have your... I have it right here there's no account number on it, it's just one of your cheap mimeographed threats to... Never mind that now Mister Lopots, just listen. If you want to go ahead with this, Mrs Booth will be glad to respond to any summons and complaint served on her in compliance with the law. She's prepared for the inconvenience of meeting your client in downtown court and any disbursements and costs if he wins his claim, which looks damned unlikely...

—No wait, please!

—I'm assuming your client's aware of how much court time of his this will involve Mister Lopots, and if you're thinking of a last minute adjournment when Mrs Booth shows up your client can expect to be served with a subpoena guaranteeing his appearance with all his records in this case, things like this so called detailed personal and medical history and this comprehensive consultation he sent to the wrong man if he sent it at all, is that all clear? If you want to confer with your client again and he decides to accept the payment she's already sent him, you should let her know promptly so she won't stop the check. Thank you Mister Lopots, goodbye.

—But do you think they...

—Forget about it... He came bent over a stove burner lighting the cigarette. —You see? They try to sound menacing but there's no malice there, just stupidity... he crumpled the letter, —just part of the trash... and dropped it in.

—You're going to stay? she said suddenly, —I mean until, if you want lunch there's nothing for lunch, I just have a glass of milk sometimes but, but supper, we could be in front of the fire like last night? I can call the store they can deliver something if we, I mean if you'll stay? Could they send up some decent veal then, he asked her, four or five veal scallops? and did she have any mushrooms? fresh ones, and heavy cream... —No but, I can order it but I mean I've only had that in restaurants I'm not sure I, I can do chicken though, if you... He'd do it he told her, and shallots, green onions if she didn't have shallots, and Madeira? was there any Madeira? —I don't think so but... A little white vermouth then, that would have to do he said turned for the door and stopped, that abruptly, with her up against him, her arm on his shoulders pulling him close, —can you? do all that?

—Of course... He let his hand close on her shoulder, —you learn to look after yourself.

—But didn't she...

—Geologists have the highest divorce rate going... close enough now to kiss the rise of her cheekbone, —even higher than doctors... and his hand lingered at her breast, letting her go. —Now, those trash bags?

Veal, she wrote on the back of B & G Storage, mushrooms, shallots, cream, Marsala was it? And she was over pulling open the drawer, digging under the placemats, a five, three singles, a twenty, before she was back dialing the phone, repeating her order —yes I know, but this time I'll pay cash... when there, straight before her, the front door shuddered open and she dropped it.

—Bibb?

—No! you, what...

—Hey... he came on, —you look really terrific.

—Wait! She settled the phone back, in to trim his embrace backed off against the love seat there —you, what is it what are you doing here?

—Man I just got back, I mean I just dropped in to see how you...

—You always just drop in! You, you just...

—Bibb like what's the matter, I mean...

—You know what's the matter! I've been getting, sit down. Just sit down.

He slumped in the wing chair. —Have you got a beer?

—No I don't have a beer. Billy honestly, how could you do a thing like that, Mister Mullins has been on the phone screaming at me he wants to call the police and have you arrested, he said he's the one who pays Sheila's rent there and if you don't give him every penny you stole from these people he'll send you to jail, is it true? Is that where this new suit came from and running off to California?

—Oh man. He's so dumb, I mean get him off my case Bibb. I give him the money and that makes him an accessory, right? So we both do ninety days at Riker's Island? I mean he's so fucking dumb he can't even...

—He doesn't want the money, he doesn't want to keep it he wants it to give back to these people you stole it from because they're all after him, they're after him and Sheila because it's her apartment, how much was it.

—I mean Sheila didn't know anything about it, like she took off for that ashram in Jersey with that skinny Tibetan two weeks ago so what's the big...

—And that's when you put an ad in the paper two bedrooms, large living room, terrace, furnished three hundred dollars a month? and then you were up there showing it and getting everybody aside to give you a cash deposit and come back next week? That's what he told me, is that...

—Oh Bibb, Bibb. I mean what's the difference, nobody got hurt did they? they didn't take anything did they? She's still got her fucking apartment and a few turkeys out on the street are out a hundred bucks man like what did they expect, I mean if they're dumb enough to think they could get a pad like that for three hundred a month they couldn't wait to hand over these cash deposits, like this one woman goes in the fucking bedroom and...

—I don't want to hear about it! And, and please stop saying fucking I just don't, why do you do things like this?

—Man like what am I supposed to do! I mean I go in and see Adolph, you know he sold Longview? and like do we see one fucking nickel? I mean it should have gone to us in the first place, it should have gone to mother if they...

—Mother hated Longview, she was terrified of it, after she saw that thing come out of the marsh and drag old Juno under she never went back, she was terrified.

—Like does that mean Adolph should hand it over to these doctors for seven hundred and fucking thirty thousand dollars? It should have brought like over three million so he does this big deal with this doctor syndicate and puts it right in the trust. He should have split it between us but it's in the trust where we can't touch a fucking nickel. It's his obligation as trustee to conserve the assets of the trust so the trust can meet its obligations he tells me, he has to guard the trust against unwarranted incursions, you know what that is Bibb? That's Paul, that's fucking Paul going around trying to borrow against it that's what he's been...

—All right! That still doesn't mean you have to do something like this with Sheila's apartment when Adolph won't advance you more money where does it go! Dope? Is it drugs is that what...

—Oh Bibb come on, I mean it just goes, I mean who's telling you I try to get money from Adolph for drugs, Adolph? Did you talk to Adolph? Because I wasn't up there trying to squeeze money out of him, I went up to see if he could get me a job, ask him. If you don't believe me ask him. I mean I just want to clear out Bibbs, I mean as far away from all this crap as I can get, Adolph knows the company operations inside out, he could get me sent anywhere. I mean the old man ran the whole show, don't I have a right to some lousy job?

—Well Mister Grimes runs it now and I don't think he'd...

—Man like there's nothing old man Grimes would like better than to see me shipped off to some burnt out hole in Africa, hand him a chuckle every time he thought of me laid out with dengue fever, he'd even throw in a little jungle rot for good...

—Africa?

—That's where they are, isn't it? And I mean that's where the action is, VCR's got a finger in Africa anyplace you look I mean that's what all this crap is about, the stock dropping and the old man's estate and these leaks, did you talk to Adolph?

—No, Paul says...

—Paul says! Man it's always fucking Paul, I mean he's the one Bibbs, he's where these leaks are coming from, he was going back and forth over there like a yo-yo carrying the bag for the old man wasn't he? I mean they kicked his ass out of the company that doesn't mean his asshole buddies in Pretoria pulled out on him does it? And I mean this old crud senator they've got on the string getting him this dismissal in these hearings Adolph told me, he's got them scared shitless even if they've got every concession over there nailed down, he's the one who carried the bag he's the one on the inside he's the, Bibbs? She was staring off at nothing, listening elsewhere, saidn't a word looking up —Is he here?

—Who.

—Paul, I mean who else. I thought I heard him.

—Oh. No, no that's just the...

—Because what I came for is that trust instrument, you've got a copy of it haven't you? I have to see it.

—It's in a box someplace, I'd have to go up and look for it but you know what it...

—It's the exact wording Bibb, I have to see the exact wording. I mean when I was talking to Adolph and I'm thinking like suppose something happened to me before this distribution and like where does that leave Paul, you and Paul. I mean your share by the time it comes through it won't be there and like if something happens to me he steps in and blows everything, could you look for it? now? I mean it's important.

—Just, all right but, but just wait there.

He watched her up the stairs, —I mean where else would I go? and he sat for a minute cracking the knuckles of one hand doubled in the other, staring blank at the odd jacket crumpled on the chair there before some sound, or second thought, or splanchnic stirring brought him to the kitchen to stare into the refrigerator, spread the last of the butter on bread he found there and come, folding it over, to stand in the open doorway chewing it, looking in. —Hi... and then again, —hi. I mean are you the guy that owns the house here?

Torn by a cough, straightening up from the bundled magazines with a hand steadied on a bookshelf, —my name is McCandless, yes. I'm the guy that owns the house here.

—Man it's some mess, I mean let me help you...

—No no no, no just leave it there... He cleared his throat of the cough and sat down, busied digging in the table's litter for the glazed tobacco envelope. —I'm just cleaning up here, there's really nothing you can...

—It's funny, you know? I mean I used to know this kid in school named McCandless. He was sort of a neat kid.

—Why is that funny.

—What? No, I mean I just never met anybody else named that, like I still owe him this two hundred dollars. I mean he was the only decent kid in the whole fucking school, he...

—Wait be careful of that, it's...

—I mean what is it.

—It's a camera shutter. It's rather delicate.

—Oh. Like if it wasn't for him I would have been kicked out. I mean I was finally kicked out anyway but not for that... and holding up that yellow orange rock now —what's this, gold?

—It's not gold no, it's something called gummite.

—Gummite? I mean what are you, like some kind of geologist?

—Yes. Yes you could put it that way, now...

—Because I mean I always felt lousy about that two hundred dollars, you know? Can I bum a cigarette?

—Well I, here... He came forward abruptly to sweep the battered State Express tin from the litter and sank back further into the chair, waving off the smoke as though searching through it those features limned in intimacy only minutes before, kissed in fact, looming over him here in this unseemly parody, that chill fragility of chin and cheekbone all untempered, unrestrained, ruminant with bread and even the hands, now the bread was gone, large, red knuckled, the very finger ends nubbed by bitten nails up shaking out a match, drawing away the cigarette, quickened by that same dread of unemployment but latent with casual breakage where one of them, cupping a dented case in general issue drab, snapped its cover open, closed, opened. —I didn't get your name.

—Me? It's Vorakers, Billy Vorakers. What's this, a compass?

—And you're her brother? Mrs Booth's?

—She's my sister.

—Yes. Yes she's very nice, isn't she... He leaned forward to stamp out what was left of his cigarette, —a very nice person.

—Nice? Man like she's the only straight number in the whole fucking family, I mean she's the only thing that holds things together in the whole...

—That two hundred dollars, what was it for.

—What, that? Man like it was for nothing. I mean we were only in second form, you know? And I mean I got busted for grass when I'm off the school grounds so there's this old locker room guy Biff we used to throw the towels to? So he gets this town lawyer he knows where before the school finds out about it if I can put up this two hundred dollars bail and then just not show up and that's it, I mean I surrender the bail and that's it. I mean he was sort of a neat old guy but like where am I supposed to get this two hundred dollars. I mean if I'd called my old man he would have told them great, put him in solitary, give him the thumbscrews so Jack calls his father and it's there the next day and I mean he wasn't rich, like these other snotty kids whose old man pulls up in a Mercedes like mine where he scribbles a check to the alumni association and then he shows up at the hockey game. I mean I never thought he'd show up at all and I'm sitting in the penalty box when I hear this fucking whisper right behind me kill them, kill them, he's

177

right behind me with his fur collar turned up where everybody's yelling and all I hear is this whisper, kill them...

—But he's dead, isn't he.

—Man, is he dead.

—Tell me something, Billy... He'd settled back digging in
the litter for the glazed tobacco envelope, —was your...

—What? Hey Bibbs, did you find it?

—I didn't find it, no. She was standing there in the doorway, quelling the tremor in an empty hand seizing it on the
knurl of the sideboard, piano, whatever it was —it's not there,
I'll have to ask Paul if he...

—Ask Paul! I mean that's why it's not there, he's check-
ing it out for the same...

—Please! rescuing calm to her voice, getting breath, looking from one to the other of them through these conspiring
planes of blue on grey, —I don't think Mis...

—I mean the shape the old man was in when Adolph drew
it up now he says he doesn't have a copy, that's just Adolph
covering his ass in case the old man screwed up, I mean like
I was just telling Mis...

—I heard you she said, her voice tight as her hand on the
dark turn of wood there —and I don't think Mister, Mister
McCandless has a lot to do here I wish you'd just come out
and let him...

—No but wait Bibbs wait, I mean where's Paul now, because I was just in California right? So somebody turns on
television and all of a sudden it's all these spaced out creeps
of Paul's. I mean this Billye Fickert is up there in this black
dress like she's in mourning only it's cut right down to her
crotch holding up this picture of her little boy that's resting
in the Lord's bosom, and I mean this huge black guy in his
uniform whipping around in this wheelchair singing and then
this creep, this redneck creep Paul was trying to fix up with
Longview? this Reverend Ude? I mean he's up there com-
forting this Mrs Fickert in the bowels of Jesus everlasting
life man it looks like he's reaching in there for a handful of
raw lung I mean you've got to hear him, like he's shouting

about these agents of Satan that have penetrated into high places trying to prevent his glorious mission where he's going even unto darkest Africa to wash them in the blood of Jesus I mean you've got to hear that voice, like he's shouting about Marxism is this instrument of Satan the father of lies and then it drops real low and slows down like he's sliding a hand right into your short hair, pray for little...

—Billy please it's, no one cares! Now...

—No no no, no in fact Mrs Booth I'm fascinated.

—But what... she broke off, suddenly deserted there against the doorframe, —Paul's not even...

—No come on Bibbs, I mean it's Paul that's running that whole freak show isn't it? like he's supposed to be this big media consultant and all that bullshit? I mean Ude's up there telling everybody to turn on their car headlights and wear a purple ribbon to show they're in this big crusade against these forces of evil infiltrating the government and the regular churches and the Jews to try to put him out of business that's got to be Paul, I mean those headlights and those ribbons that's got to be fucking Paul with his phony military school dress sabre and his box of stones and all his freaked out cheap southern bullshit pray for little Wayne, pray for America I mean that's got to be...

—Well it's not he, honestly! Paul's not even, he doesn't know any more about the Bible and Satan than you do about, about Buddhism and, and... she got breath as though to stem the colour rising in her face —why it should be fascinating to, why Mister McCandless should be fascinated by what you have to say about Paul it's not, it's just not very...

—No no I didn't mean, I'm sorry Mrs Booth... waving off the smoke, —I meant Reverend Ude. Reverend Elton Ude? There can't be two of them.

—What, I mean like you know him?

—Like the plague, yes. The Lord brought us together once in Smackover.

—Man you've got to be kidding. In what?

—In Smackover no, no you don't kid about Smackover.

179

People get up in the morning and go to bed at night in Smackover till the day they die and go someplace else, someplace that must look just like Smackover at two in the morning believe me, that's as serious as things can get, Reverend Ude in there washing them all in the blood of where are those little books, those damned little books... He collared the nearest trash bag tearing it open, pulling out pages, scraps, fragments of landscapes, coastlines, a palm size scrip of cheap newsprint stapled together in black and blue —here, here's one, Genesis to Revelation the whole thing boiled down to ten pitiful little pages of illiteracy and hideous cartoons, here's the creation. In the beginning, God created the heaven and the earth it looks like he's shooting craps, talk about playing dice with the universe. They're little comic books teaching this comic strip version of the creation, Ude was handing the damned things out all over town, here... He was back digging in the trash bag, —another one here on evolution that's even funnier he gave me a whole fistful of them, came up to me on the courthouse steps and took my arm he wanted me to get right down there on my knees with him and repent, why the Lord sent him to Smackover he told me where is that damned thing...

—Man like the Lord sent him to Smackover but I mean who sent you, what...

—Me? digging deeper, coming up with crumpled snapshots, the scanning she'd admired earlier as art, —these forces of evil in high places you're talking about, one of those brawls over equal time in the schools for teaching evolution and this laundered Genesis they palm off as creation science. There can't be a creation without a creator, if there's a clock there must be a clockmaker they've got all the answers, show them a zircon from Mount Narryer in Australia that's four billion years old, show them these fossilized skeletons of Proconsul africanus from eighteen million years ago that have just turned up in Lake Victoria, that may really be the missing link and they'll say fine, just fine, if this creator could produce the heavens and the earth and the whole shebang in just six days he'd certainly be able to produce a real interesting history to go along with it now wouldn't he? They'll point to billion year old Precambrian rocks on top of Cretaceous shale to disprove geological sequence and lump the whole thing into the flood here, it's in this same damned little cartoon book. And God destroyed the earth's inhabitants with water because of man's wickedness. And Noah only remained alive, and they that were with him in the ark and the whole geologic record goes down under forty days of rain where is it, where is it... he'd half emptied the bag by now, —how we've been brainwashed by evolution theory but can't produce the missing link and they jump on the Piltdown fraud, the Nebraska man that turned out to be a pig's tooth so the missing link is a fraud, evolution's all a fraud and geology astronomy physics all of it's a fraud, nothing in there about the fossil fragments in the Samburu hills where the strata's fifteen million years old, nothing about those fossil bones in three million years of volcanic ash up in the Afar Triangle, nothing about all those hominid fossils at that site in the Gregory Rift no, they wanted the missing link it was standing right up there in front of them, braying about the powers of darkness.

She turned abruptly for the kitchen as though she'd forgotten something there, as though the phone had rung, something boiling over, and then she stood there tapping her fingers on the empty sink staring out the window until she filled the kettle and turned on the stove.

—Here's another of the damned things here, look at this one Billy... red and black this time, —Depart from me, ye cursed, into everlasting fire prepared for the devil and his angels God, I'd like to take Ude up there with me sometime... He caught up the scanning, spread it flat —here's the top of the Great Rift, three rifts coming together in the Afar Triangle, earthquakes, volcanoes, boiling springs a hundred thirty five in the shade if you can find any, take him up there and show him where his comic books came from no don't tell me about that voice of his, I can still hear it, not at the trial no, not at the trial, they were too damned busy laundering Genesis they couldn't let him in. He'd file a brief as a friend of the court and grab a crowd wherever he could, hand them Genesis and Revelation with a little of Jeremiah thrown in, the wormwood and gall and the Lord coming down like a whirlwind, is not my word like as a fire? saith the Lord; and like a hammer that breaketh the rock? Stupidity like that, you put a hammer in its hand and everything looks like a nail, those looks we got on the courthouse steps once or twice I thought we wouldn't get out of Smackover alive.

She was back in the doorway. —Do you want some tea or, or coffee? I'm making tea if you...

—No, no we're quite well fixed here thanks... and she could see that he'd poured a dash into the dirty glass at his elbow. —Same damned thing he's up to out there in your California freak show, telling them this Full Gospel Witnessing's the only weapon we've got against the spread of Marxism even unto darkest Africa, fighting these forces of evil that want to stop his glorious mission of spreading stupidity from one end of the dark continent to the other, I'm not talking about ignorance. I'm talking about stupidity. If you want ignorance you can find it right there, that site on Lake Rudolf up in the Gregory Rift, hominid fossils, stone tools, hippo bones all of it caught in a volcanic burst two or three million years ago that was ignorance, that was the dawn of intelligence what we've got here's its eclipse. Stupidity's the deliberate cultivation of ignorance, that's what we've got here. These smug idiots with their pious smiles they can't stand the idea they're descended from that gang at Lake Rudolf banging around with their stone hammers trying to learn something no, they think God put them here in their cheap suits and bad neckties in his own image almost half the country, did you know that? Almost half the damned people in this country believe that man was created eight or ten thousand years ago pretty much like he is today? they believe that?

—Well, well no, I mean I didn't know that but, Bibbs? Wait a second, I...

—No, no sit down Billy I'll tell you something, here take one of these... he thrust over the dented yellow tin, —there's the fossil record of life going back billions of years it's got to be full of gaps, full of arguments about how evolution happened so they use those to say it didn't happen at all. We have the questions and they have the answers, dressing up Genesis and calling it science they go back from Malachi counting up all those begats, begats, begats and the creation took place October twenty sixth four thousand four BC at nine a m, that's what they call scientific method. Did anybody see it? No, no it's revealed right there in the first couple of pages of Genesis, that's what you call revealed wisdom. Talk about having business with the Bible, you walk down the street in Smackover and somebody you've never seen in your life comes right up and asks you if you've been saved as if it's any of his damned business and he thinks it is, the prevailing IQ in this country's about a hundred, did you know that? Good God, talk about a dark continent I'll tell you something, revelation's the last refuge ignorance finds from reason. Revealed truth is the one weapon stupidity's got against intelligence and that's what the whole damned thing is all about... The glass came down emptied and he looked up.

She'd come right in this time, holding out —these trash bags you asked for, and then, —Billy? where he was struggling upright from the magazine bundle, —Mister McCandless has a lot to do here he's, I don't think you should take any more of his...

—Right. Right I'm coming, I...

—No no no, no it's all right Mrs Booth, your brother just wanted to know about this trial in Smackover and that's what the whole damned thing was all about academic freedom to

teach this rickety scientific creationism and the judge saw
right through it and we won the case, talk about a healthy
attitude. We won the case and they won their equal time
because the only healthy attitude was to teach neither one
of them, wait... he was down sweeping together what he'd
pulled from the trash bag, —show you what a judge in
Georgia had to say... he dug among crumpled pages, news
clippings, —no, no this one's better listen to this. Until textbooks are changed, there is no possibility that crime, violence, venereal disease and abortion rates will decrease, this
is a charming Texas couple who keep an eye out for schoolbooks that undermine patriotism, free enterprise, religion,
parental authority, nothing official of course, just your good
American vigilante spirit hunting down, where is it, books
that erode absolute values by asking questions to which they
offer no firm answers there, you see? Same damned thing,
we've got the questions and they've got the answers, busy
in there advising the state committee, there must be twenty
of these states where local school boards can't buy textbooks
that haven't been selected by the state committee. You think
Texas wants one that talks about land redistribution in Cen-
tral America or anyplace else? You think Mississippi wants
a history book that tells the kids Nat Turner was anything
but a coon show? You talk about censorship and they howl
like stuck pigs no, they let the publishers do that for them.
Sixty five million a year, that's what Texas spends on
schoolbooks, that kind of money the edition's so big it wipes
out everything else, you think any publisher that wants to
stay in business is going to try to peddle a fourteen dollar
biology textbook to these primates with a chapter on their
cousins back there banging around Lake Rudolf with their
stone hammers? Finally repealed a law down there that evolution had to be taught as just another theory not a fact, you
think that will make any difference? No no no, stupidity's a
damned hard habit to break, if it's not in the book you can't
teach it, stupidity conquers ignorance and they all go home

and read Reverend Ude's literature here, I'll show you something Billy...

—No well I, I mean I think I better go see if, Bibbs?

—No no sit down, sit down, look at this, here's his Survival Handbook, four pages they call it a book. Keep handy for future reference, that's any minute now when millions of Christians suddenly disappear from the face of the earth and you're not one of them. They're all up there meeting the Lord in the clouds having a grand time and you're left here with seven years of tribulation but don't panic! Got your little handbook here just do what it tells you, here. Get ready for global war and global famine. Get out of the cities they'll be destroyed, stay away from mountains and islands they'll be destroyed, stay away from oceans everything in them will be killed, get in seven years' supply of food and water and get ready to fight off starving people and wild animals, fix up your house to resist earthquakes and hundred pound hailstones and watch out for demon controlled people and other creatures roaming around out there torturing and killing anybody in sight, Revelation nine, one to eighteen it says it right here, God's word isn't it? revealed to Saint John the Divine? just the way he revealed those three secrets to those kids at Fatima? Same damned thing, fire and pestilence, talk about being blown to Kingdom Come that's exactly what they mean and they can't wait. They can't wait to be snatched up to meet the Lord in the clouds and sit there watching the rest of us tormented with fire and brimstone in the presence of his holy angels and the Lord right in there rubbing his hands, they can't wait to see the sun darkened, the stars fall, hailstones and fire, the cities crumbling, the seas turned to blood I'll tell you something Billy, the whole damned thing's a self fulfilling prophecy, I'll tell you something right now. The greatest source of anger is fear, the greatest source of hatred is anger and the greatest source of all of it is this mindless revealed religion anywhere you look, Sikhs killing Hindus, Hindus killing Moslems, Druse killing Maronites, Jews killing Arabs, Arabs killing Christians and Christians killing each other maybe that's the one hope we've got. You take the self hatred generated by original sin turn it around on your neighbors and maybe you've got enough sects slaughtering each other from Londonderry to Chandigarh to wipe out the whole damned thing, here... Suddenly he was up, —give you something real to read if you want the whole story... thrusting books aside in the bookshelf —because none of it's new, none of it's new...

—No but wait man, I mean I'm not really, no wait, Bibbs? And she might have come in, she'd got as far as the doorway again standing there holding them at glare's length when the phone turned her back where she'd come from, pushing aside the tea still steeping in the cup, picking it up for —yes? Hello...? and then —oh... and —oh, and —but is everything... oh. Yes I, I'll be here yes where else would I... yes I'll be here... holding it, still, before hanging it up as though to give it time to reconsider, to retreat, retract or at the least to offer some reprieve, but the only voice to be heard was the one raised through the doorway behind her.

—talk about their deep religious convictions and that's what they are, they're convicts locked up in some shabby fiction doing life without parole and they want everybody else in prison with them it's the smugness, that's stupidity's telltale Billy, the damned self righteous smugness here, read this one. God and Jesus appear to a farm boy in upstate New York a hundred and fifty years ago out in the woods where he's praying for guidance, fourteen years old he's guilty as sin that he can't understand and just to make it worse there's the resurrection and the life starting to bulge in his pants so here comes the heavenly messenger, the resurrected angel who'd just happened to bury some plates on a nearby hill there fourteen centuries before with all the news, visions, revelations, prophecies, speaking with tongues, laying on of hands he finally gets it all down in a book that's one more recipe for bloodshed and they're off. Bloodshed in Missouri, bloodshed in Nauvoo Illinois and this time it's his, bloodshed across the Mississippi, Iowa wait, wait don't bother to read that one no, no that's just a sideshow here's the real thing, here's Runciman, three thousand years of religious slaughter have you read Runciman? Staggering piece of work, talk about having business with the Bible just try the Children's Crusade for a sideshow, thousands of kids led into slavery and death by a twelve year old with a letter from Jesus, that's one thing your Reverend Ude's learned since that trial in Smackover. Turn it into a crusade. You can't put the fear of God in them put in the fear of something right here and now, it's all fear, Satan wears a little thin so you tie him in with godless Marxism and you've got a crusade to scare the hell out of everybody, a crusade against the powers of darkness over there washing these Africans in the blood of Jesus and you'll have enough bloodshed to float the Titanic. These churches are all built on the blood of their martyrs aren't they? If Ude really wants to do it right he can always go out and get himself shot, and you know Billy? I think he'd do it...

The tea in the cup had steeped almost black and she left it there, up for a moment staring out the window again and then she pulled open the door and went out and sat on the edge of the chair overturned on the dead leaves carpeting the terrace, the streamers from the limbs of the mulberry tree drifting over her gentle as torn curtains and the lattice fence beyond like the ruptured wall of a room, of a house long since abandoned.

—You want to know what Africa's really all about here, here read this one... She'd come back in, chilled, to see him up tottering on the magazine bundle reaching down a book from a high shelf, her own hand already spotting white on the knuckles where she gripped the dark turn of wood standing there in the doorway —all four horsemen riding across the hills of Africa with every damned kind of war you could ask for. Coups d'état and you've got Somalia, Benin, Madagascar, the Congo, nationalist war gives you Mozambique, war of liberation topped off by a civil war and there's Angola, revolution and you've got Ethiopia and the tribes, the tribes. Rwanda gets its independence and the Hutus celebrate by killing a hundred thousand Watusi and grabbing majority rule, right next door in Burundi the Watusi slaughter two hundred thousand Hutus just to make sure it won't happen there. North Koreans train the Shona in Zimbabwe's Fifth Brigade and off they go in their red berets chopping up the Ndebele people in southern Matabeleland, seven hundred languages they've all been at each other's throats since the creation war, famine, pestilence, death, they ask for food and water somebody hands them an AK47 and suddenly the whole thing's a Marxist conspiracy? It's money from the West and guns from the East and they'll all sell out to the highest bidder. Somalis and Ethiopians they were killing each other up there in the Ogaden a thousand years before Marx was born. Ethiopia sells us out to the Marxists and comes out owing them two billion dollars for arms, Somalia rigs up something called scientific socialism that's just about as real as this scientific creationism, they keep it running long enough to build up a vast system of patronage and corruption when a coup d'état hands them over to us and we get to pay the bills no no no, if all this is a Marxist Leninist conspiracy to take over the dark continent it's a pretty damned pitiful show. Fifty countries over there and the seven or eight that call themselves Marxist are a shambles every damned one of them. This spectre of Marxism taking over black Africa good God, they're the best friends we've got, good healthy ignorance they believe in the same things we do, strong family ties, religion and greed.

—I, excuse me... she caught at the advantage of his efforts engrossed now in scaling down from the heights of the bookshelf, two more books in one hand and the other out grasping his balance on the table corner, wiping away cobwebs, looking over to her as though startled to see these features he'd lost sight of looming dumb over him suddenly redrawn, refined, restored in the same frail strength of her hand's restraint on the doorframe.

—No no no, it's all right yes come in Mrs Booth, come in... banging dust from one of the books and handing it over, —this will interest you too yes, come in...

Instead she sneezed. —No, I... she sneezed again.

And as though to oblige he picked up the smouldering cigarette to add to the cloud and sank back in the chair banging dust from the other book against the edge of the table —here, it's mostly statistics but you'll get the idea... brandishing it till he was disarmed —same damned thing Billy. Over there sitting on half the world's diamonds and chrome, ninety percent of its cobalt, half the gold, almost half the platinum, the whole length of the copper belt and that huge bauxite deposit at Boké in Guinea while they're starving to death who's going to buy it. Three or four centuries their main export was slaves now all they've got to sell is their minerals, they want our money, they want our investment and they want our technology call their politics any damned thing they please. Who's been guarding Gulf Oil's installation in Angola where they're pumping out millions of barrels a day, the US Marines? Cubans, Cubans, you want to see what's keeping the whole cycle of corruption and starvation poverty in business go over to Zaire and watch those South African C130s taking off at night from Kinshasa's airport packed with diamonds and cobalt, our great bulwark against the, what was it? aggressive instincts of an evil empire? the cause of unrest anyplace in the world you find it no, take a look at every country bordering South Africa you'll see who's doing the destabilizing. They've got no damned rights at all in Namibia but who's making them leave, diamond fields running up the west coast but that's not why they're there oh no, no no no they're holding back the powers of darkness up in Angola going right in there and shooting to kill. This great global Marxist conspiracy behind every insurgent movement, who recruited these wretched Ndebele for this secret Matabele brigade to destabilize Zimbabwe handing them over to rape, torture, murder by the Shonas. Who set up the Mozambique National Resistance Movement

189

in the Transvaal when Rhodesia went down, want to write to them they're at Clive Street, Robindale, Randburg, want to see a reign of terror see them raiding into Mozambique beating, raping, disfiguring the locals, teachers, health workers all the forces of darkness and the whole rickety thing collapses, Mozambique's brought to its knees like Lesotho, there's a country as big as your hat and they've ground it right into the dirt but a hundred and fifty thousand of them cross the border to work in the mines and it's that or starve. Keep their neighbors crippled and set up twenty million blacks of their own in these homelands of poverty, disease, families broken up like they were in the good old slave trading days, walk out of their Dutch Reform Church apartheid ringing in their ears and they've got as nice a slave empire as any good Christian could ask for, talk about having business with the Bible and we're right in there cheering them on. Good church going people aren't they? bulwark against this great global Marxist conspiracy aren't they? Vanadium, platinum, manganese, chromium they sell these four key minerals to our industry and defense don't they? think they're going to hand that over to the blacks? No no no, hand them the Survival Handbook and look the other way, talk about harvest time and here comes your missionary bringing Africa to the foot of the Cross with his trucks carrying the dynamite of the Holy Spirit, plundering hell and populating heaven's going to be so damned crowded it will look like the Green Pastures, here come de...

—Please... She was back with a paper napkin crushed to her face —it's, it's Paul he... and she sneezed.

—Like didn't I just tell you it's Paul? I mean Paul with this whole crusade for Little Wayne Fuckup over there harvesting souls Paul the bagman, he...

—No no no, no it's not just starting Billy it never ended, hasn't ended for five hundred years since the Portuguese heard about those great silver and gold and copper mines in the kingdoms running up the Zambezi valley and came in with a few missionaries and a free trade monopoly from the Pope, a missionary's killed and it's war for anybody opposing propagation of the true faith pouring into Mombasa and plundering the east coast, evangelism and slave trading if you want that nice line between the truth and what really happens, fighting their way up the valley five years later when they've reached the Rhodesian plateau they've been wiped out by death and disease but that doesn't end it. Here comes Doctor Livingstone opening Africa to Christianity and commerce and the British gunboats steaming up the river Niger, white missionaries in Buganda howling for protection and the British East Africa Company storming African kingdoms for trade monopolies right up to the headwaters of the Nile. Free trade and Christianity, it's the German East Africa Company, it's French Equatorial Africa, it's the Belgians cutting down the Congo's population from twenty million to ten in barely twenty years, by nineteen fourteen there's nothing left to plunder in Africa so they go to war with each other in Europe instead that's what the whole damned first world war was all ab...

—Please! will you, just let me...

—No come in, come in we...

—I can't come in! The smoke and the, the dust and the smoke I just want to tell you that, to tell Billy that Paul called that he's on his way from the, from someplace Billy... speaking to him, looking past him where her eyes were met through the petrifying drift of smoke and dust —his plans changed he's, he'll be here by...

—Man I don't believe it. I mean I don't fucking believe it Bibbs. I come in here I think no Paul, I think finally there's no big rush we can just hang out and maybe even have supper later but in comes fucking Paul with his...

—I can't help it! She broke away —if you, I don't think Mister McCandless has to lis...

—No I'm going, I'm going Bibbs... up following her through to the kitchen —I mean I'll be in New York before

191

Paul walks in the door waving his hammer where everything looks like a fucking nail and Bibbs? I mean if you've got twenty...

She'd just shaken open the drawer there digging under napkins, placemats, when —Wait. Wait, you're driving down to New York?

—Man as fast as I can get there.

—If you can just take a minute, if I can drive down with you I'll just be a few minutes.

—But... her hand came up empty —don't, you don't have to leave Mister McCandless, I mean now if you haven't finished what you...

—Never turn down a ride no, just take me a minute to tie up these bags... and he was gone through the doorway.

—Bibbs? that twenty?

—I'm getting it! She came after him into the living room, stabbing the bills out —Billy listen. You don't have to, wait for him I mean you can just leave, now right now I'll just tell him you were in a terrible hurry and couldn't, that you're not going straight to New York that you have to stop in New Jersey or someplace and...

—What's the difference Bibbs, relax... He'd already sunk into the wing chair, —I mean he's sort of a neat old guy.

—A, a neat... she came down on the arm of the love seat, —neat old guy?

—I mean he's pretty wound up but that's...

—And you can listen to that all the way to New York? He's, he's...

—He's what, I mean Bibbs what the hell is the matter? You think anybody wants to be here when Paul walks in the...

—I'm not talking about Paul! He's, he doesn't even know Paul, you and Paul, you don't know him either walking right in there telling somebody you've never, some perfect stranger telling him how awful Paul and his military school and his southern just, anything just making things up to hurt Paul when you don't even...

—Making things up! I mean are you kidding Bibbs? Like that dumb toy sword with his name engraved on it? you mean I made that up? All this military bullshit with these spades from Cleveland and Detroit in his broken down platoon out there kicking their ass to show them what the southern white officer class is all about I made all that up? I mean he's still out there on the Mekong Delta, he walks down the street everybody he sees is a gook, he's...

—Well he's not! He's, because you don't know everything you think you do, what he, how he came out what really happened you don't know the...

—Man I know he came out this same second fucking lieutenant like he went in didn't he? I mean when you told me his own father said it's a God damn good thing he...

—Well he didn't!

—I mean you told me his own...

—Because he wasn't, because I never said he was Paul's own father he was, because Paul was adopted that's what you didn't know, that's something you didn't know when you go around talking to perfect stra...

—Man then how am I supposed to know he's adopted! I mean all this time where he's putting on this good old boy bullshit like these stones? all these stones he's got numbered and crated he says they were this ancestor General Beauregard's fireplace for when he rebuilds the old family mansion? Oh man, I mean for making things up? I mean I'm the one that's supposed to be making things up just to hurt Paul? Man I mean like what do you...

—Because it's not to hurt Paul, it's me isn't it. It's to hurt me, isn't it.

—Man like wait Bibbs, I mean what...

—I mean talking about Paul and Daddy the last time you were here, how I always find somebody that's not as good as I am that it's always a, it's always somebody inferior that that's all I...

—Man like wait Bibbs, I mean wait! That's not what I, I mean it's like you've got this real secret self hidden someplace you don't want anybody to get near it, you don't even want them to know about it like you're afraid if some superior person shows up he'll like wipe you out so you protect it by these inferior types they're the only ones you'll let near you because they don't even know it's there. I mean they think they've taken over they never even like suspect you've always got the upper hand because I mean that's your strength Bibbs, that's like how you survive because if this real superior person moved in you'd be wiped out so you appeal to these real morons where they don't have a fucking clue who you really are, like how you let Paul knock you around so he thinks he owns you, I mean that bruise right there on your shoulder? did I make that up? I mean you know he's this fucking inferior person because you married the same thing you tried to get away from, the same...

—Well maybe I did! Because I, because sometimes I almost can't tell you apart you and Paul, you sound the same you sound exactly the same the only difference is he says your God damn brother and you say fucking Paul but it's the same, if I closed my eyes it could be either one of you maybe that's why I married him! If you think the only men I appeal to are fools, if all I ever look for is inferior men then maybe that's why!

—Oh Bibbs... He'd brought a hand up to his mouth as though to cover his lips, to bite the edge of a nail, suddenly he raised his eyes with a look that wrenched her square around to the kitchen doorway behind her.

—Oh I, I'm sorry, I'm sorry I didn't mean to interrupt, just my jacket... They watched his haste to where it lay crumpled in the chair there from the night before —just needed to get my jacket, almost done in there I'll only be a minute...

She watched it all as fast as a shadow flung across the room and back, leaving her staring at those hands interlacing, turned out, cracking the knuckles. —I wish you'd never said that, Bibb... and he wasn't looking at her, —I wish I hadn't made you say that... his voice as emptied as his eyes fixed somewhere on the floor between them when she got up in a turn round the end of the love seat without a sound till she came through the kitchen, a sound choked off somewhere between there and loss coming through that doorway for so long shackled closed upon everything she now knew not to be there.

—Be right with you... He came up knotting a trash bag tight, —just get these tied up and...

—What are you doing!

—Just getting these tied up so that...

—He won't be here, Paul won't be here he won't be here for hours he won't be here till suppertime you don't have to go, we've got the whole afternoon why are you going.

—I'd have to leave anyway, he's got a car out there and...

—Let him leave then, you don't have to just because he is do you? You can stay with me at least till...

—No no no, it's all right, I'm...

—It's not all right! None of it's all right no don't pat me, no! Since the minute he came in it's been look at this Billy, I'll tell you something Billy you look up at me as though you'd never, I mean what's it all about!

He had one arm in his jacket, standing there pulling it on slowly. —Something's come up, he said. —A couple of things I want to get into town to straighten out... He squared up his shoulders, buttoned a button —Elizabeth, listen...

—I don't want to listen... She'd already turned for the door —if you're going just, go.

And on into the kitchen behind her, —oh Mrs Booth? I'll leave that open, all those trash bags you've got Madame Socrate coming in?

—She's, yes, yes she...

—She can put them out then. And don't let her complain, some of it's heavy, those magazine bundles she likes to complain, have you had that?

—Your vacuum cleaner. She says it's foutu.

—You know I had to teach her how to use it? the vacuum cleaner? he came along briskly behind her into the living

room unfurling the wad of that raincoat, pulling it on.
—Came in she was dragging it around poking the brush into
corners it wasn't plugged in, just doing what she must have
seen one of those dim blondes playing housewife on television like a boy I took with me out near the Hawash river,
he'd never seen a shovel, didn't know how to use one. Not
stupid no, no just ignorance he learned how to use the damned
shovel, that's the difference. Are you ready? He shot the
frayed cuffs —wait, those books I just gave you?

—Man like what am I going to do with them now, I mean...

—What do you mean do with them. Read them! And they
started aside from his burst back through the kitchen, caught
there within reach when their eyes met and her arms came
up in a sudden embrace holding close, Billy, Billy, barely
audible in the arms sheltering her tight when he was back
calling from the kitchen, —Mrs Booth? There was a piece of
paper on the table here, a lot of arrows and crosses scribbled
on it?

—It's there somewhere... she broke away, —but why in
the world would you...

—No no no, it's just a phone number here it is, I wrote a
phone number on it... By the time she reached the door he'd
torn a finger's length from it there just east of Estrées,
—it's nothing important is it?

And from behind her, —it looks like some of Paul's crap.

—Sorry... He came out with the books, too many of them,
steeped up under one arm, reaching out the other as he passed
in a try at squeezing her hand, —afraid I disturbed you Mrs
Booth I, I'll try to call first if I come up again... He paused
there, but the front door was being held open for him.

—Billy? will you call? please? and she watched them out
only long enough to see the books tumbled into the leaves
as he came off the step, to see wind flapping the raincoat
stooped picking them up as though they'd been flung in that
boisterous climb of school out for the day and even the
laughter she couldn't hear now, getting the door closed against
it, turning away so that when the car made the turn down

196

the hill, the wave of a hand leavetook the blind windows of simply a house.

She'd walked back through the kitchen where the clock was now labouring the hour when fingertips had traced down her back, lingered at the top of the rift searching over the edge, down it, deeper, desperate fictions like the immortal soul and these damned babies rushing around demanding to be born and born again, it was all fear, standing there and looking in where the smoke had paled and the dust settled over the littered table under the dimmed panes, over the books, bundles, trash bags, all at once she stepped back and slammed the door full, jammed the padlock closed on it with the heel of her hand and turned crumpling a paper napkin to blow her nose. Stillness filled the place but she seemed to be listening, afraid I disturbed you Mrs Booth but he learned how to use the damned shovel, that's the difference. I wish you'd never said that Bibb, you've always got the upper hand that's like how you survive but he's sort of a neat old, afraid I disturbed you Mrs Booth... She turned on the radio, to be told there was a forcible rape in this country every six minutes and she turned that off, eyes fixed on the still phone till she picked it up and dialed. —Yes, hello? Let me, this is Mrs Booth Elizabeth Booth, may I speak to Adolph? It's just... Oh, oh no that's all right no, don't interrupt him. It's nothing important.

And here they came, borne up the hill on shouts borne in tatters like the leaves blown one like another, spotted, yellowed here, drawn shriveled brown there but all leaves, hats, a glove or a mitten or even a sock, was it? a book in the air spilling pages and the spill of a grin on the face of the smallest of them frozen at wide eyed sight of her there halved in the glass panels of the door where she held to the newel as though fighting for balance, still as the old man propped on his broom out there recovering his bearings, getting his footing against the threat of movement anywhere even hers, now she suddenly pulled open the door and came out for two books almost indistinct from the leaves where they'd fallen, one of them in a yellow jacket and the other, in brown buckram, Bantu Prophets of South Africa she saw when she'd got them in, got the door closed tight before she turned for the stairs.

> Où est-ce que je peux changer des dollars
> pour des francs?

She watched till the lips appeared on the screen shaping the words, drawing her own tight against their artifice, pulling up the welter of sheets, stretching the bottom one and tucking its corners, unfurling the top one, shaking it out.

> Can I change dollars in the hotel?
> Est-ce que je peux changer l'argent à...

And standing there watching it settle, smoothing the wrinkles only to see at each stroke their damp testament promptly return she tore both sheets away in a sweep and had them up the hall with the wadded socks, drawers, sodden towels on the floor of the bathroom.

> A quelle heure ouvre la banque?

Those hands disjointed, rust spotted, crumbled features dulled and worn on the page right where she'd left them, she spread the manila folder open on clean sheets, reached for a pencil and found none, and then came back slowly on the fresh pillowslip stilled in the ashen flush of those silenced lips contorting soundless syllables on the screen which gave way, as the light at the windows gave way, to a lady playing the piano, to a man playing golf as the room grew darker, to leafy vistas and soldier ants in grim procession, to shell bursts brightening the walls for an instant, dimming with stretcher bearers, men loading a howitzer, firing a mortar turned away stopping their ears against the pounding, pounding, she was up, her feet off to the floor, reaching for the light, calling out —I'm coming! to the pounding on the door below, hesitating and then sweeping the folder up from the bed and back into the drawer under blouses, scarves, before she made way down the dark stairs, got the light on under the sampler, got the door open.

—I thought nobody's home.

—Who are you!

—These groceries? you ordered groceries?

—Oh. Oh I'm sorry yes, I forgot just, just wait here.

—Only the wine, they couldn't send you no wine.

—It doesn't matter she said, back counting out bills from the drawer in the kitchen. —It doesn't matter.

She'd set out a cup, put on the teakettle and reached out to the radio which had just time to warn her that the hurdy gurdy was the King of Naples' favourite instrument when a kick at the door brought her round with —Paul?

—God damn door standing wide open Liz, did you know that?

—Oh, yes some groceries just came and I...

—Standing here wide open, he came in from the dark heaving a shoulder against it to get through with the bag he dropped on the floor, the armload of papers down on the kitchen table in his search for a glass. —Any calls?

—Yes, there was a...

—Look before I forget it, call from McFardle down in Teakell's office if he wait, wait maybe I can still get him what time is it... He looked up from the bottle pressed hard down on the rim of the glass, —God damn clock Liz you still haven't set the God damn clock? up to where she looked, to where it had just overtaken the moment she'd stepped wet from the bath, rattled drawers open holding this up to her, that, a printed chiffon she hadn't seen since this Ragg knit —any mail? He'd come down heavily in the chair behind the table there, —Liz?

—What?

—Just asked you if there's any God damn mail, ask you if there's any mail if there's been any calls we don't even know what time it is, here... he turned to obliterate Haydn's Notturno number five in C nagging at his back with a twist of the dial that brought them words of hope for hemorrhoid

sufferers everywhere, —find out what the hell time it is...
and he put down his glass but held to it, tight, against a
sudden tremor in his hand.

—The mail it's, yes it's right there it's sort of mixed up
with yesterday's but, and you had a call yes, the one you
expected from Mister Slot, from, Paul what happened! Your
whole sleeve it's, what happened! He was up again pressing
the bottle free over the rim of the emptied glass, setting it
down hard to pull off his jacket —and your arm! your arm
wait, let me...

—Don't! don't need help no just, just get the God damn
thing off me... his back turned to her lifting it from his
shoulders, parting the sleeve severed wrist to elbow —think
I dressed up like a scarecrow for Halloween you didn't even
notice it when I...

—But your shirt too the blood it's, what...

—Switchblade. He picked up the glass and drank slowly
till he'd emptied it. —Just broke the skin but there goes my
good suit. I got mugged Liz, broad daylight coming out of
that prayer breakfast people all over the place I got mugged,
that's all.

—No but was it...

—A spade of course it was a spade! Looked just like my,
see it in his eyes before he came at me, see it coming in the
yellow of his God damned eyes before I saw the knife.

—But it's, don't you want to wash it or, or some ice? put
some ice...

He was down in the chair again staring fixed at the glass,
thrusting it toward her —yes here, get me some ice. I think
he was waiting for me... He reached out to drag up the folds
of the jacket, —tried to get his hands on this I think he was
waiting for me.

She put down ice in the glass where he'd pulled out a
plain envelope, riffling the bills in it with an edge of his
thumb. —But what, where did...

—A book Liz, a book? Walked out the door I told you I
was seeing a publisher for an advance on a book? Can't back

200

me up you wouldn't believe me at least can you listen?

—But it's, Paul it's all hundreds and, and cash all in cash?

—I wanted it in cash! He'd picked up the glass again, rattling the ice in it. —Walked out the door there you didn't believe me did you, thought I just wanted to impress your God damn brother where is he, tries to clip me twenty dollars on a hundred dollar check where is he, why isn't he here pissing on the floor.

—Do you, will you want supper in a little while I...

—All you said was what's it about, don't think I can write a book so you just say what's it about... He'd dug cigarettes from the jacket's pocket and lit one —want to know what's it about I'll tell you the title, The Wayne Fickert Story that's what's it about. Sketch it out and get this writer this Doris Chin, the one on the paper, the one that did that story on him in the paper get her in for a final polish before we get into the movie tie in, already talking about a movie tie in get his mother in there to play the mother. Billye Fickert the kid's real mother, get things off the ground here send her to Actors Studio we just have to find a kid to play the kid, it's a big project. It's a big project Liz, have to start work on it tonight that's what all this is... he brushed at the heap of papers he'd dropped on the table when he came in, rattling the ice loose in the glass till it prompted him to reach for the bottle. —I think he was waiting for me.

—Do you want water?

—Saw it in his eyes, seen that look before I knew what was coming.

—I got veal I thought I'd, I thought we'd try veal.

—Put some water in this will you? Get things off the ground here before they, not so much! Before they tear him to pieces, they're after him Liz.

She put the glass down in front of him. —If it was broad daylight I should think the police would...

—What police, not talking about the God damn police I'm talking about the federal government, the ones penetrating into the top power slots in the federal government right down to the county level they're out to get him, here... dashing ashes on the papers in a sweep of his hand —see it all right here, follow up ad campaign on this big crusade we kicked off on west coast television gave them a good look at Billye Fickert back from the fat farm she's already had a few offers, get this movie tie in off the ground they'll line up ten deep she's already had an offer from somebody up in the Bay Area not exactly the kind of thing we, here she is... he held up the page, —Liz?

—Well! she's quite, I think you have a letter from her there.

—What? Where.

—It's there somewhere, you can't miss it. It's in pencil.

—Where. Ask you if there's any mail when I came in the door where, only thing here's God damn B & G Storage... paper tore. —Look at that. Sent us a check Liz look at that... he shook it free of the letter, —twelve hundred sixteen dollars eighty cents look at that, minute you don't need it they get their bookkeeping straight send you twelve hundred sixteen dollars and who the hell's Doctor Yount.

—He was a...

—Keeps sending this God damn thing OV fifty dollars? a year ago?

—No tear it up, I sat in his waiting room for an hour, there was a television set going I was watching something about grasshoppers and this awful woman came over and switched it to a soap opera doctor who's just lost his leg and I turned it off and his nurse came in and told me I had no right to deprive the other patients of their pleasure and I left, Paul this letter...

—God damn good thing... paper tore, —Doctor Yount lose his leg got what's coming to him, that's...

—This letter Paul, the one with the check it says they, no. No it says they sold the, they sold all of it Paul they sold all of it! That bill for, we owed them nine hundred and ten dollars, advertising, handling, auction expenses four hundred eighty four twenty, taxes and, they got twenty eight hundred dollars for it at their auction, for all of it! Can't we, couldn't we call them and try to, those chests and mother's beautiful old, oh Paul...

He put down his glass and sat staring at it. —He was waiting for me, Liz.

—Did you hear what I said! This letter? that they've sold...

—What I've been telling you isn't it? walked in the door ask if there's any mail that's what I've been telling you? Problem Liz sometimes you don't listen... He put down the bottle, —problem is...

—Paul honestly, don't tell me what the problem is. She'd opened the cupboard and had out a saucepan, —do you want...

—All spelled out right here see that? full two page spread pray for America right across the top see that? Somehow he'd managed to get the newspaper open wide without knocking over the bottle. —An organized conspiracy is under way to destroy the Constitution of the United States. We are witnessing a conspiracy to destroy all our churches, our free press and our rights of assembling peacefully before God. Will you let this happen? Running it in these rural weeklies out in the boondocks all these hicks read anyway, here's their picture takes up half the page here then right under it he says we are just one small church down here on the Pee Dee but these are God's people, all God's people, here on the banks of the Pee Dee and out in my radio and television audience across the land and even on the dark continent of Africa where our mission radio brings words of hope and salvation to innocent sufferers everywhere. Today we are fighting your battle single handedly against satanic powers of darkness in high places then he puts in this line from Paul to the Ephusians, gives the Bible school students time off from the bottling plant to dig up his research. For we wrestle not against flesh and blood but against principalities, against powers, against the rulers of the darkness of this world, against spiritual wickedness in high places Liz what the hell are you doing, banging pots around I'm trying to show you something here.

—I'm starting supper.

—Goes right on to the listen, we are fighting your battle for if our church, targeted for the opening attack on the US Constitution is successful, other churches will follow until not one single church in our great Christian nation is left standing. Here in our plight on the banks of the Pee Dee you are witnessing the most satanic and unconstitutional attack on the very fundamentals of American freedom, the dark . beginnings of a Marxist dictator state casting the shadow of the powers of darkness over the entire world pray for America, pray for, Liz?

—Do you want peas with it?

—With what.

—The veal, I said I thought we'd try...

—Peas? talking about peas they're down there trying to kill his Bible school wipe out his whole Christian Recovery for America's People put the skids under his Africa missions you're talking about peas? Can you look? just turn around and look for a minute?

—Paul I'm trying to heat the, you showed me her picture and I don't...

—Not her God damn picture look at it, takes up half the page it's Ude and Teakell, Senator Teakell.

—Oh? She'd half turned, —what are they doing.

—Well what the hell does it look like they're doing, think they're down on their knees shooting craps? Taken down there in that Texas hospital when Teakell went down to see his...

—To see Cettie yes, yes... she turned full —what about her.

—Who, his daughter? Suing the car company, she and the kid that was with her their lawyers are suing for twelve million, defective brakes they say the company's own tests showed the brakes could lock and kept the whole thing a...

—I'm not talking about that! suing somebody, I just want to know if she's...

—No now look Liz it's God damn serious. There's Grimes

sitting on the board of the car company, Teakell's his man in the Senate and Teakell's own daughter turns around and sues them, God damn embarrassing all over the papers moment like this the press in there driving a wedge they're going after Teakell, that's why they're going after Ude they're trying to get Teakell's what this whole God damn thing is about can you see that?

—Never mind. She'd turned back to the sink holding an empty pan, looking through darkness carved her own shape from the reflection on the glass of the walls behind her and the cupboard and the doorway, and the lamp on the table and the reach of the torn arm for the bottle beside it, through to the darkness outside.

—Liz?

—I said never mind!

—Problem Liz you just don't grasp how serious the whole God damn thing is... the bottle trembled against the rim of the glass, —after him they're after me they're after all of us... He'd slumped back against word of two tractor trailer trucks overturned and on fire at an entrance to the George Washington bridge, —fit the pieces together you see how all the God damn pieces fit together. SEC comes in claims some little irregularity on a Bible school bond issue next thing you've got the IRS in there right behind them with misappropriation of church funds for openers, problem's their new computer down there's just geared to their mailing list if they don't build their mailing list there won't be any funds what the whole God damn thing is all about, you get these Bible students they're smart enough digging up Ephusians but they count on their fingers nobody knows where in hell the last nickel went, why Ude says it's God's money in the ad he can't, get the phone there... and he had it, —hello? Who...? No now wait a minute operator can't accept the call now no, I'm waiting for an important call tell her I can't tie up the line....

—Wait Paul, was that...

—Can't tie up the line Liz... he'd put down the phone and

205

picked up the glass, —can't get him on that they want to kill his tax exempt status, bottling plant sending out this Pee Dee water join his Pray for America club he suggests a ten dollar donation they say he's running a profit making business that's where they bring in the FDA, they all know each other that's how it works down there. That's what Washington is they all know each other, get one of them he's penetrated the IRS calls his buddy at FDA and they dig up a couple of cases of typhus out in the boondocks, seize their mailing list send out agents in Georgia Arkansas Mississippi Texas digging up typhus nobody told them to drink the Pee Dee water, a lot of God damn ignorant people out there see a bottle they open it and drink it that brings in the Post Office Department and the FCC, they all know each other. Stalling his mailing permits trying to knock him off television queer his franchise with Teakell's FCC connection because they're after Teakell's the one they're after, knock out his Food for Africa program kill off donations to these missions and knock out their Voice of Salvation radio over there have you got an ashtray?

—Paul who was that.

—Who do you think I'm talk...

—I mean on the phone.

—Who do you think. Collect call from Acapulco who do you think it was. This all the whisky?

—Because if it was Edie, it was Edie wasn't it... She'd turned backed hard against her hands gripping the edge of the sink, —like Cettie I ask about Cettie I don't even know if she's still alive and you talk about a lawsuit you can't even let me speak to Edie, say hello just to say hello to her and see what she...

—Waiting for some calls Liz I've got to make some important calls I can't have the God damn line tied up all night with Edie! Want to know what she's up to this dog and pony show for Victor Sweet that's what she's up to, same bunch Liz it's the same God damn bunch in there spending her money all she's doing is trying to give her father another ulcer. Grimes in there backing Teakell and this appeasement bunch comes up with Victor Sweet you know where he takes his orders, same God damn bunch using Ude to knife Teakell any smear they can find, who do you think dug up this bag lady down there? Shows up out of the woodwork with a shopping bag full of cat food says she's the sister of that bum that drowned they buried in the county cemetery gets a court order to have him dug up, wants an autopsy says she's going to sue for negligence manslaughter every God damn thing you can think of, same list as Earl Fickert you think that's a coincidence? Running a junkyard in Mississippi who do you think dug him out of a swamp had him sign his X on a deposition charging wrongful death clergy malpractice outrageous conduct you think that's a coincidence? Tried to get him malpractice insurance they drag out some yellow newspaper clippings ten years ago in Kansas same God damn thing, thirteen year old kid comes in for counseling and Ude has him reading the Bible listening to taped sermons and tells him he's a sinner puts the fear of God in him the kid goes home and hangs himself, family's Roman Catholic they sue for negligence wrongful death same list right down the line, telling everybody Ude's a mail order minister someplace in Modesto California ordains ten million of them a year to swindle the IRS any smear they can think of, all hearsay any smear they can think of. They even put out a story teaching these six year old kids in his Bible class to obey God he hooked up a seat to a twelve volt car battery, God tells you to do something you don't do it and zap! He banged the glass down empty on the table, —same bunch out there spreading this hearsay, see the hate mail starting to come in he's even had a couple of death threats same God damn bunch, that's where Edie your great pal Edie gives a gala for Victor Sweet all they know how to do give these God damn galas... he was pulling apart the pages of newspaper —got her mother in here someplace giving a benefit for your pal Jack Orsini raising money for that foundation your old man put up eight million here it is, Halloween gala benefit Mrs Cissie Grimes, center, greeting guests the Empress Shajar, widow of the late Ogodai Shah, with her escort here's your Doctor Kissinger never sent you a bill? Doctor Kissinger, the famed shuttle surgeon, who will leave tomorrow for Johannesburg to perform a colostomy on the President of South Af, Liz? You see that doctor?

She put the pan down, a grip on the edge of the sink. —Which doctor, Paul.

—Said you were going to see this insurance company doctor get my companion suit ready for this plane crash trial when they...

—Doctor Terranova yes, I saw him. He thinks I may have high blood pressure.

—High, that's all? High blood pressure what good is that, walk down the street everybody's got high blood pressure, get up in front of a jury they've all got high blood pressure think they're going to make a half million dollar award for high blood pressure?

—Paul, I can't help...

—Probably got high blood pressure myself if I saw a doctor haven't got time, all these doctors you've got plenty of time you see all these doctors if I, probably got it myself, heart attack drop in the street and they'll just step around you. His hand wavered over the rummage of paper, found its place on the bottle —whole God damn, keep all this straight if I, big project try to keep all this straight don't even know where the, where the mail... the bottle neck clattering free on the rim of the glass —ask you any mail ask you, ask you any phone calls you...

—I told you Paul. Mister Slotko called.

—Mis, you told me? You told me Slotko called?

—Well I, yes I mean I...

—Told me Slotko called I didn't what, what did he say.

—He said you, he just said it would probably be better if you spoke with Adolph, that Adolph knows the...

—Talk to Adolph doesn't know a God damn thing that's why you get Slotko, big prestigious Washington law firm know what's going on they all know each other down there that's why you get Slotko, whole God damn thing whether the estate can pick up these shares on option before this Belgian syndicate's already taken over Lendro, buying into South Africa Metal Combine see them move in on VCR whether Grimes takes a back seat he probably knows this guy Cruikshank knows the whole God damn board ready to sell VCR out in a minute why you get Slotko down there knows everybody, what the whole God damn thing is about they all know each other why you get Slotko top of the heap that's why you what did he say.

—Well he, I told you all he said was...

—Talk to Adolph God damn it Liz what did he say! Called me here just what in the hell exactly did he say!

—He said... backed again against her hands gripping the sink, —he said he thought you were an idiot, Paul. He said you go off half cocked just because you'd worked for my father you think you, that you can call the shots he said you know as much about finance as some snot nosed sixth grader that he's sick and tired of your swearing at him on the phone if you, call Adolph if you, if Adolph can stand you let Adolph explain it. Call Adolph.

—He said that?

—Well he, you asked me exactly what he...

—He said that Liz? Slumped deeper in the chair, he sat running a finger along the clean red slit the length of his arm to the tendons outcropped on the back of his hand, —tell you what that's about... he picked up the glass, —tell you what that's all about Liz. Slotko puts on a big act he's just their Jew in the window, big prestigious law firm Slotko worms his way in they need a Jew in the window part of the same bunch, what that's all about. Same God damn bunch spreading these smear stories, hearsay rumor anything they get their hands on trying to trip Ude up now on antisemitism never met a Jew till he was twenty what do they do? Peddle some old speech they're claiming he made says the only way the Jews have survived two thousand years by being hated, move in next door buy them a drink treat them right so God damn scared they'll lose their identity so they set up Israel and think up new ways to make everybody hate them only God damn thing holds them together. Trying to get Teakell, same bunch Victor Sweet same God damn bunch using Ude to get at Teakell alienate the Jewish vote problem's somebody taped the God damn speech can't miss that voice, hear him once you can't miss that voice what are you, what's the matter...

—I just have to move some of these papers if we're going to eat, can you move your...

—Wait give me the glass, all that God damn smoke I can't...

—Oh!

—Why we've got him out tells everybody he's a Zionist right here, got it right here in the where's that ad, patch things up got him addressing these interfaith breakfasts trying to get one of their top people invite him over there take him up to the Wailing Wall have a good cry together need friends any God damn place they can, what's this.

—It's just, I thought I'd try veal but...

—What are these.

—They were mushrooms but the, I think the pan got too hot and...

—What are...

—Those are peas. Be careful!

—Just getting the God damn phone, hello ...? He held the plate up for her to free the cord, to channel peas in a rivulet between the two men knelt in prayer, —Good thing you called, I couldn't get... that's why I couldn't get there, where'd you hear about it... must have been, he must have been, people all over the place he came right at me, took him out wearing his guts for garters may have to wait before they can question him see how all the God damn pieces fit together, whole thing coming in from outside like walking in a God damn mine field over there every people's congress liberation army spade they waste he's carrying his AK47 all coming in from the... See how far they can push us, took those mission boys out every God damn boy in the mission gave him a hammer out there pounding stakes in the ground staked out the whole claim, every... their own land no, on the mission land, Metal Combine coming at them one way Lendro coming the other VCR right beside them already working a claim right to the edge of it trying to get extension rights they'd be right down there under the mission station itself chew up the whole God damn thing and spit it out that's the... No it's already registered, whole claim registered in the name of a secret nominee he turns it over to the church look around for the highest bidder probably these Belgians whatever the hell they are, syndicate registered in Liechtenstein like some Liberian freighter buying into everything they look God damn peas spilling on the, can you move this? What...? No not you talking about something else caught me right in the... Read about it in the papers I'll see you down there Liz? hang this up? Already spilled something on the God damn try to keep some order here I shouldn't have told him all that. Calls up worms it out of me I shouldn't have told him all that.

—I'm afraid the veal's not very tender.

He finished what was left in the glass. —The what?

—The veal, it's a little tough.

—Little tough... He repeated that, attacked it with his fork and then put the fork down and his head came forward into his hands, staring down at the plate, the slash a red line drawn straight up to his eye.

—Doesn't that hurt Paul? don't you want...

—Little tough that's all, little tough... He picked up the fork again —problem's the, whole God damn pieces fit them together shouldn't have told him all that... grinding the heel of the fork down, giving it up, going for the bevy of peas lost before they'd left the plate, disheveling the scorched stand of mushrooms —just like the, think he was waiting for me Liz.

She got the plate away, got her own half finished off to a safe corner and reached for the bottle —I don't think..

—Give me that!

—Paul please, you...

—I told you! and he had it by the throat, —told you... tipping it up, up, —pieces fit together problem's just too God damn many pieces, even penetrated the Vatican's true Liz, big God damn third world peace offensive Vatican intelligence network cover the whole continent even penetrated that, Jesuits speak Swahili convert a few spades in the right places get them in the confessional word goes straight to the bishop right up the God damn hot line to Rome see that? Trying to knock out his Voice of Salvation radio's why Teakell's over there fact finding tour for his Food for Africa trying to get him through Ude same God damn bunch right down to the state level, state highway department in there says that school bus brake drums rusted right through barely got them in the ground they're trying to nail him on that, county health board in there trying to close down the whole God damn operation Bible school all of it, penetrated right down to the county level says they're dumping raw sewage into the Pee Dee all their new God damn indoor plumbing, still up there in the bushes everything fine while they were still up there squatting in the bushes put in this new indoor plumbing right down to the county level what the whole God damn thing is all about. Smear stories hearsay get him any way they can, trying to smear him with Pearly Gates down there sets up his Christian survival camp out in the hills teach them weapons use, hand to hand combat, sheriff's deputies teaching kids, everybody, freeze dried foods M1A rifles target practice explosives handling same paper here, trying to smear him with that... He cleared the page with a sweep of his hand —same God damn newspaper, pay for a full page ad and they sneak in this smear story on Gates, another page and then —wait! Where is it!

—Where is...

—Envelope that white envelope, got ten thousand in it where... scattering pages —got it... the bloodied sleeve trailing from his elbow, a hand out for the bottle in a swerve to the phone —Hello...? Who do you, you got the wrong...

—Paul please, if it's...

—Hey! You old peckerhead, if it's not old peckerhead... He heaved back in the chair, —no shit. You did? Six o'clock news no shit...? you see me take him out? Cameras set up out there for some candyass politicians at that prayer breakfast two chops blew him away, that mother was waiting for me Chick. You see him? looked just like Chigger didn't he? you see his face? Same yellow shit in his eyes that last day out pouring that M60 into those hootches kids chickens pigs wasting that whole fucking ville same shit, see it in his eyes before I saw the blade, he... mother creased my arm that's all, told him that Chick when I turned him in, looking for somebody to tear you out a new asshole just step right up told him that, every mother out there got five minutes to be crazy, two weeks short Kowalski couldn't wait? walks right up route seven trying to draw fire? What? who... none of them no, why would I hear from any of them, only thing some dipshit sergeant called me come down for this Unknown Serviceman funeral be in their parade you know that mother offered me a wheelchair? tag along at the end? Military down there's got the whole thing organized, colour guards bands from all the service branches you think they want a bunch of ragass mothers in their bush caps and fatigues marching up there with the coffin? Might be Kowalski in a body bag, Kowalski's two left hands in a body bag they shut them out, think anybody wants to see the war we lost while they're dressing up to win the next one? Shut them out so they're going to fall in behind all the mickeymouse shit past that fucking wall flags flying bands playing right out to Arlington, play taps shoot a few blanks up at nowhere present, harms! shoulder, shit! See Drucker coming in with his bag of ears that's what they... All right no, no I'm fine man I'm, I'm... what? Real fine peckerhead real fine what kind of names... No I'll get some I'll get you some, straight on peckerhead I'll get you some real fine ones just watch your ass this time, you got a phone? get you some real, find a fucking pencil? Liz? his hand tearing through the papers, —find a God damn pencil?

When he hung up she was staring at him and his eyes came up sightless right on her, froze her step toward him, froze —Paul, don't... in her throat.

But he had it, had the bottle by its own hard neck coming down over the glass —sweetheart...

—Paul... she took the step.

—That's one fucking sweetheart stopped her dead. —Pulled me out of that BOQ Liz, Chick's the one that pulled me out... He brought his arm up to wipe the sweat from his face with his sleeve but the sleeve dangled loose from his elbow, drawing the length of the straight slash gone almost black where the blood had clotted and dried across his wet forehead. —Wants some names, told you he just got out? Calls me get a fresh start, wants some names problem you don't listen to me. That's my RTO, cover that radio with his life only man in that fucking outfit ever listen to me, give one of those spades an order he's stoned, they're all stoned, comes right back never happen sir. Get up on that ridgeline Beaumont, come back tell me what you see. Never happen, sir, smartass grin thought they'd show me up, thought they'd get me up on that ridgeline myself see me blown away... He stared at what he'd poured in the glass there before he drank it down, —wants some names, told you he's getting out?

—You told me that Paul.

—Problem you don't listen, told you what.

—That Chick just got out of the army and he wants, that he's making a fresh start and he wants the names of people who can get him a job?

—Told you don't listen Liz, you don't listen. Five years for robbery that's what he just got out, only one that came out with a career, army taught him a career second tour they took him out of combat put him in G2 crack any safe you show him, army taught him that in G2 get a fresh start, names like doctors cash in the wall safe hide it from the IRS Chick can spot it in the dark, mothers won't report the robbery because they never reported the God damn money in the first place he's the one that pulled me out Liz, saw it on television you hear that? Six o'clock news saw it in his eyes before I saw the blade, he was waiting for me...

She stood close enough now to put a hand on his shoulder, on the shirt soaked through with perspiration, and his shoulder sank under it as though it were a weight. —Paul I, let me help you upstairs, you're...

—Got to work, can't help you upstairs Liz too much God damn work here got to get to work.

—You can't no, you can't try to work now you...

—Don't tell me try to work! He went at the papers again, —big God damn project just get all the pieces, too many God damn pieces... and a sweep of the newspaper, —see that? Just told you, smear story about Gates see that? Christian preparedness camp he's running down there teach them to use an M2 mortar, kid gets hit by a shell fragment Bible won't let him have a transfusion he's greased smear it all over the paper see that? down in the corner here? FBI closing in Federal Marshals same God damn bunch, go after Ude trying to smear him with Gates? Buy our full page ad hand us back a smear story see that? get your ad copy in four days ahead give them time to come up with a smear story same day's paper see that? his finger running down the dry wash left by the cascade of peas —appeasement, made them mad talking about appeasement here too God damn many Christians creeping around like Jacob and Esau saying I will appease him, want to appease this evil empire because they're scared of this godless Marxism and the militant atheists who serve their evil design for Sweet, see that? all his appeasement and disarmament where he takes his orders Victor Sweet? Peace is a weapon in their offensive quotes the Bible right here again through his police his, through his policy also he shall cause craft to prosper in his hand he shall magnify himself in his heart and by peace destroy says it right here, by peace destroy many whole God damn religious awakening across the land see that?

She looked. It said it right there but —it's late Paul... her hand running across the damped fall of his shoulders, —it's too late to try to...

—Too late.

—I just mean it's too late this evening to try to...

—Too late Liz, whole God damn religious awakening across the land all out there for the kill, forty sticks of dynamite tried to blow up his transmitting tower Voice of Salvation over there why the, where's the... he had his empty glass —where is it.

—It's gone Paul. There isn't any more.

—Can't! No don't, too late isn't any more don't, don't... his sleeve dragging over the papers he caught at it and tore the bloodied thing away —don't, look just, get up there... lurching to his feet, scattering papers again looming over the table —how many times I, tell you to throw this God damn thing away! and he had the Natural History magazine tearing it across the bared chest of the Masai warrior, down the plaited hair, through the —God damn eyes, he hurled it toward the sink, seized his balance against the doorframe, turned and went down in a lunge through the doorway under the stairs heaving, gripping the seat in the dark —don't... She got the light on, wet a cloth, held his shoulder —just don't, help me!

—Be careful, Paul be...

—Being careful! He was up, heavy against the wall, out catching balance again at the newel where she stayed, holding to it herself, watching him to the top of the stairs; and when finally she climbed them herself it was to undress in the dark, to heave his half clothed weight from her side of the bed and press her face into the pillow.

Where she woke, coming over on her back, pulling away sheet and blanket for the warmth, or the sense of it, dappling the room walls and ceiling in a gentle rise and fall of reds, yellow, blazing to orange brought her to her elbows —Paul! to the foot of the bed and the window in the frolic of flames through the branches outside. She got his shoulder

216

and shook him, reached for the light, for the phone when down below the foot of the hill erupted in flashes of red, blinding white, pounding bells climbing right up to her —Paul please! both hands on him pulling him over, eyes sealed and his mouth fallen open, his hand fallen empty to the floor and she came back to the window all of it out there now light and sound, the bark of a bullhorn, hoses dragged past the fence palings as the last of the garage windows and white went in flames reaching for the branches above catching for a moment one here, one higher as though fueled to climb the firmament till suddenly the roof fell in a shower of spark and fire leaving the boys down there in silhouette on the dying light, the same boys clambering up the hill in the afternoon grown older, or their brothers, deep in fire helmets that disclosed no more than the jut of a chin, ankle deep in black raincoats fidgeting fire axes near their own height in restive unemployment till the smallest of them turned to see her in the lighted window up there and rallied the others to share his discovery, sent her back to darken the room, to pull up the sheet, to lie still with the heaving calm beside her, and the smell of smoke.

Climbing the hill, waiting for breath, the old dog had fallen in beside her where she stopped again almost to the top, her hand steadied on a scorched fence pale drawing deep on the smell of ashes that still tinged the air, looking up to the house before she stepped out into the black gape of the road. The front door stood wide open. She'd barely crossed when the dog blundered past throwing her off balance in its own haste up the step where she stumbled, recovered in a reach for the doorway holding to it, looking in, backing off, breaking into a voice gone hollow with —Who...

—Out! damn you get out! and damned the black dog came

past her, ears laid back in a transport. —What happened here.

—I don't, what...

—And over there... He'd come out as far as the newel, his hand thrust past her from the frayed cuff pointing —there, what happened.

—It, it burned, it just burned down last week the night that day you were here and, but what... far enough in now to see the silk flowers scattered among pieces of the vase smashed on the floor, —how did that...

—I just got here, front door standing wide open somebody broke in, somebody in a hurry, here... he had her arm, took her hand firm in one of his but she pulled it away, coming down on the edge of the love seat. —How long have you been gone? Just this morning she told him, since early this morning, she'd had a call from a Mister Gold at Saks telling her they'd found her purse and she had to go into town anyway, she had to sign some papers for a lawyer and then when she went to Saks to claim her purse they'd never heard of Mister Gold, there was no Mister Gold, and —Yes, and while you were there to see Mister Gold they were here to rob the house, they had your keys and your, what is it... She'd come up in a sharp turn for the kitchen to pull open the drawer there digging under napkins, placemats, —something missing?

—No... she got it closed —it's, nothing no.

—Ripped the lock off the door to my room there it wasn't even locked, I left it open didn't I? for Madame Socrate to get the trash out?

—I locked it.

—You, why. Why did you lock it.

—I don't know.

He stood there pulling off the raincoat, looking into the room's disarray as though matching it to memory, and then —Elizabeth? without turning to her —I'm, it's very difficult to say anything that's, that I'm very sorry about what happened, to say anything that would help... She didn't say anything to that, bent down freeing a crease in her stocking from the bite of her shoe, hair spilled away from the white of her neck as she straightened up suddenly caught with his arm around her, his breath close —that I've felt very badly...

—Mrs Booth? twisting sharply away from his hand grazed at her breast —I've felt very badly Mrs Booth, isn't that how it goes? I'm sorry I disturbed you Mrs Booth? Then why haven't you even called.

—I tried to call you this morning when I...

—I wasn't here! I just told you I wasn't here, I just told you I was in New York if you think I, if you thought I'd just be sitting here this whole horrible week waiting for you to call?

—I didn't mean...

—I'm going to make some tea. Do you want some tea?

—I, no... He pushed the wad of the raincoat from the chair where he'd dropped it and sat down, digging out the glazed envelope of tobacco, watching the shape of her back to him where she made busy filling the teakettle. —Has she been here? Madame Socrate?

—Well she, not exactly.

—Not exactly?

—I mean she's not very dependable she, I should call the police shouldn't I. To report it.

—I'd just, maybe later... spilling tobacco as his thumbs brought the paper together, —let me look around my room in there first, there might be...

—I mean it might just have been those boys those, awful boys... she broke off for the phone, tensed for the second ring and then, with the third —no don't answer it!

—But I thought you...

—Because they keep calling, those newspapers I mean how they even got this number they even came up here, the front door, the back door looking in the windows, I mean I had to hide in that little bathroom for hours under the stairs they think they have the, they think people have the right to know everything about you, that they...

—No no no, they just have the right to be entertained,

that's all it is... He'd reached over to lift the phone breaking off its ring, dropping it back —why they go to the movies isn't it? why people read novels? Get the inside story, explore the dark passions hidden in the human heart and the greater the invasion of privacy the better, that's what wins prizes. That front page picture of your Reverend Ude huddled down with Senator Teakell? passing him that ten thousand dollar bribe for his television licensing? That's what gets the Pulitzer Prize it's not about art, it's not about literature, about anything lasting, it's the newspaper mind, what's here today and you wrap the fish in tomorrow, it's just...

—That's not what it was.

—What what was, the...

—I said that's not what it was! And he's not my Reverend Ude no I've seen it, I've seen that stupid picture before that's not what it was.

—Never seen two faces so engrossed in conspiracy.

—That's because they were praying... The cup rattled the saucer coming down from the shelf —it's not funny! What are you laughing at it's not funny it's, it was just like him coming up to you on those courthouse steps, when you said he took your arm at that courthouse in the, in Slopover kneeling down with him to repent it was in a hospital, Senator Teakell's daughter was in the hospital you can even see the hideous flowers behind them it's right there, look at it. That pile of newspapers, it's under there with the rest of the trash all those pictures of, they get a picture and then make up a story to go with it. Paul said it was all Victor Sweet, those people behind Victor Sweet that they fixed up that bribe story just to smear Sen...

—Where did they get the picture?

—I don't know, I don't know who gave them the picture I don't...

—Then how do you know what the...

—Because I know who's in the bed! because it's Cettie in the hospital bed you can see the corner of it behind that hideous that, that cross with all those hideous flowers because I know Cettie! Because we were all best friends Cettie and Edie and I, Edie Grimes her father was this close friend of Senator Teakell's and Edie's been raising money for him, I mean for Victor Sweet she thinks he's charming then she ran out of money, I mean it was mostly her own money she was raising she thought her father would be furious. He calls Victor Sweet a black marshmallow she thought he'd be furious but instead he just gave her more money right out of her trust and, because that's...

—Because they were setting up Victor Sweet, and that story that he's a jailbird I'll tell you where that came from. He was dumb enough to park his car in some two bit town in Texas and a couple of good old boys set fire to it, he reported it to the police and they jailed him for littering the street. They were setting him up.

—I mean that's what I just said! that that's where Edie's money went setting him up so he could run against Cettie's father in the Senate and...

—No no no. Grimes, that whole wing of the party out here on the front page this morning howling for blood, planned to set up their black pacifist marshmallow with the nomination and then wipe up the floor with him suddenly the whole damned thing moves faster than they expected. Draw the line, run a carrier group off Mombasa and a couple of destroyers down the Mozambique channel, bring in the RDF and put the SAC on red alert. They've got what they want... He finally lighted the cigarette he'd made, brushed a speck of tobacco from his tongue on the back of his hand.
—How he happened to be on that same damned plane with Teakell...

—I thought you'd know she said, steaming water into the cup there.

—Well, yes well of course there aren't that many flights out of a place like that, maybe two a week. One like this comes through and if you've got any connections, if you've got a name you can throw around you can usually...

—That's just the papers, the story they put in the newspapers no, I mean one of those fine phrases that you, that
doesn't mean anything. The unswerving punctuality of chance,
one of those.

He pulled on the cigarette, drew it away in a cloud of
smoke. —There's not a drink, is there?

—You can look.

—Where would it...

—I don't know where! Over there, on the counter behind
all those newspapers if there is any. Paul would keep getting
it and then there never seemed to be any, behind that bag
of onions... pulling up sharp —please! twisting from his
hand's surprise at her waist behind her —there, you've made
me spill the tea... from the apologetic haste of its retreat
down the swell of her thigh, —honestly!

—No I'm sorry, Elizabeth lis...

—And stop calling me that! That's, what's sorry no, that's
what my father always did, saying I'm sorry and he'd pat
me and try to give me a kiss no, it's always something else,
saying I'm sorry it's always for the wrong thing that's why
people say it. I'm sorry I disturbed you Mrs Booth, loading
all those books on him and driving away filling his head
with, with I don't know what; that whole show you put on
for him in there from the minute he, the minute you found
out his name, that his name was Vorakers. Fossils and brimstone and calling Reverend Ude the missing link so he could
make fun of Paul why, why. Just to make it all worse between him and Paul? yes, and me?

—You've been the only thing that held them together.

—Me? do you, when you said when you feel like a nail
everything looks like a hammer if that's what I, if you think
that was holding them together is that what he told you?
taking him out to dinner, taking him out drinking in New
York asking him all kinds of questions about my father and
the company and Paul and the whole, because he was up
here. He came up here the night before he left and it wasn't
even him, it wasn't even Billy he'd picked up your no no no

223

and your Belgians chopping off hands and your comic books about the Bible and Reverend Ude, that the church is built on the blood of its martyrs you said that, didn't you?

—Well I, actually it's a loose translation of Tertullian's the blood of the martyrs is the seed of...

—No you said it I heard you, and if Reverend Ude wanted to do things right he'd go out and get himself shot? that the Crusades were nothing but slaughter and that's what his is going to be too? Turning his harvest of souls into this crusade against the evil empire like Lincoln turning the war to save the union into a crusade to free the slaves after the battle of Antietam I mean where did he get all that. Billy never heard of Antietam no, it was all just to start a fight with Paul because of Paul's southern, about the flower of southern youth what did Billy know about it, that it was Lee who wiped out the flower of southern youth keeping the war going when he knew he'd lost it that that's what the south still is? a paranoid sentimental fiction? a bunch of losers where the degraded upper classes go around with their crackerbarrel talk like they're all these poor cousins blaming the rich part of the family up north for stealing their birthright? Keeping the memory fresh till somebody gives them a war they can win, that that's why there's so many of them high up in the army? A war to restore the national dignity because they lost theirs a hundred years ago and nobody's let them get it back and that's what the war Paul was in, that they wouldn't let them win it I mean what did Billy ever know about the Civil War and all that, that he thought all that up himself just to make fun of Paul with? How the south is this cradle of stupidity where they get patriotism and Jesus all mixed up together because that's the religion of losers where they'll get their rewards someplace else so they're the only real good Christian Americans still living down there in this sentimental junkyard of the past where there's strength in stupidity and this mushmouthed vulgarity like Reverend Ude's, taunting him with Reverend Ude but it was you, wasn't it. It was really you all the time.

224

He'd crushed the cigarette in a saucer, not a coal, not a wisp of smoke left, crushing it there till it crumbled between his yellowed finger and thumb. —Your tea's getting cold there, he said finally, and then —you know, I didn't take him out drinking he took me out drinking. I didn't sit him down and question him I didn't need to, I could hardly get a word in, he...

—That Paul wasn't even a southerner? that I, that somebody'd just told him Paul was adopted so he was probably really a Jew and didn't even know it? Paul the bagman? that it was Paul who made all these payoffs for Daddy and the whole...

—No no no listen, it was all in the papers wasn't it? I didn't have to ask him, you saw the papers didn't you?

—That's what I just told you! They're right there, that pile right there I just told you with those old pictures of Daddy and Longview and the, and that picture of Billy from his school yearbook they even found that. They even found that.

—I'm sure they had it... He'd started making another cigarette, dashing the spilled shreds of tobacco off the table, off his lap, —in the morgue, must have been in their morgue.

—But what morgue where no, no... blanched, hands gone white as the sink they clung to behind her —there wasn't a picture in the morgue they...

—The papers I mean, the newspapers, it's what they call their files, that story on Paul, the big Lightning Division hero blown up in a...

—Because they had that picture that's what I mean, so they could put it all over the front page and make up a story to go with it just because they had that picture...

—It was quite a picture.

—And make him a killer? a killer without a war to go to who told them that.

—Well good God, he killed him didn't he?

—He didn't mean to.

—Didn't mean to? a skinny nineteen year old kid tries to

225

mug him he couldn't have just knocked him down? But she'd turned away looking out on the fading turmoil of the terrace, the overturned chairs and the leaves and doves, three or four of them, picking indiscriminate, specked like the leaves in the sun still casting a warmth, or the look of it out there, like her voice when she'd spoken just beginning to fail. —Tell me... he'd lit the cigarette, and he coughed. —Why did you tell me your father had been pushed off a train.

—What's the difference... She hadn't moved, her back to him rigid as the table between them —he was dead, wasn't he?

—Going over a trestle? off the roof of the train? Because I remember it, I remember that scene. I saw the same movie.

—That wasn't kind, was it... and her shoulders fell a little, —because when people tell a lie...

—No I didn't mean, I didn't say that you'd...

—I'll tell you why yes, because why people lie is, because when people stop lying you know they've stopped caring.

—Wait... but she'd made a sudden move for the door, pulled it open and was through it out to the terrace where, before he could follow, she'd come down sitting alone on the edge of an upturned chair and he stopped, looking out at her, at her hair smouldering red in the sun and the yellow green of something she was wearing, a sweater? he hadn't noticed, even the pale arch of her face protesting the drab of the leaves dead around her and he coughed again, cleared his throat as though about to speak, to arrest a shudder turning away to pace the kitchen floor looking out there each time he passed, finally reaching the phone, dialing it, speaking in blurred tones of —en désordre, la maison oui... demain? tôt le matin, oui? certainement... before hanging it up and stepping out to the sun's pale warmth.

She'd looked up, not at him but right past him at the house, at the roof peaked in this outward symmetry over twinned windows so close up there they must open from one room but in fact looked out from the near ends of two neither of them really furnished, an empty bookcase and sagging daybed in one and in the other a gutted chaise longue voluted in French pretension trailing gold velvet in the dust undisturbed on the floor since she'd stood there, maybe three or four times since she'd lived in the house, looking down on the greens of the lower lawn and the leaves before they'd cried out their colours, before they'd seized separate identities here in vermilion haste gone withering red as old sores, there bittersweet paling yellow toward stunted heights glowing orange in that last spectral rapture and to fall, reduced again to indistinction in this stained monotony of lifelessness at her feet where a dove carped among last testimonies blown down from somewhere out of reach, out of sight up the hill in its claim as a mountain, leaves of scarlet oak here and there in the blackened red of blood long clotted and dried.

—Here... he'd come down to right an overturned chair, —sit here... brushing the leaves from it —I, I've thought about what you said and, I hope you don't think I...

She hadn't moved. —I've never really looked at it.

—At what... looking where she was looking.

—At the house. From outside I mean.

—Oh the house yes, the house. It was built that way yes, it was built to be seen from outside it was, that was the style, he came on, abruptly rescued from uncertainty, raised to the surface —yes, they had style books, these country architects and the carpenters it was all derivative wasn't it, those grand Victorian mansions with their rooms and rooms and towering heights and cupolas and the marvelous intricate ironwork. That whole inspiration of medieval Gothic but these poor fellows didn't have it, the stonework and the wrought iron. All they had were the simple dependable old materials, the wood and their hammers and saws and their own clumsy ingenuity bringing those grandiose visions the masters had left behind down to a human scale with their own little inventions, those vertical darts coming down from the eaves? and that row of bull's eyes underneath? He was up kicking leaves aside, gesturing, both arms raised embracing —a patchwork of conceits, borrowings, deceptions, the

227

inside's a hodgepodge of good intentions like one last ridiculous effort at something worth doing even on this small a scale, because it's stood here, hasn't it, foolish inventions and all it's stood here for ninety years... breaking off, staring up where her gaze had fled back with those towering heights and cupolas, as though for some echo: It's like the inside of your head McCandless, if that was what brought him to add —why when somebody breaks in, it's like being assaulted, it's the...

—Listen! The phone had rung inside and she started up at the second ring, sank back with the third. —All I meant was, it's a hard house to hide in... Raising her eyes up to the twinned windows again, —seeing it from outside, looking up there and seeing myself looking out when everything was green, it all looked so much bigger. Like Bedford. The last time my mother came out to Bedford she just sat in the car with the chauffeur. She sat there for two hours and when we left, all she said was I never realized there were so many shades of green.

—What was Bedford.

—A big country house we had. It burned.

—When you were a child? was that...

—Last week... She thrust a foot into the leaves bringing the dove nearest up in a flutter, and down again, bleating. —That was the last thing she said that made any sense... looking down off the terrace —and now it's, look at it, it's just a horrid little back yard.

—Well it's, yes of course that's what happens isn't it, he said as though again called on to explain, pursuing it as he had the house itself, welcoming facts proof against fine phrases that didn't mean anything with —all those glorious colours the leaves turn when the chlorophyll breaks down in the fall, when the proteins that are tied to the chlorophyll molecules break down into their amino acids that go down into the stems and the roots. That may be what happens to people when they get old too, these proteins breaking down faster than they can be replaced and then, yes well and then of

228

course, since proteins are the essential elements in all living cells the whole system begins to disinteg...

—Why did you ask me that.

—Did I, about what I don't...

—About my father.

—I don't know, I... He'd settled on the bare rungs of the chair, rubbing a thumb over the back of his hand as though to rub away the spots there, —I don't know.

—Then why did you. Because you knew the whole thing anyway, you knew what really happened Billy'd already told you every...

—Can't you, please. Just listen to me please. I didn't need to hear it from him. I didn't have to read it in the damned papers I was out there when it happened, good God. You know the name Vorakers out there like you know the name De Beers, you know Vorakers Consolidated Reserve like the name of a country and it's bigger than most of them, buy and sell half of them out of its back pocket and that's all he was doing, that's what your father was doing it wasn't a secret, it wasn't even a scandal till these big bribe cases like Lockheed came up and the politicians and papers over here turned it into one and what happened then, I didn't need Billy to tell me what happened then did I? Took him out drinking half the night no, no I told you he took me I hardly got a word in, you think you have to teach the young outrage? Not just Paul not just your father no, he was outraged at everything, everybody who came before him you think he left me out? that he had some kind of romantic picture like the, like you did? finding gold out there when I was his age do you know what he said? Just one more four fucking thousand foot hole in the ground they'll pack with black skins to dig it out for them oldest damned story there is, the new generation blames the old one for the mess it inherits and they lump us all together because all they see is what we've become, lying in wait for you out there one misstep and they pounce, grab one straw of expediency and they're on to you for betraying yourself, betraying them, selling out like the ones writing bad books and bad everything who are doing the best they can? when we thought we could count on civilization? Two hundred years building this great bastion of middle class values, fair play, pay your debts, fair pay for honest work, two hundred years that's about all it is, progress, improvement everywhere, what's worth doing is worth doing well and they find out that's the most dangerous thing of all, all our grand solutions turn into their nightmares. Nuclear energy to bring cheap power everywhere and all they hear is radiation threats and what in hell to do with the waste. Food for the millions and they're back eating organic sprouts and stone ground flour because everything else is poisonous additives, pesticides poisoning the earth, poisoning the rivers the oceans and the conquest of space turns into military satellites and high technology where the only metaphor we've given them is the neutron bomb and the only news is today's front page... He'd been up kicking paths through the leaves until one of them led him to the edge of the terrace where he stood looking down toward the river. —Have you ever seen the sunrise here? and as though she'd answered she hadn't, as though she'd answered at all —especially in winter. You'll see it in winter, it's moved south where the river's its widest and it comes up so fast, it's as if it just wanted to prove the day, get it established so it can loiter through the rest of it, spend the first damned half of your life complicating things in that eagerness to take on everything and straighten all of it out and the second half cleaning up the mess you've made of the first, that's what they won't understand. Finally realize you can't leave things better than you found them the best you can do is try not to leave them any worse but they won't forgive you, get toward the end of the day like the sun going down in Key West if you've ever seen that? They're all down there for the sunset, watching it drop like a bucket of blood and clapping and cheering the instant it disappears, cheer you out the door and damned glad to see the last of you.

But the sun she looked up for was already gone, not a

trace in the lustreless sky and the unfinished day gone with it, leaving only a chill that trembled the length of her. —He'd never have gone, she said. —All your talk trying to, whatever you were trying to do turn him into some kind of a, like a disciple somebody who'd be no, no he'd never have been on that plane.

—I don't, what do you mean. I didn't even know it, I didn't know that's what he...

—Listen! It rang again in there, and then she was up in the silence that followed and through the door, standing over it, waiting, a hand on it giving its new ring no more than a moment for —Paul yes, yes I'm so glad you... Yes what happened... leaning back against the table's edge looking out, looking at him out there kicking a path away from her. —who did! But he, how could he do that! They can't... but they wouldn't come here would they? to arrest you here? They can't... No but who would believe him, who will believe him Paul there's no way they could prove it now anyhow even if it, if it's only you and him now your word against his and who would... and he'd already denied it hadn't he? When that picture came out in the paper and he issued that vehement denial the day that he left? They can't... well he's dead isn't he! She was watching him out there hands come up behind him, one twisting in the other as though to break free —Paul it doesn't matter! It doesn't matter anymore any of it if we can just, if you can just get them all out of our lives this loathsome little Reverend Ude and Edie's father and all of them, you've done what he wanted haven't you? testified like he wanted you to and saved the whole... no well then I'll call Edie I'll call Edie, if only I could call Edie if I only knew where she was, she can tell him that she can... staring out there where that one hand broke free of the other only to seize it and renew the struggle —it doesn't matter! It doesn't matter Paul none of it matters anymore, the way you were before you left that night with, I, I can't no I can't ever see you that way again I can't, if we can just... And out there now both hands were suddenly gone from sight, brought round in front of him in what, from behind, was a clear demand for their cooperation, where he stood pissing off the corner of the terrace onto the sodden leaves below. —Paul? Paul please listen, I... no I went down there this morning I signed the deposition yes, that I've, that I haven't been able to fulfill my marital obligations the way they put it all in that legal language but, I mean I know I haven't done things very well all the things that I, the things you've tried to do and how hard you've worked for all these hopes that you've, that we've had and now, if we can get a fresh start Paul if we could go away, if... of what? Seven hun... no you didn't lose it no, don't you remember? just before you left you gave me seven hundred dollars for the rent? to pay the rent? And it's... yes I've paid it and... No, no I stopped answering like you told me there was only one it was... no it was, it was Chick it was, Chick it was only Chick he called last night and I, that's all he just, he just called Paul? When will you be here tomorrow? because none of it, if we could just go away? because none of it... no I will Paul, I will...

He'd come in behind her down at the table there, a napkin wad crushed in her hand over the dead phone and he brought up both of his to close firm on the crests of her shoulders, moving only so far that the tips of his thumbs met facient on the rise of her neck, and again —if we could just go away... the lengths of his fingers slipping over her collarbones, down coveting the warmth of her breasts.

—I've been thinking about it, he said.

—About what.

—Clean things up here and leave, pack a few clothes and we're gone. You won't need to take much.

—But I meant... her eyes fallen fixed on these hands harbouring her breasts as though to restrain their rise and fall dextrous and effortless as art in that deceit, vein and tendon standing out yellowed, rust spotted as she'd left them in her own cramped hand on the lined paper safe under blouses, scarves, her breasts rose on a deep breath —I don't...

—Light things, summer things, a sweater or two and a raincoat, you'd need that... his fingers preying closer as though to calm what they'd provoked there —those hot places, that's all you'd need.

—But we, for days even a week I...

—A week? his hands gone from stealth to possession, —what good's a week, no. For good.

—Gone, for good? She turned so sharp his hands lost custody. —There's no, no...

—Why not! He'd stepped back dispossessed, hands flung out in all their emptiness —the whole damned thing flying to pieces, madness coming one way and stupidity the other? to just sit here and be crushed between them? There's no...

—They're going to arrest him.

—Who, who's...

—Paul. That was Paul.

—He called? I thought you weren't answering the, what for, arrest him for what.

—For bribery.

—He's not surprised is he? Grimes finally threw him both ends of the rope?

—It's not Mister Grimes no, it's...

—Of course it's Grimes. What they had him down there testifying about today isn't it? that little piece in yesterday's paper hidden back in the business section? If he told them these bribes were common practice and the whole board knew about them this lawsuit would hit VCR right between the eyes and Grimes with it, triple damages and all, of course it was Grimes. I told you Billy took me out drinking I couldn't get a word in, that's what he talked about he couldn't stop talking about it, that Grimes and Teakell had Paul by the short hair and he'd get up there and testify it was all your father, that your father arranged those bribes and was the only one who knew about them and that's why he shot himself when it all came out, the stockholders would turn right around and wipe out his estate and Paul would walk away clean because Teakell was going to lead him through his testimony and get him a dismissal. With Teakell out of the picture Grimes throws him both ends of the rope and he's up for bribery.

—But that's not what the...

—Why isn't it, he's up to his neck in this mess in Africa isn't he? with all of them down there right now howling for war? this mission tract where they're drawing the line against the evil empire, he set this idiot Ude up for them in the first place didn't he? had that whole tract staked out so Ude's mission could file a mining claim on it and name him secret nominee to hand it over to the highest bidder for the money to pour into his damned crusade? And who's the highest bidder. VCR running shafts right up to the edge of the mission's land when Grimes took things over and tied in with this Belgian consortium, a promoter showed up with word of a big ore find on the mission tract, they bring in Cruikshank with his scenario and the Rift turns into an inferno from one end to the other. Does Paul know him? Cruikshank?

—I don't know who Paul knows! And I mean that's not what it's about anyhow, if you think Paul wants to have a war whoever made up these stories you don't even...

—You remember Lester? came up here once looking for me and you wouldn't let him in the door?

—I mean that's what I mean, the kind of friends you have if you'd trust him, if you'd trust anything he...

—I told you they weren't all friends didn't I? I've never trusted Lester a damned inch, black suit black tie and the black Bible he showed up over there paying his own way, they don't send them out like the Catholics do, one look at him and the locals took him for some kind of intelligence so did the Baganda, out there trying to sell them on the Second Coming next thing there he is in the New Stanley bar drinking orange juice and no Bible in sight. They'd recruited him. Cruikshank spotted the cold blooded fervour in those hard little eyes, he was Chief of Station, set up a Somali they had ten years on for stealing some truck tires and when Lester woke up he knew he was finished, homosexuality's the bottom of the pit out there, everybody taking him for an agent he might as well be one. All the discipline, obedience all the missionary zeal put a gun or a Bible in hands like that and they're just as deadly. They brought him in working on a contingency plan, they do them all the time just to generate paper work, cable traffic, show Langley they're on the job writing these little scenarios, setting up these confrontations till somebody draws the line. It was all routine but finally Cruikshank was so damned well known, he ran a cover as a dealer in local artifacts but you'd see him sitting alone at the end of the bar nobody would talk to him, they shipped him to Angola and when the mess they made of things up there was over they brought him home and gave him a medal he can never wear anyplace. One of those childish secret rituals they hold down there at Langley, put him out to pasture and he set himself up as a consultant like all these dreary faceless sons of bitches the one thing they know is how to survive. Hundred thousand dollar retainer the one thing they've learned is where the money moves and who's got it and the one thing they've cornered is how to get in on it, call themselves risk analysts and the bigger the mess they've left behind them the higher the fee. Iran, Chile, the Phoenix program, Angola, Cambodia, one monstrous miscalculation a few thousand body counts later and they're right there holding their heads up in Le Cirque and Acapulco, obsequious interviews in the Times and discreet dinner parties comparing their little black books with the other black tie refuse, even an expresident or two or their dazed widows, a few decorators, haute couture, any transient damned joke on reality while he's peddling the thing itself on the side in a poisonous little package like Lester. All that disenchanted missionary fervour would never lie steal or kill except in the name of a higher cause, doesn't smoke or drink or chase women all the damned fruits of youth gone bitter like the, like what falls from that old wild cherry down here at the foot of the lawn. Like the Zen master pointing to the forest

235

and asking the acolyte what he sees. Woodcutters. And what else. All the straight tall young trees are being cut down. And what else. Well nothing but, no there's one twisted, rotting, bent old tree they're leaving alone and that's Cruikshank, that's the successful survivor. Grimes brings him in as consultant, he brings in Lester and Paul brings this idiot Ude blundering into history with his battalions of ignorance hell bent on confronting the powers of evil with the cross of Jes...

—And that's where you've got it all backwards! I mean if you think Paul knows what the, if you think Paul and Mister Grimes that he likes Paul? If you think Paul and Lester that they, that Mister Grimes never liked Paul no, no he never trusted him he always thought Paul was just out for what he could get and he, that he wasn't even...

—Nobody likes Paul no, no that's not the point. If you don't own them you can't trust them that's Grimes isn't it? he owned Teakell didn't he? Get down to these hungry low level agents it's better if they don't like each other because the whole damned thing's based on mistrust, better if they don't even know each other people like Paul and Lester, they're just pieces in a puzzle who suddenly get grand ideas and take off on their own. They'll get credit if it works and they know damned well they'll be covered if it doesn't. Paul thinks he's been using Ude but Ude's been using him and Lester's been using them both because he wrote the scenario, set up that site get a few missionaries killed and then that plane gets shot down, Cruikshank pulls out the scenario dusts it off and we're all back in the sixteenth century copper, gold, slavery sanitized in what they call the homelands and the cross of Jesus going on before. That speech of Teakell's in the Senate when he left on his so called fact finding tour, this great threat to the mineral resources of the entire free world? That dusty little sliver of land it could have been anywhere, we must face up at last to this conspiracy casting the shadow of evil over the face of mankind, preserve the nation's honour, pledge ourselves unflinchingly to defend the vital interests of the United States wherever they are threatened that's his seed company, the family seed company, that's his great Food for Africa program. Starving countries get US aid credits to buy US products and the Teakell family seed company's got the patents on hybrid corn strains so they buy that and it blows their planting schedules to pieces even now, I liked that even now. Even now the wanton killing of two young men of God venturing forth from this mission for water, water which we take for granted with the turn of a faucet good God, this mission bringing the message of Christian love that was the scenario, get a few missionaries killed and draw the line. You wonder what the hell he thought sitting there five thousand feet up with a drink in his hand when he saw that missile coming in and the end of the world in smoke and fire, talk about meeting the Lord in the clouds he, he... He turned to see her numbed. —I didn't, I, I didn't mean... his hands clenching nothing —I didn't mean, sorry's no good no you're right but I'm so damned, damned sorry! And he stood there hands drawn in fists. —I didn't think. I didn't think because he, why he was on that plane, why Billy was on that plane!

—But he was.

—No but that's, a flight out of a place that you take what you can get, everybody knew Teakell was coming through on his phony fact finding trip that's what it was for. Everybody knew things changed course when the President got him and sent him down for the funeral of South Africa's President as his personal representative you grab some bush airline and Billy got on it, they don't even know who brought it down. Look at the paper it says new information indicates the flight was targeted by one of those black left resistance movements because of Senator Teakell's outspoken position on the aggressive instincts of this evil empire and the whole damned, not for attribution, new information from intelligence sources not for attribution you know damned well who that is, Cruikshank earning his fee and Grimes' syndicate damned glad to pay it, this plane strays into the wrong airspace anybody could have brought it down. South African missile batteries all the way through there they'll shoot at anything that moves and they'll hit it. They'll hit it and they hit it this time and sucked us right in, this carrier group off Mombasa and destroyers running down the Mozambique channel they've sucked us right in. Restore the national dignity with a war they can win this time and the chance to move up a few grades, peace time army they'll sit there for twenty years without making colonel but combat brings that first star so close they can taste it. Billions of dollars in fancy weaponry finally give them a chance to see if it works, turn the Great Rift Valley from Maputo right up to the Horn back to the hellfire time it came into being, up the Jordan valley through the Dead Sea where the Lord rained brimstone and fire on the cities of the plain and lo, the smoke of the country went up as the smoke of a furnace they can't wait listen, Elizabeth listen. I meant it. Pack up and we're gone there's nothing to keep you here now, nothing you can do, it's done. Playing out their scenario over that little scrap of land and every pygmy in Congress with his tribute to Teakell up defending the mineral resources of the free world where there's nothing but thornbush. It's as good a place as any, that was Lester. I told you madness coming one way and stupidity the other, put the house here on the market I've already called the agent, pack up and leave.

—I didn't mean you, she said finally. —I meant Paul.

—Paul what, you mean to stay here for Paul? Hasn't, good God hasn't Paul done enough? Bringing in Ude to stake out this mission site that's the excuse for this whole damned scenario? The papers playing up the threat to this key mineral reserve where there's nothing but bush?

—But bush? what...

—Bush, a few thorntrees. Nothing.

—But if they knew that why would...

—Nobody knew it. Klinger knew it and he was gone, do you think this Belgian syndicate would be backing a war over a few thousand acres of dirt, a little quartz, not even enough copper to pick up a shovel for? The vein runs out. It's the last exploration I did out there the mapping, the field notes all of it, Klinger blew it up into a big ore strike that Lester got hold of for his scenario and I got out, things went bad and I got out.

—But why didn't you tell them... her voice protesting less his failure of enterprise than her own of comprehension searching, like her eyes on the grain of the table, or the back of her hand there, for some relevance in the smallest particular, finding wood grain and skin follicle all the same, looking up —if you knew all the time?

—Tell them what, tell who. No no no, I've been there, show them the fossil record and they reach for Genesis, show them war being jammed down their throats and they read you Revelation, what the whole point was setting up Ude with his missions and his crusade in the first place wasn't it? One thing that Cruikshank and the rest of them learned from this string of disasters they've pulled off, you can't get a good war going without support back in Smackover that's what Paul brought Ude in to stir up. Godless Marxism attacking his holy mission even unto darkest Africa wash them all in the blood of Jesus give them a good hot bath, pray for America and every sad little frame house where they'll hang a gold star in the window when it's over. The car headlights? the purple ribbons? pray for little Willie Fickert he's got a war he can win this time, the big Lightning Division hero he'll get out of this bribery charge don't worry, they'll get him out, Reverend Ude in his pocket and...

—You're wrong, aren't you.

—About what. About Paul? He's...

—I think you're, maybe you're wrong about everything.

—That he's not a bagman? that he's not a killer? that he's...

—That he's got Reverend Ude in his pocket no, because it's Reverend Ude. That's what this bribery's about it's Reverend Ude, he just told them it was Paul, that Paul said he'd have to pay a bribe for his television station so he gave Paul

239

ten thousand dollars to pay Senator Teakell that's why he just called, that they're going to arrest him for interstate travel with intent to bribe a public official.

—There. Fine. You think he didn't? you think he...

—Because he's not a killer! Because he, all the things you don't know like you didn't know that, like you don't know anything! That he's this big Lightning Division hero looking for a war he can win you never saw that scar, that terrible scar you've never seen it you don't know the, all your grand words about the truth and what really happened that don't mean anything because it was one of his own men that's the truth, that's what really happened. He was fragged. Do you know what that means? he was fragged? His crew chief he'd turned in for heroin rolled a hand grenade under his bed and that whole story they made up, that the enemy got into their Bachelor Officer Quarters and blew them up with mortars and Chick pulled him out because it was Chick, it was Chick who just told me and he kept saying, he kept saying oh shit Mrs Booth I thought you knew. I thought you knew...

He stood there for a moment before he said —It's madness then isn't it, it's just madness... Backing off to the counter, spreading the newspapers heaped there aside —madness coming one way and...

—That picture, is that what you're looking for? Well look at it! Find it yes, look at it if that's what you, with the mugger yes because that's why Chick thought I knew how it happened, that nineteen year old kid when Paul saw him coming that was what he, his crew chief was nineteen and they covered it up, he just passed the word that he'd fragged the old man and they covered it up, the old man! He was twenty two! Find it yes, look at it if you...

—No, no I was just, bag of onions back here you said, I was just...

—Why do you want a bag of onions!

—No a drink I, you said... But she was up coming toward him reaching out, suddenly holding to the handle on the refrigerator door and he caught her elbow —what is it, what's...

—I don't know! She freed her arm —sometimes I, maybe I've got high blood pressure, walk down the street what good is that, get up in front of a jury they've all got high blood pressure what good is that... She'd reached past him into the corner to bring out the bottle —because you don't know what happened, you weren't here the only way you were here was your no no no and your stupidity conquering ignorance that night Billy came up here before he left, Reverend Ude with the Lord in the clouds and your Portuguese chopping off hands steaming up the Niger river trying to start a fight with him?

—Well that wasn't, it was the Zambezi in fact, the king-doms along the Zambezi... He watched her pour an ounce, two ounces —that's enough I, no ice just a little water in it... his hand out, open.

—A killer without a war to go to? that Clausnitz was wrong, it's not that war is politics carried on by other means it's the family carried on by other means? just looking for a war he can win?

—Well I think, I think... his hand falling empty, watching her raise the glass and take a good swallow from it —it was von Clausewitz what he said was...

—That's what I mean! Where did he ever hear of Claus-nitz, that that's what our family was all about now, Paul the bagman, Paul the Jew who didn't even know it, Paul the killer, just a nineteen year old kid? you couldn't have just knocked him down? And Paul said, he barely whispered he said Billy, don't you see? They never taught us how to fight, they only taught us how to kill he, they only taught us how to kill! and he, his hands were shaking, he couldn't... like her own, raising the glass again, the white of her throat rip-pling till she lowered it —and when Billy still kept after him that he was going himself, that he was going to Africa he was getting Adolph to send him to Africa while Paul and

Mister Grimes and all of them sat here and started a war there jabbing at him, jabbing his shoulder till Paul grabbed him and, and held him, he just stood there holding him with his arms pinned like a child shouting God damn it Billy listen! *These are the same sons of bitches that sent me to Vietnam!*

—No now wait, I didn't...

—No I won't wait, no... but she did, getting breath, the corners of her eyes tearing from the whisky —because what Paul told him that's what really happens isn't it, not a lot of your whatever you were trying to make him some kind of disciple you don't have to teach outrage no, no but using it to give him some dumb kind of strength that wasn't real to try to destroy Paul with? to make him suddenly go to Africa the next day just to prove that he, he'd never have gone...

—Yes but, what it was... and he found the cigarette he'd made earlier on the table there by the phone, where he'd left it looking out at her sitting alone on that chair upturned in the drift of leaves dead on the terrace in that last light of the sun looking up, when he came out, now as though all that had happened long before because of all that seemed to have happened since, getting past her to light the stove, to bend over the burner there for the time to muster —if you want to think that, creating a disciple, the better the job you do of it... he straightened up with a choked puff of smoke, —the better you've created an apostate, I'll tell you, the...

—No you've told me, you've told me, lying out there ready to pounce while you're spending the second half of your life here cleaning up the mess of the first? While you talk about isn't it awful how we've handed these kids a trashed up world from all those great ideas of progress and civilization and you knew all the time? About not leaving things any worse at least if you can't leave them any better, that you're the only one who still has these great ideas and you're standing here just, in this house in this kitchen standing here smoking and coughing and talking and letting them all go out and kill each other over something that's not even there?

—Well good God! They've been doing that for two thousand years haven't they? And you think I, you've seen the paper this morning's paper? and you think I could stop it? Go out to Smackover knocking on doors of those little frame houses and tell them there's been a big mistake? down to that Christian survival camp where Ude's gospel singer is holding off the Federal Marshals with an M16 did you see those pictures? Stars and Bars flying overhead and the place packed with crates of fragmentation grenades, grenade launchers, M2 mortar shells, show him the proof there's nothing there and we've got a new game plan? He's read Ude's little Survival Handbook hasn't he? tells him to establish tight security against demon controlled creatures roaming the earth to torture and kill? He knows damned well that every marshal and FBI moving in on him is part of the conspiracy, that they worship the beast and wear his mark on their foreheads and they'll drink the wine of the wrath of God, says so right there doesn't it? His Commander in Chief tells him there's sin and evil in the world, that we're enjoined by Scripture and the Lord Jesus to oppose it with all our might and he's taking his orders now just like he did from Tiger Howell in the 11th Cav. The Lord is a man of war, that's Exodus isn't it? the voice from heaven telling him blessed are the dead which die in the Lord says it right there, doesn't it? Meet him in the clouds? No no no, talk about disciples there's your prize exhibit, that that's what I tried to do with your brother that's what you've been saying? turn him into a, gets it into his head to take off for Africa because of me? Because I said they're hell bent on a self fulfilling prophecy and every stupid, ignorant...

—Because you're the one who wants it, she said abruptly in a voice so level he stopped, simply looking at her, at the glass coming up in her hand and her head thrown back for the last of what was in it, the full swell of her throat rising in the hollowed arch of her jaw's line hard as bleached bone, as he'd seen it only once before. —And it's why you've done nothing... She put down the glass, —to see them all go up like that smoke in the furnace all the stupid, ignorant, blown up in the clouds and there's nobody there, there's no rapture no anything just to see them wiped away for good it's really you, isn't it. That you're the one who wants Apocalypse, Armageddon all the sun going out and the sea turned to blood you can't wait no, you're the one who can't wait! The brimstone and fire and your Rift like the day it really happened because they, because you despise their, not their stupidity no, their hopes because you haven't any, because you haven't any left. Because when I woke up again that morning after I'd loved you and I knew you were in the house, I heard you cough downstairs and I knew you were here and it was the first time I, when I came up the hill that night in the dark and the lights were on and you were in there in front of the fire, sitting reading in front of the fire because it had never been mine, it had never been like coming home. Because we've never had one. Because Paul it was just a place to eat and, to eat and sleep and fuck and answer the telephone because he'll never have one, he'll never have a home and when I came down that morning and I knew you were here and I thought, and I felt safe. That one night and then the morning and all those babies demanding to get born out there on a star someplace with a telescope watching what was already gone? Because it was wasn't it, it was already gone, look at this one Billy here's the missing link, talk about a dark continent they think God put them here in their bad suits and cheap neckties no no no sit down, I'll tell you something, it's all just fear you said, any fiction to get through the night when you think of all the people who are dead? It's being the prisoner of someone else's hopes but that was, but that's not being the prisoner of someone else's despair! Because it was all your, I'm not a writer Mrs Booth no because it was all your despair locked away in that room there with the smoke and the cobwebs, pouring a drink with that old man and his dustpan pretending there was some reason to get up in the morning? locked away from her hopes all out here in the open? The silk flowers and the lamps and the gold draperies all her own hopes spread out like she'd be back in the morning until they were mine, spread up there in her bed?

He'd opened a cupboard, looked for a clean glass where he might once have kept them but come down with a cup holding the bottle straight up for little more than the half ounce or less left in it, no more than enough to warm the mouth not even a swallow. —I, incidentally I called Madame Socrate she'll be here first thing tomorrow to, to clean up...

—All your gentle, your hands on my breasts on my throat everywhere, all of you filling me till there was nothing else till I was, till I wasn't I didn't exist but I was all that existed just, raised up exalted yes, exalted yes that was the rapture and that sweet gentle, and your hands, your wise hands, meeting the Lord in the clouds all these sad stupid, these poor sad stupid people if that's the best they can do? their dumb sentimental hopes you despise like their books and their music what they think is the rapture if that's the best they can do? hanging that gold star in the window if, to prove that he didn't die for nothing? Because I, because I'll never be called Bibbs again... He stood there holding the empty cup as though looking for a place to set it down, for some refuge: she was looking straight at him, and then —I think I loved you when I knew I'd never see you again, she said, looking at him.

—But that wasn't...

—And you're going.

—I, yes... he put the cup down on the counter, —yes, I told you.

—Summer things, hot places, an umbrella that's all you told me.

—Where there's work... He started making another cigarette, spilling tobacco off the paper, —New Guinea, Papua there's a big strike back in the mountains there, a million ounces of gold when their smelter's set up, half a million tons of copper, up the Fly river from Kiunga... he twisted the paper and it tore, —or the Solomons, they're all the same these hot places, only difference is the diseases you pick up and even those... crumpling paper and tobacco together —listen, I meant it I, I've got some cash, got my hands on about sixteen thousand dollars and a ticket to anywhere, we can... he reached out to break off the phone on its first ring, —we can...

—What are you doing!

—But I thought... he dropped it back, —I thought you weren't answering, I...

—Just, just leave it alone!

—But...

—Because it might have been Paul again, when it rings twice and stops and then rings again no, a ticket to anywhere? to some hot place where the only way we know where we are is the disease we get? Just pack up and go when you're the only one who could stop it? who could tell everybody there's nothing there but some bushes? that you don't even care if they...

—Don't you see I, good God. And you really think I can stop a war? I told you, try to prove anything to them the clearer the proof and the harder they'll fight it, they...

—You could try!

—It's not, it's late... but she wasn't even looking at him —I, I'll do what I can. He caught up a sleeve of the raincoat, pulling it on —I can't get into town before dark. I'll call you.

—No wait, wait just...

—I said I'll do what I can! And I'll call you, I'll call you tonight that same two rings, two rings and hang up, will you pack? get a few things together if I can...

—Just hold me she said, and she already had his wrist tight.

—When I call... and he held her, —and if anything goes wrong...

—No, just hold me.

She stood still as her gaze fallen on the empty chairs out there on the terrace till the snap of the front door brought

246

her round with a broken sound that scarcely left her throat, left her searching the kitchen's silence as though for some provocation square into the ambush strewn there on the counter in the rag ends of headlines, **SENATOR DEAD IN RED PLANE SHOOTDOWN   VIET VET KILLS MUGG   TRAGEDY STALKS**   all starkly relevant in their stark demand to be read again for what they'd already demolished in their confusion, a wingcollared senator waving from the window of a bright red airplane or Doctor what was his name, might still be for he'd been quite young, the vet who'd wormed and dieted those Jack Russell terriers at Longview where she stood now jamming the black headlines together in a crush of newsprint as though to destroy their tyranny once for all, passing the kitchen table there with the heap clutched high against her so not a page, not a paragraph, not a word paralysed in cliché or sprung into odd company through the first enthusiasm of a byline or even, as she'd remarked herself, in the servitude of a caption which made the picture, for that day's paper, news, would fall to the floor, coming on to heave the armload through the opened door and with it her language in the printed word itself.

At the top of the stairs she paused, gripping the rail, before she went in to wet a cloth in the basin and hold it to her forehead coming down the hall that way to the bedroom to cry out —oh no! as though there were someone to hear: scarves, sweaters, smalls, papers, the chest's drawers themselves lay flung out on the bed, the floor, the closet door standing wide and even a shade drawn against the view from below. She came in slowly picking things up, dropping them again with a sense of something missing but apparently none of what it might be, finally settling to gather up the pages as though, righting them in their folder, here in her own hand at least lay some hope of order restored, even that of a past itself in tatters, revised, amended, fabricated in fact from its very outset to reorder its unlikelihoods, what it all might have been if her father and mother had never met, if he'd married a chorus girl instead or if she'd met a man with other lives already behind him, crumbled features dulled and worn as a bill collector on through the crossings out, the meticulous inserts, the wavering lines where her finger had run over cut-rate, curt, in pursuit of cunning and on to collisions of only days before, seeking the spelling of those Jack Russell terriers running down jackleg, jack mackerel to trip on jack off (usu. considered vulgar); seeking, for some reason, loose for its meaning as slack here cited in the sex roles of shorebirds with the author's name misspelled; confusing rift for cleft, and there waylaid by the anal ~ of the human body or here was livid, bypassing ashen, pallid, for the perversion she sought and found licensed by a sensitive novelist as reddish (in a fan of gladiolas blushing ~ under electric letters) for this livid erection where her hand closed tight on its prey swelling the colour of rage when she looked up sharp, straight before her: the television set was gone. It was simply not there; but her stare where it had been was as simply one of a blank insistence that the furnishings of memory prevail as though, if it were so abruptly nonexistent as to never have been there, then neither had the man flung from the train on the trestle, nor everything in shadow while wind roared in the laurel walk, near and deep as the thunder crashed, fierce and frequent as the lightning gleamed striking the great horse chestnut at the bottom of the garden and splitting half of it away.

The shrill of a car's horn brought her over to snap up the shade. In what light remained out there two waist high boys sat sharing a cigarette under the bare tree on the corner where a battered station wagon lurched to a halt bringing one of them to his feet and then she saw both of them pointing at the front door, her front door, and the car glided stalled past the crumbled brick and stopped. By the time she got down the stairs there was already someone there knocking, peering in, and when it came open —yes, I'm looking for Mister McCandless?

—Oh. I mean he's not here, he left a little while ago, he...

—I was just passing through the woman said, and then,

248

in the door held wide open —no no no, no I needn't come
in... but she did, just inside as the lamp came on under the
sampler there catching the faded blonde of her hair, the whole
spent fragility of her features turned looking over the room,
sounding almost as an afterthought —I'm Mrs McCandless.

—Oh I didn't, come in yes I'm afraid it's all a little dis-
organized if you, I mean is it about the furniture?

—About what furniture.

—No I just meant about all the furniture, if you've come
to, oh oh the flowers yes... looking there where the woman
was looking, —I'm sorry, they got knocked over I just
haven't had time to clean up but they're all right I think, I
think it's only the vase that's broken we'll replace it but, I
mean do you want to take them?

—Take them? The woman looked at the wilted silk, the
spatter of porcelain on the floor. —Take them where.

—No I just meant, with you, I mean if you'd like to sit
down? If you'd like some tea?

—Thank you. I would, yes, I'm really quite tired... but
she came following on into the kitchen. —I really just stopped
to see if he'd heard anything from Jack.

—Oh. I don't know. I mean I don't know Jack, who
Jack is.

—Jack? Jack is his son.

—His... she half turned from filling the tea kettle, —but
I thought, he said he didn't have children.

—Children, no. That's the way he'd say it of course, he
doesn't have children... The woman was over looking into
the dining room, at the plants there in the windows, —no
other white ones that I know of, at any rate... and she drifted
back into the kitchen, past the table there, to stand in the
doorway looking into the room. —Quite a mess.

—Yes he, he's just been cleaning up, in there cleaning up.

—That's really all he ever does, isn't it... and, a step into
the room, —and it's always once for all isn't it, to get things
cleaned up once for all... out of sight, only a voice now from
the near darkness in there —all his books, what he'll do with

all his books they might as well go too, once for all. He probably hasn't looked into one of them since he stopped teaching, has he.

—I don't, teaching? I didn't know...

—And he's throwing this out too? this old zebra skin?

—Well he, I don't think so I mean he brought it back from Africa, I don't think he'd...

—He told you that?

—Well yes, I mean I think so, I...

—No no no, he bought it from a young Nigerian who was emptying bedpans in the hospital, he'd come over here to study medicine and brought a whole stack of them to pay for medical school. A hundred dollars, he gave the boy a hundred dollars for it and I was quite annoyed, a hundred dollars was a lot to us then. He'd just come out of the hospital and there were still all the bills.

The empty cup rattled its saucer in a tremble of her hand putting it down on the table where she reached for the light. —Was it, what kind of hospital... She put down the other cup. A wisp of steam came from the teakettle, and she reached for it carefully —I mean, it wasn't a...

—He's probably told you all those stories hasn't he, came through the dark doorway, —finding gold when he was Jack's age and nobody believed him? up above the Limpopo? It was always up above the Limpopo... and a sound as though she'd stumbled over something in there. —Or that boy he taught how to use a shovel?

—Do you need a light in there? It's over...

—No no no, just a look around... stepping over the newspapers flung on the floor there —he'll save anything, won't he... and coming out into the light —you can tell he's been in there can't you, the smoke, it clings for ages. And if you know that cough... She sat down and turned the cup's handle to her. —He doesn't much like getting old, does he.

—I hadn't really...

—That arthritis in his hands, it's been there since he was

thirty. Like his father... she sipped at the steaming cup.
—If you'd seen how he acted when he lost those teeth in
the front, good God it was like they'd taken his balls all that
Freudian stuff, you know, but it was a shock getting used
to. He's not one for smiling much is he, but when you've
been used to that broken grey Protestant smile and suddenly
here's this row of neat even white teeth? That was just before he met you, the same Freudian stuff I guess... she picked
up the cup, —because you're young. Just to prove he still
had them.

—But I don't...

—And I don't mean his teeth.

—I don't quite, I mean I didn't know you'd be old enough,
to have a son twenty five I mean.

—I didn't know you'd have red hair the woman said,
looking at her all appraisal as she'd looked over the living
room when she came in, as though that's what she'd come
for, putting the cup down. —Is there a drink?

—It's, no I'm sorry there's not no... following the woman's eyes to the bottle empty on the counter —I mean there
was but...

—No no no I understand, good God I understand that!
She was standing, —it's just as well, really...

—Wait, there's a cobweb wait on the back of your skirt
they're just everywhere in there, in that room... coming down
to brush it away to be met with a knee come up, with the
skirt raised skewed, with an indelible glimpse of flesh sagging these inner lengths of thighs she'd in that bed upstairs
inhabited surging to meet him for as long as it lasted, until
he came down fighting for breath himself, until she backed
off unsteadily straightening up there against the sink —I, let
me get something to...

—It's all right no, they're nasty aren't they... the hairy
wisp of the thing hung black from her fingers —why they're
so sticky, it's the smoke isn't it, it clings to everything for
ages... dropping it into her teacup up with the back of her

hand brushing her skirt smooth again, her shoulder, her sleeve as though brushing away her question, —he's not teaching now, is he?

—Well he, no, no I mean I don't really know what he...

—I don't think anyone does... she went on toward the front door, —anything he could get his hands on, even Greek drama and you can imagine that, but he didn't even really teach history no, no he wanted to change it, or to end it, you couldn't tell... and she had the door open, —to clean it up once and for all, like that room in there. It's getting dark... she'd stepped out, but she stood there. —If he hears from Jack, but he won't, will he. They just both finally felt like they'd let each other down, like they'd asked too much of each other and there was nothing left to, but he knows how to reach me. I'm sorry I disturbed you, I don't like to drive in the dark, I just spent ninety six dollars to have a new fuel pump put in this old car and it still stalls when you never expect it... and she suddenly put out her hand. —You look pale, she said, and then looking back into the room —you have lovely taste... squeezing the hand clutched there tight to the doorframe before she turned away.

The streetlight had come on out there on the corner. The door of the car slammed, and then it moved silently, dark, onto the road, coughing, moving faster down the hill, and then it was gone as though it had never been there at all.

When the phone rang she'd just picked up her own cup, back in the kitchen gazing down over the dark terrace where the twisted limbs of that naked scarecrow of a tree stirred their frayed reach as though in sudden torment to be gone but she'd filled it too full, and it spilled, catching that first ring before she could stop and then holding the phone like a weight unsteadily, listening, and then —oh! gripping the edge of the table —Edie! Oh I'm so glad you... no but you're right here! You could hire a car it's less than an hour, you could be here in less than... No I, I'm all right Edie I, I don't know it's all, everything, wonderful I, I can't tell you all, beautiful yes... yes tomorrow then, early? I can't wait... and she hung it up to get both hands gripping the table, coming up slowly as though fighting each moment, fighting a hand free to turn off the light and then stand, breathing deep, breathing deeper, before she turned back for the living room toward the stairs, toward the newel in flashes of colour caught in the glass on the sampler.

The front door hadn't closed, and through its glass panels the bare shadows of branches in the streetlight rose and fell on the black road out there in a wind scarce as the gentle rise and fall of breathing in exhausted sleep. For a moment longer she held tight to the newel as though secured against the faint dappled movement of the light coming right into the room here and then suddenly she turned back for the kitchen where she rushed into the darkness as though she'd forgotten something, a hand out for the corner of the table caught in a glance at her temple as she went down.

Some time later, and well up beyond reach where she lay with her head fallen on her shoulder, the telephone rang and a choked bleat of sound came lost from her throat in a great sigh as her knees drew up sharply turning her on her side, an arm flung out and her thumbs still crushed into the palms of her hands, the uneven trembling of her lip abruptly stilled spilling the tip of her tongue, and it rang again and was silent, and then it rang again, and it kept ringing until it stopped.

The red glare in the alcove windows spread through the cold living room setting the walls ablaze with the sun's rise red on the river below, gleaming in the emptied bottle and glass beside the wing chair where the hand stirred seizing its arm with the sudden blare of the Star Spangled Banner from the kitchen heralding another broadcast day. He opened his eyes and closed them immediately, and the blaze of the room fell away to a pink, to rose, till by the time the phone's ring brought him up in a stumble banging his shin on the coffee table it was all simply daylight.

—Hello? He sat rubbing his shin, staring at the broken

trace of the line drawn in chalk on the floor there, —well what about the phone bill, I don't... No this is not Mister McCandless, I don't know where the hell Mister McCandless is look I've never even met him, I'm just... Look, I just told you I've never met him, how can I tell you whether he's sent you a check for the God damn phone bill, I don't even... Good I'll tell him, if I see him I'll tell him, if you don't receive payment by five p m today you'll discontinue service, that's the... no goodbye, there's somebody at the door...

Somebody hunched down, peering in, snapping open a wallet on an ID card bearing a photograph similar in all undistinguished respects to the man standing there when the door came open. —God damn early aren't you? He tucked down a tail of his shirt and fastened his trousers, —told you everything I know on the phone yesterday didn't I? same statement I signed for the police? All right here in the God damn newspaper isn't it? He'd led through to the kitchen where he brought up a headline from the heap on the table, **HEIRESS SLAIN IN SWANK SUBURB** —House ransacked? Apparently interrupting a robbery in progress at her fashionable Hudson river residence, the daughter of late mineral tycoon F R Vorakers was found dead this morning by a childhood friend FBI doesn't read the God damn newspapers? Mrs Jheejheeboy where they got hold of that, must still be her married name that Indian in the dirty diapers look, whole God damn story's right here isn't it? Police said the victim, a stunning redhaired former debutante from the exclusive Grosse Pointe area in Michigan, had suffered a single blow from a blunt don't step on that! He'd seized the man's arm with an intensity locking them in an embrace of violence so pure that his hand came down trembling the whole length of his arm.

—Don't ever do that again.

—I, God damn it I, I don't... and the hand that had caught his wrist eased away to his elbow where they'd broken back from that line chalked on the floor —think I'm crazy don't you, probably read that in the paper too, look. Look, you said you just wanted to come in and look around what's the, whole story's in my statement to the police isn't it? you people don't talk to the police? Time I got here that morning the whole God damn place was a media circus out there, Edie, that's her friend Edie showed up here early front door standing wide open, I always told her to keep the God damn doors locked, lying right here on the floor drawers dumped out napkins, placemats, spoons all over the place God damn woman out front there pushing a microphone in my face. Can you describe your feelings when you arrived home to discover your wife's body on the, God damn lucky it wasn't hers look. Tell me why the FBI's suddenly so God damn interested? you think I, look I can prove I was on that noon shuttle from Washington, airport limousine they call it that it's a God damn bus by the time I got here the whole place was a, get the phone here... He went down in the chair, —who? Look I can't... Look Sheila what in the hell are you talking about! It's God damn well not going to be a Buddhist service for him no, and don't... Look I'm telling you Sheila, send one of your God damn skinhead rimpijays out there in his little red mantra ringing bells chanting umm umm and I'll serve you up a good monk barbecue, that's the... God damn it Sheila listen nobody gives one good God damn about his karma getting him off the wheel whether his next incarnation is a look, look there's a God damn fly just landed on the table here you think that's him? just went up to the ceiling doesn't know where the hell he's going you think that's him? Crazy as he was coming in here pissing on the floor he God damn near killed me once, you know that? Down under the car out there jacked up on a stick of wood he gave it a kick the whole God damn thing came down I could have been, could have, I, I... the phone shook in his hand, holding it further from him, holding it away, hanging it up and staring at his hand until it came up wiping the perspiration down his face. —What? Suddenly he was up, —said you wanted to come in and look around what the hell do you think you're going to find in there, never been in there it's been locked up since we moved in, you looking for clues? What they pay you for isn't it? look for clues? Clues to what... he stepped aside, —don't ask me that's all, what the hell's in there don't ask me... coming on behind him for the front door where the man stopped, looking the room over, looking him over.

—You'd better shave.

—Always told her keep the God damn doors locked, I could have hired somebody to do it for me is that what you think? Read the God damn papers how much money she had is that what you think? And he stood there filling the doorway until the undistinguished grey car turned down the hill, knocking over a broom leaning there against the staircase and picking it up, standing there looking up the stairs and finally dropping the broom back to the floor and climbing them, down the hall where scarves, sweaters, papers, the chest's drawers themselves still lay flung out on the bed, on the floor as he'd found them, and the manila folder where he'd found it spread open on the bed to pages in a hand he knew spelling little more than bread, onions, milk, chicken? here drawn out in whole paragraphs and crossings out, marginal exclamations, meticulous inserts, her tongue tracing the delicate vein engorged up the stiffening rise to the head squeezed livid in her hand, drawing the beading off in a fine thread before she brought him in, surging to meet him for as long as it lasted, standing there numbed and then replacing it carefully in the folder, and then he stooped to pick up his shoes and hurried from the room, down the hall where his same numbed look met him now in the mirror over the basin, the white wisps he'd found there dangling from his hand as though he didn't know what to do with them before he turned on the water full and held his head under the tap, finally coming out shaved, scarred and shirtless where a movement no more than the flutter of a wing caught his eye through the glass at the foot of the stairs, someone on tiptoe, peering in, and he came down them.

—A what? She was barely his waist high, standing there in the doorway all timidity and he bent down, —Look little girl I don't know where he went, see that old man over there with the broom? He's the one who watches out for black doggies with red fingernails, only God damn thing he's got to do you go over and ask him... and he watched her hesitant step down into the road, calling after her —and that goes for his cat too... before he closed the door muttering —God damn cold in here... twisting the thermostat coming through to his suitcase opened on the dining room table where he pulled out a shirt, where he'd stood reeling the night before, or the night before that or it might even have been dusk, clinging for balance to a chair there when he'd shouted out her name, standing here heaving as though that cry of outrage still hung in the air, pulling on the shirt, down on his knees on the kitchen floor now with a wet rag scrubbing again at that chalk line's amorphous enclosure but for what might have been an arm flung out toward the sink, when the phone rang.

—Adolph? this you? Been trying to reach you where the hell have you been... All right, look. God damn State Department shipped him back with Teakell they want three thousand some dollars carfare before they'll release the body, get on them and tell them if it's not there for this funeral in Michigan Friday Grimes will have their ass. Now this trust instrument, you found your copy yet? What... Look I've got one, I've got a copy right here in front of me and I've got a copy of the will only God damn question is when his half goes into her estate with this delivery delayed, you... He went first didn't he? What do you... Look God damn it Adolph get one thing straight, you're working for me now I don't give one God damn what you think, you can't handle it I'll talk to Slotko, that's... what the hell do you mean her mother's claim, down there with Uncle William in that thousand a day nursing home your God damn doctor syndicate Orsini Kissinger and the rest of them set up at Longview the old lady's a vegetable, what do you... No what else then, read it to me... He snapped his hand ridding it of the fly that had lighted on a knuckle, veered off over the sink and come down to his knee where he slapped at it —wait, what? What do you mean a dollar... The fly paused on the corner of the table, came up in a fast turn and down in a zigzag march across **10 K 'DEMO' BOMB OFF AFRICA COAST War News, Pics Page 2** —what the hell do you mean went in legal fees, insurance company settled for four million she and everybody else on that plane get a dollar and the rest went in legal fees? His free hand crept across **PREZ: TIME TO DRAW LINE AGAINST EVIL EMPIRE** and he slapped it down —look, Grimes is on the board of the God damn insurance company isn't he? get in there and tell him to fight the... partner in what, what legal firm... Well God damn it! You call that ethical? Those sons of... what about mine then, my suit for... on what grounds, threw it out on what grounds God damn it she signed a deposition didn't she? said she couldn't fulfill the... All right get on it then and look. One more thing, what the hell was this in the paper about the house in Bedford being burned down by the fire department up there as a training exercise, any God damn reason the estate can't get in there and sue them for... Well just do it! Look, car coming for me any minute for a flight out to Michigan this afternoon, when you hang up call this guy in the State Department and chew out his ass, I'll call you when it's over... and he hung up, —Liz? you hear that? God damn court threw out my companion suit for, for, Liz! and his hands came up against his face savaging its features as though to do away with them, coming down to leave him shuddering, staring at the fly's course over **SURVIVAL CAMP SHOOTOUT NETS VET** and seizing it, tearing open its pages, dialing the phone —Hello? Look, this ad you've got in the paper, picture of these two marquetry chests thirty eight thousand the pair? Where did... no I don't want to buy them I want to know where the hell you got them. Whose... what do you mean an estate auction whose estate, what... look what else was in it, was there... Because I want to know if there were stones, boxes of stones that were... I said stones yes what's so God damn funny about... Well why in the

259

hell can't you give me that infor... See what's so God damn funny about it when you hear from my lawyer! and he banged it down, pulling a deep breath and then taking the newspaper, rolling it stealthily, raising it over the fly's new foray across **PREACHER SHOT IN BRIBE CASE** and bringing it down hard, up slamming it at the refrigerator, the counter top, the table, finally standing there wiping his hand down his face and slumping back in the chair, sweeping up the pile of envelopes, spurious salutations, bills, staring at the top one Professional services rendered... $4000. and he had the phone again.

—Hey, peckerhead? Told you I'd get you some good names didn't I? He squared the bill round in front of him, —Kissinger, he's... straight on, he's going to be out of the country, paper says he's going over to ream out the Pope tear him out a new... get you that in a minute here's another one, Orsini, Jack Orsini... he went on, buttoning his wilted shirt, names, numbers, up jamming it into his trousers —God damn nightmare, I'll tell you one thing Chick one, just one thing, what really happened in that BOQ God damn glad she never knew about that she, she wouldn't have... didn't know about that either no, letter from some refugee camp in Thailand finally got to me here but nobody did. Nobody knew till those God damn pictures in the paper, some dogood agency spotted me on television just got to me here and laid it on, would I put up their passage money guarantee their entry into the US her and the boy, it was a boy, try and make you pay with the rest of your God damn life for every mistake those mothers handed you over there? God damn VA sees that picture in the paper cuts off my disability? you see yesterday's papers? Same shit all over again, same mothers pissing up everything this time it's blacks instead of gooks, waste their hootches burn out their crops whore up their girls blow your gut I'll talk to you peckerhead, get your shit together I'll talk to you... and he'd barely hung it up when it rang.

—Hello...? Hey Bobbie Joe, what's the... hey now slow

down Bobbie Joe, just slow down, now why would I want to go doing a thing like that look. Now this old senator he denied it now didn't he? before he went down? You saw that in the paper now didn't you Bobbie Joe? and maybe I just kep it for my own use? Now why would I want to go and get your daddy shot over a thing like that, why he's... Well now I wouldn't go making accusations like that in public if I was you Bobbie Joe, say maybe the Roman Catholics was behind it because he was in there harvesting their flock that could get you in a lawsuit where you'd... no I know all about your juries down there but that's not the... No now listen here Bobbie Joe, you just listen here. Your daddy's all right now isn't he? took one in the shoulder I've put men right back in combat with worse than that. Now this black boy they brought in that he says he did it? made up that story somebody gave him a hundred dollars that said they were a friend of your daddy's and your old daddy he wanted to be this old martyr for the blood of the church and all? Now here's what your daddy's going to do Bobbie Joe and you tell him, hear? This little old boy he's going to get twenty years consider where it happened and what your daddy's going to do, he's going to forgive him, just like he did when Earl Fickert came after him with that ax? But he's not going to plead mercy for him either, he's going to go right ahead with these charges just to show the liberal press he don't make exceptions for a man's skin. He don't press charges that sounds like he thinks all the blacks will go do a thing like that where a white man would go to jail shooting another white man and he just wants this boy to be treated fair like anybody else, go do his twenty years and your daddy will pray for him? Now one more thing here, you know Billye called me up here? Billye Fickert? thought I'd gone down living in Haiti because some check she wrote me came back cashed in some bank down there in Haiti and my name signed on the back of it looked real funny? Now you just tell her that's true, I've gone to living down there in Haiti and I won't get to see her for a while because... well I'll just do that Bobbie Joe, see how many of them down there's been harvested I'll just do that you tell your daddy now I've got to hang up, car just pulled up outside I've got to go, somebody at the door...

Someone standing out there looking down the black stream of the road, looking down where no flashes of colour, of those reds and bright yellows were left to break the still light on the river below and he got to the dining room to pull his jacket off the back of a chair, to snap the suitcase closed and get through the front door with —you didn't need to get out, Edie... pulling it closed behind him for the snap of the lock, taking her arm by the mailbox there in the sudden chill, holding open the door of the dark limousine until she was in and settling in beside her as it moved almost silently down the road scattering boys on both sides into the banks of dead leaves, his arm resting across the back of the seat behind her turned looking away from him out the tinted window when he said —got plenty of time... and then, —you know? settled closer, —I've always been crazy about the back of your neck

For a complete list of books available from Penguin in the United States, write to Dept. DG, Penguin Books, 299 Murray Hill Parkway, East Rutherford, New Jersey 07073.

For a complete list of books available from Penguin in Canada, write to Penguin Books Canada Limited, 2801 John Street, Markham, Ontario L3R 1B4.